Praise for *Catalyst*,
the first tale of the Barque Cats

A *Wall Street Journal* science fiction bestseller

"A fun, madcap adventure with tongue planted firmly in cheek.
Even this non-cat-person liked it. We can only hope that more
tales of the Barque Cats are forthcoming."
—*Analog*

"A full-bore action-adventure novel. The complicated relations
between humans and animals will remind McCaffrey's readers of
her dragon books, to my mind an excellent recommendation."
—Sullivan County *Democrat*

"With youthful protagonists and an incorrigible cast of cats, this
lighthearted sf tale is a good choice for cat lovers as well as fans of
the authors."
—*Library Journal*

"The human-feline interactions work well, and the intriguing plot
is sure to entertain genre readers."
—*Booklist*

"This is magic . . . science fiction at its most primal and at its best."
—*January Magazine*

CATACOMBS

CATACOMBS

A TALE OF THE BARQUE CATS

ANNE McCAFFREY

ELIZABETH ANN SCARBOROUGH

BALLANTINE BOOKS TRADE PAPERBACKS

NEW YORK

2012 Del Rey Trade Paperback Edition

Copyright © 2010 by Anne McCaffrey and
Elizabeth Ann Scarborough
Illustration on p. 113 by Justin Batten

Published in the United States by Del Rey Books, an imprint of The Random House Publishing Group, a division of Random House, Inc., New York.

DEL REY is a registered trademark and the Del Rey colophon is a trademark of Random House, Inc.

ISBN 978-0-345-51379-3
eBook ISBN 978-0-345-52478-2

Printed in the United States of America

www.delreybooks.com

9 8 7 6 5 4 3 2 1

Book design by Karin Batten

*For Cisco and Pancho and all of our friends at
UnitedCats.com, some of whom were recruited, with a
slight change in breed, to fight the good fight as
Barque Cats and handlers.*

— Elizabeth Ann Scarborough

ACKNOWLEDGMENTS

I would like to thank Lea Day and Tania Opland for early reading of the manuscript and for research assistance. I would also like to acknowledge the work of Paul Gallico, who in his cat book *Jennie* (*The Abandoned* in the United States) coined the phrase "When in doubt, wash," and featured the first cat washing lessons.

For the latter part of the book, inspiration for a critical mission for cats in space came from Cordwainer Smith's short story "The Game of Rat and Dragon."

CATACOMBS

Pshaw-Ra the Spectacular, Mariner of the Stars, returned to his world in what he fondly imagined as triumph, bearing with him the seeds of salvation for his race, if not his entire planet.

Were he not the bold, heroic, cunning, adventurous, incredibly brave, fast talking, quick thinking, highly skilled, and of course devastatingly handsome cat he knew himself to be, all would have been lost. But thanks to his daring, his farsightedness, his willingness to spend month after solitary month in alien space cleverly tricking passing ships into unwitting participation in his master plan, his race would be saved. And so, more or less, would the remnant of the once-proud Barque Cats, now beaten and broken, bewildered by the betrayal that had befallen them at the hands of those they had once loved and served. It had been a useful object lesson that would make them, Pshaw-Ra thought, much more amenable to the plans he had in store for them.

Unfortunately, he had been obliged to accept the assistance of a crew of cat-friendly humans in transporting his cargo. He didn't see them as a major obstacle. In time they were bound to acquiesce to their place in the feline scheme of things.

Chortling behind his whiskers, Pshaw-Ra steered his pyramid craft to land upon the sands of his beloved homeworld. "Go, now," he said with uncharacteristic thoughtfulness to his recently recruited assistant, the only cat among his cargo he thought might cause him any difficulty. "Be with your boy. He is no doubt frightened and will need you to comfort him."

The half-grown kitten, whose long black coat with white chest and paws resembled an antique version of male human formal dress, flicked his fluffy tail, turned around twice to look at the hieroglyphic controls he was still far too ignorant to understand, and bounded back down the cat-sized corridor leading from the pyramid ship's nose cone into the larger portion of the ship.

Once the youngster left, Pshaw-Ra activated his communication device and announced his imminent arrival to his planet's people and especially to his queen. "Bring healers and groomers, bring the eligible queens and virile toms. Bring the most biddable and best socialized servants that they may choose among the new ones those most worthy of honor. For my part I bring kitten-capable breeders of great size, many toes, and somewhat regrettable furriness. Also, for my queen, delectable fishy treats."

He didn't listen for a response before darting out to wait for the triumphal procession that would escort him and his prizes through the city, according him a hero's welcome.

CHESTER, AS PYRAMID SHIP LANDS ON PLANET MAU

Entering the atmosphere of Pshaw-Ra's planet, it occurred to me that while we Barque Cats had been preoccupied with escaping death in the labs of Galipolis, perhaps we should have spared a thought for where we were going afterward.

Because now, here we were and there was no going back.

Our host, the tawny short-haired big-eared Pshaw-Ra, pilot of the pyramid ship, was the only one among us who knew anything about this mysterious world. And he had been far too busy smiling into his long black whiskers to provide a narrative preview of the place that he had promised would be our new home. All he had confided in me was that cats here were very advanced, worshipped as gods, and were bent on universal domination.

That was fine for him. Most of the other feline passengers who came with us were still in a state of shock from recent events. In the past weeks my race, including my mother and two of my brothers, had gone from being valued crew members—guardians of their ships' safety and beloved fur-coated surrogate children of their human crewmates—to being labeled the vectors of an unknown disease, incarcerated in dirty cages in a crowded laboratory, and threatened with mass extinction. Several Barque Cats, it was rumored, had already been sacrificed on the altar of scientific inquiry, and the others feared they would soon follow.

Then Pshaw-Ra decided that we two, who were traveling together at that time, should rescue them, not because he was such a benevolent cat but because (a) we fit in with his plans for the previously mentioned universal domination, (b) it was the fault of him and his accursed kefer-ka, the delicious keka bugs we all loved to eat, that we were mistakenly thought to have a disease in the first place, and (c) Jubal and I wouldn't have stood for any other course of action.

But once we were inside the ship, and the other cats had time to absorb the fact that they were no longer in cramped dirty cages in a strange place, but were now in cramped quarters, rapidly getting dirty, aboard strange space vessels, they immediately wanted to find something to hide under or to attack, each according to his or her nature. Desperation clawed every available surface, including some human ones, desolation yowled in ear-splitting decibels throughout the ship, despair shed carpets of hair that floated through the air as if fur could bond with oxygen. My fellow cats—cats who had saved a thousand ships (okay, maybe a slight exaggeration, but LOTS of ships)—were thoroughly bedraggled, bewildered, and frustrated.

Fortunately, thanks to Pshaw-Ra's mouse hole, a cat-created shortcut through space, our trip was not a lengthy one.

One moment we were fleeing with Galactic Government attracker ships hot on our tails, the next we were surrounded by space empty of other ships, with a sandy-colored planet looming ahead. In the far distance were one large star and two smaller ones, but no other ships that we could see. We passed a moon on our left. It seemed to be circled by a bristling cloud of something or other.

"What's all that?" I asked Pshaw-Ra, indicating the cloud.

"State-of-the-art terraforming equipment in its day," Pshaw-Ra replied. "It transformed Mau from an uninhabitable chunk of rock to the paradise you see before us."

I beheld the big planet, most of it a nondescript beige, growing ever larger in the view port. It continued to fail appearing any more impressive. "Mrrrrumph," I said. "Some paradise."

"Once great cities and pyramids rose from the sand, but that was in ancient times. Ours was among the earliest colonies to be set-tled, and when the great colonial corporations decided they could do better elsewhere, they took many of our people to newer worlds. Mau serves its purpose quite adequately for the rest of us, however, at least until we are ready to rule the universe."

"Rrrrright," I said.

"Do not judge a planet by its surface, catling," he said sharply. "I have many wonders left to show you."

"I can hardly wait," I said, cleaning delicately under my tail.

"Just wait until we are given our heroes' welcome, the choicest tidbits placed before us, the most alluring mates offering them-selves, our two-legged slaves providing every imaginable comfort."

What's that about two-legged slaves, Chester? My boy, Jubal, sent me the thought privately. The short-furred tawny cat couldn't have heard it because he was too busy gloating about the joys of his planet and all he expected to find there. *I don't like the sound of that.*

The boy and I can share senses, he seeing through my eyes, hearing through my ears, smelling, tasting, and feeling what I smell, taste, and feel, and vice versa.

He sat just on the other side of the hatch that separated the cats-only bridge of the pyramid ship from its docking bay. We were the only creatures remaining on the ship since our escape from the Galactic Government. Once Pshaw-Ra had threaded us through the mouse hole, we had entered the docking bay of the *Reuben Ranzo*, the ship Jubal had served on. The hatch was opened and the dozens of Barque Cats who had been packed around my boy inside the pyramid ship were released into the *Ranzo* to join the throng of cats who had been transported to the larger ship after being crammed into two other shuttles.

This was the result of our daring rescue.

As soon as we had unloaded our passengers into the *Ranzo*, Pshaw-Ra launched the pyramid ship into space once more, leading the way to his planet. "Why do they call your planet Mau?" I asked Pshaw-Ra.

"They didn't call it Mau, we did. The humans named it Bubastis, but that's not a word easily spoken by their gods—namely us—so they had to change it," Pshaw-Ra replied.

Pshaw-Ra dismissed me shortly before we landed so that I could be with Jubal. Though I was somewhat surprised by the tawny cat's consideration, I was quick to take advantage of it.

I bounded down the catwalk leading from the bridge in the nose of the pyramid cone, leaped onto the deck and made for the small ship's tiny docking bay to share first impressions with my boy.

I sprang onto Jubal's knees shortly before we landed, and my boy unstrapped himself from his seat.

The *Ranzo* landed beside us. In a moment Pshaw-Ra paraded into the docking bay and activated the paw-pad control for the pyramid ship's hatch.

A few of the rescued cats peered curiously around the humans emerging from the *Ranzo*, but the rest, I suspected, were hiding under bunks and in ventilation ducts and the other places Barque Cats normally patrolled. They weren't in a trusting mood, hardly surprising under the circumstances.

My mother—Thomas's Duchess, aka Chessie—stood beside

me. "It's so open," she said when her paws touched the ground. We looked out over a landscape more featureless than an empty cargo hold.

Toward the south, though, the endless expanse of golden brown sand and white-hot sky was interrupted by a strip of silver-green river, lined as far as we could see with a fertile strip of trees, grass, and some mud-brick structures, most of which were in ruins. A single yellow sun burned overhead, the heat soaking through our dense fluffy coats. We all had long beautiful fur, being descended from a feline race once known for some arcane reason as "Maine coon."

"How would you know where you were out there, away from the river?" Mother asked, nervously surveying the surrounding fields and sand.

"That's why we don't go away from the river!" Pshaw-Ra told her. "The river is life. And it is long. But the city is large enough for most of us, and that is where my people await your arrival and where your new lives and families will begin."

"I kind of like the wide-open spaces myself." That was my milk brother, Bat, racing toward us from the *Ranzo*. Bat and his brothers were born to be wild. Their mother was Git, a barn cat who befriended my mother. The two queens had birthed their litters hours apart, Bat and his brothers only slightly older than my siblings and me. When Git was killed, Mother nursed Bat and his brothers Doc, Wyatt, and Virgil, alongside her own. Jubal's father then took all of us into space to serve aboard different ships. All except Mother and me, who were sold back to Mother's original ship.

Bat plowed sand until his paws came to a stop, whereupon he stood stiff-legged and lashy-tailed beside me. "I've got your back, milk bro," he told me. "In case the locals don't all share old Sandy Britches's enthusiasm for us."

"It's too big," said Hadley, the *Ranzo*'s ship's cat who was still in the arms of Sosi, Captain Loloma's daughter and the ship's self-appointed Cat Person. The *Ranzo*'s passenger hatch was still open, and while a few more cats and crew poured out, Hadley suddenly wriggled from Sosi's grasp and bolted back inside the ship, leaping over the cats coming the other way. "I'll just be in here when we're ready to leave," he told us.

Pshaw-Ra spat, "Foolish feline, do you think I have led you all this way to the promised place for you to leave? You are all here to stay. This is the planet of the cats and you are a cat. Accustom yourself to your new life."

"It's very warm," Mother said, and she was right. The humans, who had no thick fur coats, were leaking water from their pelts. Sosi's face was wet and Beulah's was as red as her hair. None of them spoke cat, however, so they were merely uncomfortable, not alarmed by Pshaw-Ra's words.

Jubal of course understood him as well as I did.

The Ranzo *can go whenever it wants to though, right?* he asked me openly enough that Pshaw-Ra could hear.

Pshaw-Ra turned with twitching tail to regard my boy impatiently. He had heard the thought through me but was becoming adept at sorting out whose thoughts were whose. And no wonder. The kefer-ka, the shiny beetles that had caused our psychic link, were his creatures. I didn't fully understand what they were— other than delicious—or what all that eating them could do, but Pshaw-Ra claimed they were responsible for the link between Jubal and me.

"Ask the boy where he thinks the ship that allowed diseased cats to escape the clutches of the tyrannical Galactic Government can go," Pshaw-Ra said. "Our other human minions have been sent for. They will assist the *Ranzo*'s crew in acquainting themselves with their new homes and duties."

"See here, Pshaw-Ra," I said. "It's good of you and yours to hide us here until the Galactic Government humans come to their senses. But you can't make the cats stay here if they don't like it. And you are not going to force the *Ranzo*'s crew to—"

"Calm yourself, catling," Pshaw-Ra said. His tail had stopped twitching and he sat calmly grooming his paws. They needed it, surely. All that sand blowing around out there made us all instantly very dusty. The coats of the horde of cats milling around outside the ship had all begun to look almost as tawny as his, with a coating of the surrounding environment. "I was merely pointing out that they will need refuge from their authorities until further notice, and the resident humans will be happy to offer them accommodation. Human food is less plentiful than ours, however, so the duties I spoke of will involve acquiring that as well as helping their hosts tend to our needs."

"What are they to be then?" I demanded. "Bringers of food we can hunt for ourselves and litter box changers?"

Pshaw-Ra snickered behind his whiskers, then planted his front paws wide and stared out into the vast tawniness that so closely matched his coat.

"Behold the desert!" he said. "The largest self-changing litter box in the galaxy!"

CHAPTER 2

*T*he arrival on Mau turned out to be a nonevent. For a half hour or so everyone followed Pshaw-Ra's gaze as he stared expectantly across the desert, waiting for the welcome wagon. Then the cats from the *Ranzo* returned to the shaded interior of the ship, followed by the humans, Captain Loloma, Beulah, Sosi, and Felicia Daily.

Pshaw-Ra's tail began twitching, then thumping the sand. Then, abruptly, he darted back into the pyramid ship. Chester hopped down from Jubal's shoulder and started to follow, but a shrill whistle from the *Ranzo* made both of them look up.

Captain Loloma beckoned. "Jubal, we got ourselves a situation over here. Sosi says to have you bring your cat." He sounded as if he thought that was a bad idea.

Jubal half expected Chester to decline in favor of his original course, but his tuxedo-furred friend had decided that while something had clearly gone wrong with Pshaw-Ra's plans, the tawny short-hair wasn't about to discuss it with them for the time being.

Without a further word to Chester, Pshaw-Ra took off across the burning sands in the general direction of the river.

By the time Jubal and Chester boarded the *Ranzo*, the place was a cacophony of yowls, howls, hissings, spittings, and snarls. Sosi was screaming, "Hadley! Stop! Other kitty, let Hadley alone!"

Mild-mannered Hadley, in full-furred battle dress, straddled his food dish as three other Barque Cats, including Chester's sire Space Jockey, challenged him for the right to eat from it.

"Mine!" Hadley snarled. "My food. My bed. My ship. My crew. My girl. Mine!"

The others lashed their tails and closed in.

Space Jockey leapt into the air and Sosi screamed, "No, kitty, no! Hadley!" Hadley seemed to levitate to the top of Sosi's head, where he clung while she screamed, now in pain.

Hadley's remaining food was the only cat food on the *Ranzo*. The river wasn't far; maybe it contained fish. Jubal saw himself with a line and a pole catching endless fish to keep the cats fed. That could work out. He liked to fish, though he'd never had much time to do it.

Fish would probably be about all they could get for the cats, though. He didn't think a mouse could survive here.

"Does Hadley have any extra food?" Jubal asked Sosi.

She shook her head.

"There's not much," Captain Loloma said, correcting his daughter and giving her a stern look. "We were going to restock at the next station and then we were diverted to Galipolis for the catty call."

If Pshaw-Ra had it wrong and they weren't welcome on Mau, the Barque Cats could be in for a bad time. Gentle as they were with their human crews, they were used to situations in which one cat inhabited one ship. Right now there were probably more than 150 of them stuffed into every available cat-sized spot aboard the *Ranzo*. Somehow, Jubal just couldn't see this working out long-term. But now that they'd lost the attackers, maybe Captain Loloma could find some not-so-law-abiding place to take them until the plague scare blew over. Meanwhile, some of these cats at least were going to need other accommodations.

He looked up into the ventilation duct and saw two cat shadows arched and bristling at each other. "Hey, you two, cut it out," he told them. "This is only temporary, you know." But the cats either didn't hear him or didn't care.

A larger, older cat dabbed a clawed paw at Chester, who sat calmly except for the switching of his tail. Jubal understood him to say, *Come off it, old man. You can't fight your way out of everything. I'm younger, stronger, and I take after you so go scare someone else, or better yet . . .* Chester gave Jubal a significant look. Jubal, still in his shipsuit, grabbed the larger cat, Chester's sire, Space Jockey, known as Jock. It wasn't the smartest thing he'd ever done. Jock clawed and bit and squirmed. *I'm starving!* Jock snarled. *At least in the lab we got fed.*

"We'll take care of it," Chester said. "My boy will bring food, right, Jubal?"

"There's an extra bag back on the pyramid ship," Jubal said alone. "We can go get that. But let's split up the rest of Hadley's chow to calm everyone down first. We can put the ginger momcat and her kittens in a separate cabin so they'll be safe."

By the time Jubal and Chester set out for the pyramid ship to retrieve the food, the battle cries and yowls had been replaced by the happier sound of kibble being crunched as whiskered faces dove into dishes of it.

While Jubal dragged the large bag of cat food toward the outer hatch, Chester sprang up to the cat ramp and darted inside, his paws retreating into the cabin in the nose cone. He reemerged with a bag of fishy treats clenched in his teeth.

The sun was setting, painting the sky in gaudy pinks and oranges. The light faded, then darkened to navy blue as Jubal and Chester returned to the *Ranzo*. Jubal had been hoping Pshaw-Ra might reappear but wasn't terribly surprised when he didn't.

He hauled the bag of food to the bridge, where the officers were all in conference.

"Unless help comes, we should all remain inside for the night," Captain Loloma was saying. "The cooling system is overtaxed as it is."

"Even so, we won't be able to maintain a comfortable—or even habitable—temperature much longer." The engineer, Denny Gregg, spoke in a clipped, no-nonsense voice. "We were running low on fuel when we got to Galipolis. Since we didn't refuel there, we're dangerously low now. By my calculations, we haven't enough power to break atmo. I assumed we could refuel here but have seen no signs of a proper station."

Beulah, with sweat rolling down her heat-reddened face, said, "If we don't maintain the climate control, we'll die from the heat, and the cats will go first." She wiped her face miserably.

"How does anybody live here, Dad?" Sosi asked.

"I'm not sure, honey. I hope we'll have a chance to find out soon."

Jubal felt frustrated and guilty. He had trusted Pshaw-Ra, and the wily old cat, maybe intending to save them, stranded them in this predicament. Didn't he realize it would be too hot for the Barque Cats? Or that the *Ranzo* would need refueling sooner or later? He was the pilot of his own ship, after all. He ought to be aware of these things.

Chester sat down, dropping the fishy treats at his front paws long enough to yawn. *He's not what you'd call a thoughtful cat. I doubt it occurred to him to think anything about anyone but himself. He's probably telling all his mates about his adventures and has completely forgotten about us.*

Realizing at last that his summons for a welcoming party was going unheeded, Pshaw-Ra set off for the city to see what catastrophe could have possibly led his race to neglect to greet his return with the appropriate display of joy and gratitude. Had he reflected a bit more on what had actually occurred and a little less on his reception as he imagined it, he would have realized that no one had actually answered his transmission.

Which surely meant that something dire had happened.

Presiding over the lesser structures, the ziggurat temple/palace loomed as serrated and sharp-fanged as he fondly remembered. And yes, there were the guards, looking like stone cats sitting on the steps at each level. He padded down the dune and leapt the city wall that in olden days, before the force fields were perfected, protected the streets from the worst of the sandstorms.

As he strolled through the streets, passing and being passed by cats coming and going to their duties, it occurred to him that he'd been in space longer than he realized. When he left he had known almost everyone, their list of mates, whose offspring were whose, and who had secrets they'd rather not have made public. He'd also known which cats he could thoroughly trounce in a fight, and that had been most of them.

Now he noticed some younger, stronger-looking toms and queens he thought might give him a spot of bother. But there were also a few likely looking clueless specimens who could prove useful later.

He was sure the failure to answer his summons was the fault of some newcomer to the Office of Communications. Queen Tefnut would hear of this!

But when he entered the temple, as all citizens of Mau could do at any time, he recognized the cats resting in the sleeping platforms along the temple walls and also, to his shock, the cat sprawled across the head of the sacred statue of the Mighty Mau.

He hadn't counted on a total regime change!

"So," the queen on the head of Mau—none other than one of his own offspring, the troublesome Nefure—trilled down at him. "I heard a rumor that you had returned, Pshaw-Ra. If you're looking for my mother the former queen, she doesn't live here anymore. The queen is dead. Long live—me!"

Diplomacy was not Pshaw-Ra's greatest skill, but he knew enough not to say what he was thinking, which was something to the effect of "easy come, easy go." He was disappointed that Tefnut was gone, however. She had been unusually reasonable and cooperative for a highborn female, and he was rather fond of her. However, he was a very old cat, older than almost anyone realized, and had been the consort of previous queens. They did not tend to last very long. Tefnut was a good ruler, more throne than kitten oriented. And she'd had the intelligence to understand the brilliance of most of his schemes. He hoped this chit of a kit would as well.

Bowing over one extended front paw, he said, "Indeed! Long live you and glorious your reign. Speaking of which, my mission was successful beyond even my expectations. I have returned with a great number of exceptional felines from the outer galaxy, each of them having devoured quantities of the kefer-ka and ready for our accelerated breeding program."

"Why should I want an accelerated breeding program?" the queen asked. "My own kittenhood would have been idyllic had it not been for the presence of the one other kitten born on Mau during the late queen's reign — Renpet. Bringing more kittens into our world would only clutter it up. We have plenty of grown cats here now."

"Grown cats, Your Majesty, who live quite extended lives thanks to my longevity and rejuvenation treatments, but cats who have not been able to procreate with each other for some time. Our gene pool, it seems, has become too shallow and we are now too interrelated. Bast, in her wisdom, has therefore decreed that we can no longer produce kittens within our community. Thus our females are fallow and our males uninterested in the gentler forms of combat. However, with the arrival of these newcomers, and the help of a bit of chemical stimulation, our numbers will once more increase."

Nefure considered this as she toyed with a golden mouse that lay beside her. "Hmmm, more kittens would eventually mean more subjects under my rule, hence more power. Tell me more about these newcomers."

"Your Majesty, they tend to be very large, intelligent, and I have noticed that many possess the coveted papyrus paws with extra toes."

"How nice for you. But other than increasing our numbers with half-breed kittens, what have their characteristics to do with the greater glory of my reign?"

"Majesty, when these cats have served their purpose, and our offspring—your loyal subjects—have spread throughout the galaxy, they will conquer other peoples and other places in your name, expanding your realm so that in a very short time it will be not merely this sparsely catted planet, but the known universe!"

CHAPTER 3

CHESTER: FISHY

Humans sleep for long periods at a time. It's a wonder they ever get anything done. Cats sleep, hunt, eat, groom, sleep, patrol, eat, groom, and sleep again—interspersing other activities between sleep sequences as required. The point is that with nice naps punctuating every other thing we do, we are always able to give our full alert attention to each waking task.

Cultural differences. I'm not judging. Jubal was very tired and so I lay on the pillow beside his head for my first nap, woke to visit with the family and do a bit of mutual grooming, ate some of the crunchies before the others gobbled them up, and took another nap.

There was no porthole in Jubal's cabin, but somehow, even on this alien planet, I knew that the sun was rising and time was wasting. Jubal's dreams and my dreams were the same and they both involved rivers and fish.

Of course, Jubal had been alive for ten years and I had been alive only about six months, so he had the opportunity to read a lot more books and watch a great many more informative programs than I did.

His dreams were of the two of us on the bank of a placid body of water, him in overalls and a straw hat, with a cane pole dangling an intriguing string into the water. Mine were less complicated and featured me and a big fish. When I finished my dream fish, I woke, stretched, and just happened to stick a paw in his face, incidentally waking him too. Funny how that happened.

He did his usual waking up stuff, washing his face, slicking his hair back with water, brushing his teeth, but then he departed from his routine and, still in his pajamas, went on a scavenger hunt among the storage lockers. He stuffed his away bag with a strange collection of items, including a fist full of salt packets from the galley and the sheets he'd stripped from his bunk. Instead of replacing his pajamas with his shipsuit, he reached for a bag that contained the kind of coverings he'd worn back on Sherwood, where I was born, only these were a little nicer than his overalls. Pants, a shirt, socks, and low shoes instead of the slick boots he often wore in the barn. Leaving off the socks, he put on the clothes and added a collapsible cloth hat. Then he left a message on the console that connected each crew member to the bridge. *Gone fishin'*, it said.

Unusually, the entire crew except for the watchman was sleeping at the same time, so the ship was dark. Together we padded down the darkened corridor. Three other cats passed us and one peered out of the ventilation duct, watching curiously as we made for the forward hatch, but I pretended not to see. If I let them know where we were going, they'd all want to come, and while most were trained ship's cats, they might get lost or otherwise be a bother. This mission was for me and my boy alone, and if I happened to get the first fresh fish, well, someone had to test and make sure they were safe for off world cats, right?

The sun hadn't made much of an impact on the sand yet, and the air was much cooler than I expected, quite comfortable enough for me to ride on top of Jubal's pack and watch his back. There was no sign that Pshaw-Ra had returned to the pyramid ship.

The lovely quiet cool period didn't last, however. The river was farther than it looked, and the closer we got, the brighter it got, until before we knew it the sun had zipped up into the sky and made the sand shimmer and the water dazzle.

Jubal stopped and I hopped down while he pulled off his pack. The sand was not yet as hot as it had been the day before, and the extra fur between my toes protects my pads. My extra toes make my feet broad too, so I could mostly walk on top of the sand instead of sinking down into it the way the boy did with every step.

He smeared some stuff over his exposed skin and pulled out the sheet and put it over his head. I saw then that he had cut a hole in the middle, so it draped over him. Humans! If he was hotter, why was he putting on an outer coat?

He tried to put some of the cream on my nose, but I jerked out of the way. *Chester, your nose will burn out here.*

I'll take my chances, I told him. *That stuff smells so strong I wouldn't be able to smell danger before it pounced on us.*

You think there's danger? Did Pshaw-Ra say there were dangerous things here?

No, but he did say there'd be a welcoming committee of friendly cats bearing food and drink for everyone, and that didn't happen, and if there's no danger, what happened to him?

Good point.

We were walking again then, Jubal's sheet flapping around him as he moved, creating a slight breeze that tickled my fur in a pleasing fashion.

I tried to run ahead but quickly stopped, waiting for my boy to catch up. The heat made me want to pant like a dog, but my mouth was so dry! Jubal picked me up and I crawled under the sheet and back on top of his pack.

A couple of winks later the air cooled and a welcome scent of greenery awakened me. I peered out of the hole in the sheet, to the side of Jubal's sweaty neck. We stood in the shade of a tall tree looking out over the river. Around us grew tall reeds and trees.

The reeds were strong enough for Jubal to attach a line with a shiny thing weighing down the end so with a flick of the cane it carried the line far out into the water.

I hope these fish are dumb enough they don't know a lure from live bait, he said. And he sat. And sat. And the nice shade we had been under when he first sat down moved as the sun scaled the sky, and still we sat.

My belly on the grass, I scooted forward under paw power until I peered down into the brownish flow before us. There were fish in there, but they must not have been stupid enough because all of them were swimming right past us and nobody was stopping to see what was at the end of Jubal's line. Through the wet wild scent of the water, bearing tidings from every creature that had taken a drink from it, and every place it had been before this one, I smelled the deliciousness of fishes. At least one of them needed to get caught.

No, don't go, I commanded them, not that I speak fish. *Lookit the shiny thing! Yummy yummy shiny thing.*

I stuck my paw into the water and waved it toward the lure. The nearest fish didn't swim to the lure, though, it swam right up to my paw, taking it for the live bait Jubal didn't have. I let it get within biting distance but I wasn't about to lose my paw. I didn't have to think about it. As if the paw remembered something the rest of me hadn't learned yet, it swiped from the fish's head to its belly, claws came out, paw scooped up the fish and flipped it wriggling onto the bank.

Jubal grinned. "Good work, Chester!"

I was occupied with watching the fish trying to flop its way back into the river. At the last moment I would pounce it and foil its attempt to avoid becoming my breakfast.

So intent was I on the fish that I didn't smell trouble until it bounded down from above and snatched my fish from between my front feet, then streaked away with it in a tawny blur.

Two could play at that game. I shot after the streak before Jubal could open his mouth to call me back, his thought hanging between us.

The tawny blur was another cat—one of Pshaw-Ra's kind but not him, as I clearly smelled. *Hey, you, come back with my fish!* I snarled so ferociously I almost frightened myself. That was my very first fish ever, and I wanted it back. The cats who lived here probably caught their own all the time. Why take mine?

Mine! The other cat's thought seemed to echo the end of my own, mocking my anger and fish-hunger.

She—I could clearly smell that she was a she—darted into a thick stand of reeds and I dove in after her. Dimly, as if he was very far away, I heard Jubal's feet swishing through the grass and clattering through the reeds behind me, not calling, but listening for my thoughts, watching through my eyes, smelling through my nose.

Suddenly the other cat bounded to a halt and crouched over the fish, her fur spiking up all along her back, her tail twice its original size.

Fearlessly, I leaped on top of her, snarling and biting. *It's mine, you fishy thief!* I growled, and she yowled as my teeth penetrated her short fur and found flesh, surprising me almost as much as it did her.

Then something whipped down across my ears, then whacked the bridge of my nose, driving me off my enemy and my prey.

A female human voice was screaming, *Let her alone, you monster!*

I was so surprised I crouched back, spitting and hissing and crying all at the same time. No human had *ever* struck me or spoken to me like that, not even when I peed on the captain's bed! Who was this crazy girl bending over the still battle-ready tawny cat, who nailed her with bared claws and growled over the fish.

Look what you've done! the human cried, and struck at me again with the reed, but I dodged her and backed against a comforting pair of legs.

"Cut it out!" Jubal hollered at her. "Don't you dare hit my cat again or I'll—"

The girl's mouth fell open and she dropped the reed. I thought she was just surprised to see a strange boy wearing a sheet and waving what had been a fishing rod at her, but she fell to her knees, staring at me horrified from black eyes with whites showing all around them. "Cat? That's a cat?"

Jubal knelt beside me and patted my bristling back. "Of course he's a cat—half-grown kitten really." Jubal was less challenging now. This was the first native human we had encountered, or native cat for that matter, if you didn't count Pshaw-Ra.

"Kitten? But he's *huge!*"

"His breed is large. He's a Barque Cat, a very well-bred one too," Jubal said proudly.

"And he's got so much fur!"

"They're like that," Jubal agreed, continuing to stroke me. Against my inclination I started purring.

The other cat had turned away from me and was tearing into my fish. I looked up at Jubal and meowed, as if he couldn't understand very well that it was *my* fish, my *first ever* self-caught fish, that the creature was devouring before my very eyes. I tensed, ready to spring again, but Jubal restrained me by holding onto my ruff in a very pushy fashion.

Hey! I protested.

"That's his fish your cat is eating," Jubal told the girl. "He just caught it and she swiped it before he got a bite."

"She is a sacred Mau. All things Mau are hers."

"Then she should have caught it herself," Jubal said. "I have a vessel full of cats bigger than Chester, hungry and stressed out from their trip."

"No one said you could take the fish of the Mau."

"Maybe not, but I'm not real impressed with your hospitality at the moment. One of your Mau, a cat named Pshaw-Ra, brought us here and said that you all loved cats—worshipped, was what he said, actually—and would help keep ours safe until we could work things out back where we came from. But he disappeared and nobody else has showed up to help us, so Chester and I figured, being near a river and all, we'd catch some fresh fish to supplement the little bit of food we were able to bring with us."

"Why were you not better prepared?" the girl asked. Like Jubal and Sosi, she was little more than a kitten, with wide dark eyes and a wild curly black coat of head fur, her skin two shades darker than the coat of the thieving cat eating my fish.

"We—uh—we had to leave in a hurry, before we could provision ourselves properly. And the extra cats were what you might say emergency passengers who came with nothing but the fur they were wearing. I used to fish back home but I guess Chester just figured it out because he was hungry."

I growled to reinforce his argument, but it was futile. My fish was down to skeleton and the other cat was making small growling noises as she gobbled up the last bits.

"Renpet is hungry too. She does not fish. I do not fish. Offerings had always been made to sustain her before our banishment."

"Banishment? What for? Did she get busted for stealing some other cat's fish?"

"Certainly not! Renpet is a princess among the divine ones, progeny of the queen herself."

"All kittens come from queens," Jubal told her. "That's just what you call a mama cat."

"Queen Tefnut is—was—ruler of the divine ones," the girl said stiffly.

Renpet, full of my fish, turned back to face us and began washing herself. *Ummm,* she purred. *That was luscious. Got any more?*

I had relaxed a little under Jubal's touch but now I narrowed my eyes, flattened my ears, and swore at her. The girl took a step so that she stood over the cheeky beast, one foot on either side of her while the fish thief licked her haunch, pausing once to look up at me and make sure I was watching.

I wasn't really mad anymore. No use fighting over stripped fish. But I did want to catch more and Jubal had yet to catch any. I reminded him of this.

He took another look at the girl. By his reckoning she was on the thin and ragged side. "What was that about being banished? If your cat is royalty, how come you're out here?"

"I fled to save her from certain death," the girl said. "When the queen died, Renpet's litter sister Nefure declared herself queen and drove Renpet from the temple."

"You look hungry. How about you tell us what happened while I try to catch another fish for you. Have you got enough pull with Renpet to get her to lay off anything else Chester might catch?"

"Renpet does what she will," the girl replied with a lift of her chin.

Renpet rubbed against her ankle and purred.

"Cats are like that," Jubal agreed.

Keeping to the shade as much as possible, for by now it was stiflingly hot, especially for someone as well endowed with fur as I am, who had just been in a strenuous battle, we resumed our fishing posture. Jubal cast his line and I watched—first the water, then Renpet, who appeared to doze, though I *saw* her eye open a slit to spy on me. Turning my tail to her, I dipped my paw into the water as before. As before, a fish swam up to see if my cat's paw was tasty or not and I snagged it and flipped it up on the bank.

And—I couldn't believe this, after all the peacemaking my boy was trying to do—that rotten Renpet pounced my fish again.

"Hey, you had one!" I yowled, and she pounced me! She wasn't fast enough this time—I sprang backward and into the river.

"Chester!" Jubal cried as I went under, and waded in after me. The water wasn't all that deep at this spot, for a human.

He didn't have to worry. I surfaced again without effort. It seemed I was naturally buoyant. My fur was wet but it did not soak up so much water as to weigh me down. I *liked* this. Though it wasn't any cooler than cat pee, it smelled better and cooled me off.

Fishing was easier in the water. I could chase a fish and bite it and drag it up with me. The first time I did this, I didn't know what to do with the fish, but Jubal swam up beside me and cupped the fish in a bag he made from the bottom of his sheet.

I had to swim away from him to catch them, and then swim back. The fish weren't afraid of me, more fool them, but Jubal cast a longer shadow.

When I'd caught three or four, Jubal took them back to shore and gave two to the girl, trapping the others in a netted bag he extracted from the knapsack and sinking it with a rock. "Why don't you cook these up for us and we'll have fish for breakfast?" he suggested.

Nice of you to give our fish away, I said. *Especially since I, who have caught all of them, have yet to do more than taste one!*

Yeah, but you know how to get more. I don't think that fool girl even knows how to cook them. Look there, she's just staring at them like she's starving but doesn't quite want to eat them raw!

I have no interest in the female human or her wretched female cat, I told him.

Awww, Chester. They're hungry.

Not that cat. She ate my first ever fishy I caught, I said. *And she pushed me in the water.*

I think that might mean she likes you, Jubal said. *Dad said girls get ornery when they like you.*

Why shouldn't she like me? I replied. *I'm a source of delicious fish for her!* I grabbed another of the slippery little devils.

As long as I was in the water, I was fairly cool, but when I looked around at Jubal, the parts of him not covered by his sheet or his hat were red. The sun was two whiskers away from the middle of the sky.

Jubal waded back to his submerged fish trap and the place where we left Renpet, the thieving "princess" cat, and her girl. They were gone.

I suppose they took the rest of our fish, I said, cat-paddling back to shore.

No, no, the fish are still here. I'm not sure that girl knew what to do with the ones I gave her, and two fish for that cat must have been plenty, no matter how hungry she was.

Good, I said, and hunkered down to growl over my last catch, covering it with my body lest any passing feline royalty swoop down and snatch it.

While I gobbled it up—the most delicious meal I had ever had including the tasty keka bugs or the mice in Jubal's barn when I was a young kitten—Jubal cleaned and filleted our fish and tucked them into a thermal pack in his bag.

Then we returned to the ship. I was almost comfortable for about a quarter of the trip and trotted ahead of Jubal until the sun evaporated all the water in my fur and started broiling cat meat.

Then he tucked me under the sheet and on top of his very fishy smelling pack again. I slept. It was all I could do in the heat. I wasn't sure if I would wake up or not and I was too miserable to care.

CHAPTER 4

The heat was so intense Jubal was sure the fish must be already cooked by the time he carried them into the ship. There wasn't enough for all the cats to have much, but if he chopped it up and divided it, everyone could have a taste and maybe some of the others would go fishing with them the next time. He intended to speak to Captain Loloma about the girl and her cat—maybe they could join the *Ranzo*'s crew. They didn't seem to be welcome here anymore.

He was certainly welcome on the *Ranzo*, however. The minute he stepped through the hatch, he was surrounded by, almost engulfed by, cats tangling themselves in his flapping sheet and under his feet. Chester, still exhausted from his swim, slept through the chorus of hungry cat noises, chirrups, mews, meows, short yowls, rumbly purrs, and hungry growls, but Jubal was in no doubt about their meaning.

A cat leaped up onto his shoulder and others immediately tried to climb him. Claws dug into him and *he* yowled. Chester woke up and looked straight into the face of the cat on Jubal's shoulder, none other than his milk brother Bat. "Back off!" Chester hissed.

"Cranky, aren't we?" Bat asked.

Jubal tried to bend over without losing Chester or the fish and smack the paws off his legs, but the cats acted as if they hadn't eaten in months. "Help!" he yelled.

Human help was already on the way. Beulah, Captain Loloma, and Sosi were calling the unheeding cats, and when they were close enough, began dragging cats off Jubal, whose legs and arms were bleeding freely now.

"What's wrong with them? Have they gone nuts?" the captain asked, and Jubal laughed.

"It's the fish in my pack. They want it, and they can have it but we gotta divide it up first. Take my pack and run. They'll follow you."

Sosi reached for the net. "The kitties won't hurt me."

Her father grabbed it instead. "I'm taller," he said simply, and broke into a run.

The cats abandoned Jubal and bounded after the captain. He ran pretty fast for an old guy, and of course he hadn't been in the sun all day long either so he raced the cats to the galley and slammed the hatch in their whiskery faces.

Die-hards scratched at the door and yowled their protests, but others among them, whose bellies were after all still filled with kibble, sat down and washed or wandered a few feet away.

The hopeful few who tried to linger near Jubal, still smelling the remnants of the fish on him, were warned off by Chester. In the infirmary, the medical specialist cleaned and medicated his scratches and applied a couple of strategic bandages.

"Better wash and change clothes," Beulah suggested when he'd been treated. "Get rid of the fish smell. But Jubal—go easy on the water."

Jubal nodded. He had some experience with that when the well back on the farm went dry a few times. He could take a bath in half a cup of water, but here he had disinfectant soap to use as well.

Chester had no faith in the soap or the medic and kept trying to wash Jubal's scratches cat-fashion, with his rough tongue, and asking if the boy was okay, was he really okay? Even though the cat could tell what Jubal was thinking and feeling, he followed him anxiously, mewing aloud and inwardly asking what hurt, where it hurt, who had made this or that particular scratch.

"It's okay, Chester," Jubal said aloud, finishing his washing and changing into his shipsuit again, but when he turned around, Chester wasn't there anymore.

Silly boy, I'm with my fish, Chester said, and through his eyes Jubal saw the interior of the mess cabin.

The ship's cook—a rail-thin man named, appropriately enough, Cook—chopped fish at a small table while Sosi put it onto plates. A mass of quivering fur waited with what seemed to be amazing patience, until Jubal realized that Chessie, Bat, and Sol were facing them down. Chessie's ears were flat and she was flipping her tail in an angry way. Bat and Sol were each twice their regular size, showing their teeth and growling menacingly. Chester was under the table, gulping gobbets of fish as fast as he could.

CHESTER: ROYAL WELCOMING COMMITTEE

I finished gobbling my last bite and sat back to watch the fun and lick my whiskers. Jubal had come in and was watching with his mouth wide open. I walked over to him and twined around his ankles, making him flinch a little.

"Nyow? Nyow?" the crowd asked.

The cook finished cutting, and the girl set dishes in front of Mom, Bat, and Sol. I strolled casually in front of them and sat down, spreading my paw so my claws popped out in full array. I licked my pads and glared over my arsenal at my former cellmates.

The humans, including Jubal, quickly began setting down plates for the others.

The fish disappeared as if the morsels had been teleported to some distant planet, and the humans disposed of the plates while we cats, happy with the world and each other once more now that our appetites had been satisfied, stretched out or cuddled up for naps.

Wake up, Jubal said. *Pshaw-Ra must be back.*

Sure enough, outside the ship, bells tinkled, chimes chimed, rattles rattled, and drums thumped, accompanying the laughter and singing of human voices mingled with occasional feline remarks. The noise blew toward the ship on a cat-mint-scented breeze.

A number of long white-shaded pallets borne by bronze-colored, sweaty humans barely clad in scanty white garments snaked through the desert. On each pallet sat, reclined, or stood many more cats. As they drew nearer I saw that some were tawny like Pshaw-Ra, others were black, and still others had wild looking dark spots on pale tan fur.

An unmistakable tawny form lounged at the front of the foremost pallet. As soon as it had been borne close enough to the tent, the cat leaped down and bounded toward me, heedless of the heat.

"Your transportation awaits you," Pshaw-Ra told me. "You may summon the others."

"I expected something more airborne," I told him.

"Why waste expensive resources when the manpower is so pathetically grateful to serve?" he asked. "Now then, darkness will fall before we reach the city again if we don't commence."

I turned to call the others but they were already emerging from the tent, investigating the commotion.

"Pshaw-Ra is here with an escort to his city," I explained.

Mother took one look and backed off, saying, "I prefer to stay with the ship. How will Kibble know where to find me if I go wandering off dirtside with strange short-hairs?" Mother wasn't bonded to her lifelong Cat Person, Janina Mauer, in the same way Jubal and I were bonded via the keka bugs, but she was devoted to her nonetheless. She didn't seem to grasp that Janina would not be able to find us here. I conveyed this too, but Mother just said, "I'm staying where I'm staying and that's the end of it."

"Oh no," Pshaw-Ra told her. "As Chester's mother, you have a place of honor among us. And I have arranged hospitality in private homes for each and every one of you. Messages to your ship can be relayed to our communications center, and I assure you, madame, you will be alerted immediately if any come for you. Your crew must also join the procession, though of course they'll have to walk. But we will not insist that they relieve the bearers this time."

The rest of the group drew nearer and we were scrutinized by many pairs of copper and peridot eyes.

From the middle pallet sounded an imperious meow, and a bearer stepped forward and reverently lifted a tawny beauty whose coat matched Pshaw-Ra's but whose form was more finely made and whose bearing, if possible, was more arrogant. Around her neck was what at first appeared to be a broad flat collar of turquoise, red, and blue stones but proved to be some sort of coloring process applied to her fur. A multicolored tiara was painted onto the fur of her head, dipping under her ears. She regarded us with a slit-eyed look that did not bode well for future relations. So: Renpet's sister, the self-appointed queen, had joined us.

"You call those cats?" the queen demanded of Pshaw-Ra, her voice expressed in a low hiss. "They look like bears. Those hairy ears and huge hot coats with fur sticking out everywhere. And the size of their paws!" She gave a little shudder. "You have exceeded your authority bringing such inferior beasts among us."

"Majesty, they grow on you," he answered in a calming purr. More loudly he said, "They are refugees from the corrupt system that stripped our planet of many of our ancestors and the servant class." Lowering his tone again. "And remember what I told you about my plan."

"Oh, very well."

And she turned away from us, her tail high over her sleek-furred rump, and permitted her bearer to return her to her pallet.

"That's some female," Bat said. "Who is she?"

"That is my queen, Nefure," Pshaw-Ra said.

"Your mate?" I asked.

"My daughter," he replied, giving his shoulder a self-satisfied lick.

"So by queen you mean she's the boss of you?" Bat asked.

"Just climb onto the nice pallet, kittycat, and don't ask impertinent questions," Pshaw-Ra told him. "Chester, you too. Quickly. It is too hot for you here. Refreshments await us in the city."

The people carrying the pallets looked hot and uncomfortable, but smiled and waved to the crew to join them.

Captain Loloma walked up to the most important looking man and inclined his head in greeting. "We're very glad to see you. We seem to be stranded. One of your—well, one of your cats led us here but we are about out of fuel and hope you can help us. We don't actually have enough for the life-support systems to function for long, but if we can work out a deal, we will refuel and be on our way as soon as possible." Jubal noted that the captain said nothing about them being on the lam.

The man smiled broadly, and a woman stepped forward and inclined her head as the captain had. "We welcome you and the wondrous creatures you bring in such quantity. Never had we dared hope for so many. We have arranged accommodations for each of them and each of you, where your every need will be provided. You must not stay aboard your ship. It would be unbearable during the day, whereas our dwellings are well equipped for Mau's climate. Please, be our guests."

The captain looked around as if for transport. "Uh, you walked?"

"Yes, it is warm but it is only a short distance. The sacred ones of course must ride, but it is tradition that we walk."

"We should help you load the cats," he suggested, though to Jubal he sounded extremely unsure how that was going to happen.

"It is not necessary. They arrange themselves," she replied. And indeed, with a little prodding from Pshaw-Ra and Chester, the Barque Cats each found a pallet. To Jubal's surprise, there was no squabbling, hissing, spitting, or fluffed fur, mostly because the native cats were almost uncatly in their gracious welcomes, offering grooming and nose kisses, and showing their guests to the dishes of water and food set into the pallets for their use. Women, sweating themselves, wielded feathered fans to keep the cats cool.

The young mother cat, Flekica, and her seven-week-old kittens rode on a pallet with several other females who seemed to admire the kittens. The humans carrying that pallet spoke soothingly to the mother cat.

The captain signaled to the rest of the crew to fall in behind him, then assigned them each a position and told them to make friends. "We need their help," he said. "You've got your marching orders. Go!"

Sosi and Hadley stayed with him and the first man he had addressed, who accompanied a pallet of six cats, two spotted like leopards, two tawny like Pshaw-Ra, and two black. Space Jockey rode with the queen, Jubal noted, and Chessie, Bat, and Sol rode with Pshaw-Ra and a group of four or five native cats. A boy about Jubal's own age waited beside the pallet.

Jubal decided he wanted to meet the boy and went to greet him. Chester jumped onto the pallet, accepted a grooming from his mother, had a drink, and lay down to rest.

"I am Edfu, keeper of Bahiti," said the boy who accompanied the pallet, gesturing to a large and rather wild looking spotted cat, who used the boy's gesturing hand to rub against his ears in an affectionate way. Edfu's Standard was heavily accented but understandable. "Welcome. We have long waited for the Grand Vizier's return, but little did we imagine he would bring with him such bounty—so many beautiful new cats!"

"We didn't have much choice," Jubal told him. "There was sort of a—misunderstanding with the government."

"Your government does not like cats? Or are these cats perhaps exiled members of a larger royal family?" Edfu's voice dropped when he asked the last question.

"No, no, nothing like that. Our cats don't have a royal family—neither do the people, actually—but these are very special cats just the same."

"So have we heard! It is said that the Grand Vizier told the queen that each cat among them has extra toes and that they hunt among the stars!" Said by whom? Jubal wondered, but then he realized that the kind of bond he had with Chester was commonplace here, where cats and humans routinely shared communication. If the cats wanted to, of course.

"Well, a lot of them have extra toes. My kitten Chester does. This is him, here." He reached over and scratched Chester's ears and was given a brief *prrt* for his trouble. "But not all of them. They are all good hunters, though, and all of them come from ships where they were sort of security and morale officers, I guess you could say. It's what their ancestors have been doing for a long time. Chester's supposed to look like the very first Barque Cat of all, his own many times great-granddad Tuxedo Thomas."

"Ahhh! So these cats help you to hunt?"

"No, they do the hunting," he said. "Don't yours?"

Edfu looked a bit puzzled. "It's much too dangerous."

Jubal thought that was pretty odd but it would be rude to say so, and besides, he was tired and hot, and to his surprise, Edfu seemed to be too. Beulah offered her sunscreen to the woman she walked beside and rubbed some on Sosi. The woman was fanning the pallet full of cats just as another woman was fanning Bahiti, Chester, Pshaw-Ra, and the others on that pallet.

"Is it always this hot?" he asked Edfu.

"Yes," Edfu said.

"How do you stand it?"

"Our houses and the temple are cool. Our work is done under the city."

"Do kids work too?"

"There are not many. I tend to Bahiti and that is my work. That is my mother, Eshe, wielding the fan."

"Is fan wielding a part-time job or what she does for a living, besides being your mom, I mean?"

Edfu gave him quizzical look. "Part-time? Living? Oh! Oh no. My mother is an engineer who designs and maintains the underground structures." When he saw Jubal still watching the fan going up and down, he said, "What she does—what we all do at this time is strictly ceremonial. We seldom stray far from the city."

"How about your dad? What's he do?"

"He is a medical assistant," Edfu said. "That's him at the front of the pallet, on the right side." He pointed to one of the bearers. His father was dripping sweat and panting. They were climbing a tall dune now and it was slippery.

"If this is the welcoming ceremony, it's a good thing you don't get visitors more often," Jubal said, starting to pant a little himself. "I thought you might send flitters for us."

Edfu looked a little confused, but before Jubal could explain, the other boy pointed. "Behold, Bubastis!"

Spread out below them was a city shaped differently than any Jubal had seen before. In its center was a tall stepped pyramid—ziggurat, he thought they were called—and around it was a road with houses lining the far side. But then there were more circles of houses attached to the central circle, like the petals of a flower, and in the center of each of these was another pyramid structure—Jubal thought they might be pyramid ships similar to Pshaw-Ra's.

Bahiti *mrowled* up at Edfu. In turn the boy told Jubal, "We go first to the temple so that each of your passengers may meet a host family. This is a great honor for us."

As they proceded through the city, they were met along the roads by people banging on things like drums or cymbals, rattling can openers, and sending wind chimes swinging. With each house they passed, the occupants fell in behind them and followed them to the temple.

CHAPTER 5

CHESTER IN THE TEMPLE OF MAU

We entered the temple, a comparatively cool shadowy place dominated by the fangy openmouthed face of a huge golden cat statue. The queen and two of her feline attendants were already installed between the statue's ears, presiding over the welcome. Well, presiding after a fashion. The two attendants sat beside her with paws crossed and faces impassive. The queen, evidently fatigued from her earlier exertions, lay splayed on her tummy, paws curved down onto the forehead of the golden cat, head cradled against one leg.

"Come with me, catling," Pshaw-Ra said. "Your assistance is required to get our guests housed. It will perhaps expedite matters if you inform them that more food and water awaits each of them in the new quarters, as well as two-legged servants who will devote themselves to the happiness of each cat."

"I'll tell them, but some of them aren't going to want to be split up," I said. "And I hope you're not thinking of trying to keep Jubal and I apart."

"Perish the thought!" Pshaw-Ra said with mock horror. "In fact, I am housing you in my old home, where I used to live with my senior servant before my journey."

"Where will you stay?" I asked him.

"Oh, I will be nearby. But for now, we will place the others. Of course, the humans think they are making the choices, but I have some very specific ideas regarding who I want to stay with whom."

That surprised me. Pshaw-Ra usually didn't concern himself with the comfort or welfare of others.

"The girlchild, her father, and her old tom will be lodged with Heket and her family. Heket is a physician and is out a great deal, taking her assistant with her, so they will have privacy."

"Heket is a vet?"

"Heket is a feline physician. We have several such. The humans may assist with tasks requiring thumbs, but who better than a cat would know how to tend the needs of a fellow feline?"

Jubal caught that. *Wow, a cat cat doctor! That's great.*

Pshaw-Ra ignored him. After all, *he* was the cat pilot of a space vessel. "Your mother will stay with Bahiti and his family. He is also a physician. Your boy seems to have made friends with his boy and their lodging is next to yours, so you may easily visit your mother. From what you have said, she is the sort of cat who may be able to learn something from observing Bahiti's skill.

"There are, I believe, two pregnant females among the ranks," Pshaw-Ra continued. "They will be staying with Bes, the top cat physician, so he may be within paw's reach when they are ready to deliver."

Wait a minute, Jubal said, having heard all of these arrangements through me. *I've heard that strange toms will kill kittens.*

I passed this along to Pshaw-Ra, who said, "Ah, but Bes is, as male physicians always are, a eunuch. It is not a profession that runs in families."

Jubal was not entirely reassured, probably because he didn't trust Pshaw-Ra. Neither did I. I found his sudden interest in the pregnancy of the two females especially suspicious; I hadn't even known about the coming kits. But perhaps the native cats who rode on the pallets with them had passed the information to him.

"The young ginger mother and her kittens will stay with the woman Mesi and her lamentably catless family, who dwell in the circle nearest the temple entrance. It will be such a blessing for them to have kittens in their midst."

He went on and on, sometimes putting Barque Cats with native cats, sometimes in catless homes with humans he said would feel honored to finally have a sacred feline, even one of an inferior species, gracing their home.

Jubal and I took our fellow refugees to meet each host. The human hosts promptly carried our cats off to their homes. I expected a certain amount of protest from the cats whose abodes were being invaded, but Pshaw-Ra told me he had picked each home specifically because of the hospitable nature of the resident feline deity. Again I was surprised he had been able to see beyond the end of his own whiskers long enough to figure out who had hospitable natures and who didn't.

My sire Space Jockey was invited to stay with the queen. Better him than me.

The communications officer, Beulah; the second mate, Felicia Daily; and the medic, Guillame Pinot, were assigned quarters at the edge of town with three different catless families so as not to burden any one family unduly, Pshaw-Ra explained.

"*Divide and conquer?*" Jubal muttered under his breath when I transmitted the last instructions to him.

Pshaw-Ra, who had been prancing, tail curled high over his back, to and fro, from cat to human and back to another cat again to indicate his choices to us, finally relaxed and sat down to wash his feet.

Most of the Barque Cats and a lot of the native cats and people still milled around the temple. "What about the rest of them?"

Pshaw-Ra kept washing. "What of them? I have made the special assignments. Everyone else can pick up a guest and go home. I suggest we do the same."

———

By the time they left the temple, the outside was as dim as the inside had been. Pshaw-Ra did not leave with them, Jubal was somewhat relieved to find, but the round man the captain had first approached led them to the house where they'd been assigned. He stood outside the door opening, which was covered with a beaded curtain, and gestured that they should go inside. "Thanks," Jubal said.

"It is nothing. Make yourselves comfortable. This house is for you," he said, looking at Chester. Soft lights bloomed from unseen sources as he entered. The little house was wonderfully cool and its furnishings pretty simple—a bed, a chair and table, a little round bed on a sisal-covered pedestal, and four blue pottery bowls, two on the table holding what seemed to be dried fish and fruit, and two on the floor, one that held dried fish, the other water. There were also a few storage baskets and bowls lining the wall.

A small enclosure held a fairly conventional toilet and sink and a box of sand.

There was a real door as well, and Jubal closed it. The beaded curtain appeared to act as a kind of screen door.

Toys! Chester cried delightedly, and began scrabbling through a basket until he dumped it onto the floor. Balls and wiggly things spilled out. Around the top of the room was a long shelf. Chester hopped onto the cat bed and from there leaped to the shelf and peered down, chin resting on paws, at Jubal. He rubbed his face against the ceiling, both marking it and pushing at the boundary. *I smell air*, he said.

With a nudge of his nose, he opened a hole in the ceiling and slipped through it. He stood with his front paws on the roof, his back paws still on the ledge. His tail flicked back and forth as he looked. *There's one of those ship things on the side. Looks like all of these houses have a personal pyramid ship, like a smaller version of Pshaw-Ra's, in the yard. And there's the temple over there.*

He drew himself back inside and began washing his white paws, which were now a dusty tan. His chest, only a little whiter, was next.

Jubal yawned. The excitement had worn off. *You go ahead and take a bath. You've had a few dozen naps today but I'm getting tired. We had an early morning. I'm turning in.*

Chester looked down. *You're right. I'm not tired. I'm going to check out the places Pshaw-Ra sent our friends and make sure everyone is comfy.* And he disappeared through the ceiling flap.

Jubal turned on his side, away from the door.

A few minutes later he was awakened by a yowl and a cat's scream. He sat up. *Chester?*

Janina Mauer, former Cat Person to Thomas's Duchess aboard the *Molly Daise*, had felt like cheering when the ships carrying the fugitive Barque Cats, including her Chessie, blinked out of sight and out of reach of the pursuing Galactic Government attracker vessels. She'd felt like cheering again when the council ruled that the epidemic had in fact been caused by premature panic among the overly cautious and that all of the animals that survived their quarantine in good health would be allowed to return home.

Then the loneliness set in. Chessie would not return home— maybe not ever. Would the *Ranzo*, the ship of her rescuers, stop running long enough to discover that it was safe to bring back the cats? Would they fear prosecution for the illegal nature of their rescue mission and just stay hidden? That would be terrible. Without Chessie she felt incomplete. To her surprise, the new closeness she shared with the young veterinarian, Dr. Jared Vlast, was no substitute. In fact, it was difficult to enjoy at all when she always felt there was something missing—the part of her that Chessie had filled for most of her life.

Jared was kind and caring about the animals, but he didn't quite understand what the loss of a cat meant to a Cat Person. And it wasn't *only* Chessie—she missed the *Molly Daise*, her home for so many years, and the crew who had been her family. Hers and

Chessie's. She had lived with them since the age of ten when she first came aboard to care for her special kitten.

It didn't help Jared or her either that they were right when they exposed—or caused the authorities to expose—the recent epidemic as a hoax. Quite the opposite, in fact. While the council admitted to each other and even to their accusers that mistakes had been made and wrong had been done, they did not quite come clean publicly. To do so, Jared told her, would have cost the government far too much money in reparations to farmers whose livelihoods had been destroyed, not to mention everyone else whose valuable and loved animals had not survived the council's little "oops" moment.

Jared was allowed to return to Sherwood Station, but at first there was little work for him there, since many of the animals he would normally have screened or treated had been destroyed.

Janina, shipless and catless, found work at the same station with a maintenance crew. Since she was needed only part-time, she was sometimes free to accompany Jared when he flew down to the planet's surface. This had been the case when he was called to leave the space station for George Varley's ranch. The trouble had actually started there, through no fault of the rancher or his animals.

Nevertheless, they had suffered for the greed and foolishness of others.

Mr. Varley's extensive herds were no more. The relief vets who replaced Jared when he was sent to Galipolis had disposed of all but a few of the beautiful horses, condemning them for the glitter in their secretions, which was nothing more than a by-product of the shiny beetles they'd ingested.

Now, Varley came out to meet them when they arrived. His step was as vigorous as ever but there was a hardness in his face Janina hadn't noticed before.

"Glad you're back, Doc," he said, and nodded to Janina. She

wasn't sure he actually knew her name, but he did not seem to mind her presence. "Those butchers who replaced you ruined my spread."

Jared just shook his head. "Are the horses you want me to check in the barn?"

"Yeah, and believe it or not, they're more of the ones that started this whole mess. They must have hid themselves someplace until the search and destroy parties were gone. Doc, they have the fairy-dust slobber and manure but they're healthy as—well, horses."

Jared nodded, carefully not saying anything to agree or disagree with Varley. What could he say, after all?

"So were the others, of course," Varley said bitterly. "But they're gone now—my breeding stock, my daughter's pony, the caretaker's dog Rollie, my Roary and Rowan . . ."

Janina felt tears stinging her eyes and looked away. Jared had told her before that in vet work a soft heart sometimes could be a liability. Hers felt like it was breaking all over again. Those horses and dogs had been so beautiful, so full of life. But they were just *things* to the government. People had the glittery secretions too, she knew, but nobody had suggested murdering humans. Come to think of it, nobody had suggested hospitalizing even a single two-legged person for so much as observation.

"How will you survive?" she asked Varley, although she hadn't intended to speak.

"Oh. I'll get by, young lady. I can sell off some acreage if push comes to shove. But I have other resources and I intend to use them to bring down the criminal idiots who allowed this to hap-pen. I never wanted to use my family's money, never wanted to go into politics. But I am going to now, and all I'll say is there are some bozos in Galipolis who will be real sorry they drove me to it."

The grounds and buildings were as neat as they had been before all the trouble started, but they looked bare without the dogs in the yard. No horses were pastured beside the pad where the trackers, flitters, and shuttles landed. The pasture grasses were tall, waving in the breeze.

As they entered the barn and her eyes adjusted to the dimmer light, Janina saw a pair of glittering eyes, low to the ground on the far side of the barn. A rat. A large one, watching them from beside one of the stalls. It seemed unafraid. Well, why not? None of the fat sleek barn cats that once prowled the premises were to be seen. The Galactic Government's efforts had succeeded in controlling only the domesticated animals—apparently not the wild rats and other vermin, left free to roam without predators to check them. The darn rat could thumb its nose at them if it had a thumb.

The broken-colored horses that now occupied the stalls in place of the beautiful thoroughbreds that had lived there before looked as if they felt out of place. They shook their manes, stamped and snorted, obviously restless, wanting to be elsewhere. Jared spoke to each one, checked its mouth, and moved on. Janina thought that all of the strange horses had been tagged when she and Jared last came to Varley's ranch, but apparently some of the beasts had hidden from them then. These horses were not tagged.

The blaze-faced black and white Jared had just finished checking suddenly screamed, reared, and shot out of the barn at a gallop.

"What got into him?" Varley asked. He had been in the entrance when the horse bolted, and was lucky he wasn't trampled.

Janina pointed to some red dots on bits of straw. "He's bleeding!"

"I just checked—" Jared began. A rustling noise came from the back of the stall.

"I'll bet that rat bit him," Janina said.

"That's not very likely," Varley told her. "There's plenty of grain and that sort of thing for the rats to feed on. They've never gone after the stock before."

But even as he spoke, three large rodent forms darted across the open door at the other end of the stable.

"Of course not. They were afraid of the cats, I'm sure."

"We're short on those since the government stepped in," Varley said. "I'll have to put out traps or poison, I guess."

That was only the first instance they saw of the growing problem with the vermin. Soon, Jared was being called upon to treat bites and infections on what seemed like every remaining farm, ranch, and town on the planet.

Back on Sherwood Station, a familiar figure made an informal visit to the clinic. "Captain Vesey!" Janina said, delighted to see her former boss. His eyes warmed when he saw her but he didn't look happy. "What brings you here?"

"I was hoping you might be willing to help me find another cat. You could have your job back."

"Captain, the Barque Cats—"

"It doesn't have to be a Barque Cat. I just need a cat to catch mice and bugs. We're overrun with them. They're somehow getting into sealed cargo containers and have even bitten crew members. Dr. Vlast, I don't suppose you could recommend a good poison that kills rats without getting into the ventilation system and doing in the entire crew?"

"I am in the business of healing animals, not killing them, not unless absolutely necessary," Jared said stiffly.

"Of course, of course. I just thought you might know . . . how about it, though, Kibble? Any barn cats had litters lately that you know about?"

"Sir, the barn cats were also caught in the epidemic scare."

"Yes," Jared told him. "And because nobody set a high monetary value on them, they were disposed of much more casually."

"We should unload all the rats into the council chambers on Galipolis," Captain Vesey said bitterly. "Dammit, I miss Chessie. I even miss that rotten kitten of hers."

CHESTER: EXPLORING BUBASTIS

Oh this was fun! Over the rooftops and through the town, looking down on the streets below and peeping into the houses through the little cat flaps they all had in the tops.

I left my boy sleeping, but it began to look like ours was the only quiet house in the whole city.

The night was much cooler than the day had been, and a breeze carried the fishy smell from the river. It blew right up my tail and seemed to penetrate my whole body, enlivening me to the tips of my whiskers. They vibrated with the excitement of exploration. No ship, no cage, not even my boy to restrain me. I was a free wild cat stalking his new domain. I tried roaring but it came out as a yowl.

Another yowl answered, I thought, but then realized the remark hadn't been addressed to me.

Chester? Jubal's sleepy inquiry sounded alarmed.

No fight, just high spirits. Sleep!

Poor boy, he worried about me. But what he didn't realize was that though he remained a human child, while we had been separated, I almost became a full-grown cat. I could look after myself now.

And interesting things were happening in the streets below. I saw the rather ugly black cat Pshaw-Ra had called Bes, the feline physician, scratching on a door two down from the one behind which Jubal slept. I backtracked to sit on the roof of that house. The human inside opened the door and murmured something respectful to Bes. Behind the cat was his human assistant, carrying a little basket full of tiny wrapped packages. I sniffed the air to see if I could pick up the scent. Catnip? No. Something much different. Muskier. What was it?

I trotted back to the upper cat flap, similar to the one I'd used to exit our lodgings, and pushed it in enough to see into the room below. Bes rubbed noses with a cloud-gray female who had arrived on the *Ranzo* and sniffed her tail. She reciprocated. They were establishing rapport in the way of our species.

"Pshaw-Ra told us the tale of the awful treatment you endured at the hands of those you trusted," he said soothingly. "I have brought a little treat for you that will undo any exposure you may have had to disease or illness there, and also calm you so you can sleep well and begin adjusting to this, your new home."

The human assistant folded the contents of the packet into a gobbet of fish and offered it to her by setting it before her. "Please partake," Bes invited, and with a little trill, she did.

Bes and his assistant departed and the physician scratched on the next door. If they were going to visit each of us, they had a long night ahead of them. Boring!

Jumping from one roof to the next and the next and the next, I was sure I'd left them behind, and had paused to survey the situation below me when I heard, quite nearby, another scratching. This time, though, in addition to the physician's greeting, I heard a familiar voice—my mother's.

Once more I peered down through the roof flap. The old chap Bahiti, his boy, Edfu, and my mother were entering. A gray and white Barque Cat sat up from his nap. "Hello, Skitz," Mother said, as Bahiti and Edfu consulted with the resident humans. "We just came to check on you. I am staying with this cat Bahiti. Isn't it amazing? They don't have vets here! They have cats who take care of other cats when they're sick or might get sick. Bahiti brought you a treat that will counteract any bad things you might have picked up in that awful lab. It's delicious too." She ran her tongue around her teeth for emphasis.

Trust Mother to have a job an hour and a half after she arrived! She was a great one for making herself useful.

I thought about popping in to surprise her, then decided against it. I wasn't ready yet to give up being the Night Stalker Who Pads on Invisible Paws Through the Darkness.

As I leaped from roof to roof, toward the outskirts of town, I saw the two other cat physicians, first Heket, then Hathor, doing the same thing as Bes and Bahiti.

Much as I enjoyed exploring, I didn't want to miss out on a treat, so I turned around and roof-hopped back to the house where my boy slept.

It was noisier on the way back. From the inside of the houses came the strangest cries: moaning yowling, singing. Peeking through one roof flap, I made sure that no cats were being hurt. On the contrary, the resident cat, a spotted fellow, and Ti-Min from the *Ontario*, before he was incarcerated in the lab in Galipolis with the others, were becoming very friendly indeed. Assured that all was well, I popped back into our new house and hopped onto the bed where Jubal lay.

Miss me? I asked.

Yeah, Jubal replied sleepily, raising his arm to let me snuggle. *What's going on out there? Are the cats sick?*

No, just making friends. Where did you put my treat?

What treat?

The cat doctors brought us all treats.

Sorry, Chester, nobody came.

You should have got up when you heard them scratch at the door. It could have been me, you know.

I would have! Of course, I would have. He stroked me. *But nobody came.*

I was left out at treat time? After all my hard work? The management was going to hear about this!

CHAPTER 7

Three nights after the Barque Cats settled in the city, the first catastrophe happened. It was at night, and fortunately just after the feline physicians began making the rounds they had made both of the previous nights.

On the second night Jubal had been amused, as he watched through the beaded curtain, to see the cats scratching at the doors, as Chester had described it. The phrase "wandering mendicants" came to him from one of his old books. Chester pawed at him. *Why am I being left out? It's not fair!*

Keep your tail on. I'll ask Edfu. Maybe they just forgot where we are. You said he came with Bahiti last night. Let's go find them.

He rushed Chester past the house where Bes and his servant had entered to minister to the cats inside.

Two looped streets later they saw Bahiti, Chessie, and Edfu emerging from one of the houses. When the door had closed behind them, Jubal ran forward, waving. "Hey, Edfu, how's it going?"

"Going?" the other boy asked. "We are going from door to door, as you see, where Bahiti passes out these packets."

"Yeah, well, about that? Chester saw the packets being taken to the other cats and wondered why he didn't get one. I told him our house probably just got overlooked."

Edfu looked a little shifty, like his old man did, Jubal thought, when he was trying to think of a good excuse for doing a bad thing. "Yes, yes, that must be it."

"Can I have one for him now?"

"Oh, I am sorry but there are just enough doses—I mean, treats—in this basket for the cats we must see tonight. I'll tell you what, though. When we are done with rounds, I will ask Bahiti if we can make up another treat for your Chester and bring it to him." He gave both Jubal and Chester an inquiring look, and Bahiti purred something soothing to Chester.

Chessie gave her son a nose kiss. "Bahiti is not really assigned to your house and has been very busy, but I will remind him about your treat. You have grown into a very fine cat and should not be left out."

Chester purred and rubbed his head against his mother's cheek. "Thanks, Mother."

He jumped up onto Jubal's shoulder. *Let's go back to our house now. I want to be there when they bring my treat. I thought those were fish but now I wonder if they might not be ground-up keka bugs. It's funny. I haven't seen any keka bugs since we left the ships, have you?*

Jubal allowed as how he hadn't and agreed that it was kind of strange. *Maybe Pshaw-Ra exported all of them,* he suggested. *Didn't you say they're part of his plan for universal domination? He might have used them all up.*

He intended to ask Edfu about it when the other boy came by with Chester's treat, but Edfu didn't have time to talk then either, just handed him what seemed to be a gob of rolled-up fish and left. Neither Bahiti nor Chessie were with him.

Chester nibbled at the treat, then batted it around with his white stockinged paw. *It's just fish.*

You like fish.

Yes, but there should be some powder or something rolled up in it. I thought it might be powdered keka bugs. Whatever the others got, I don't think it was only fish.

Judging from the increase in wildly operatic cat song issuing from the neighboring houses, Jubal was inclined to agree. Maybe the other cats had been given some really good nip. In which case Chester's complaint was justified. He was the best and brightest cat there, Jubal felt sure. If the others got good nip, Chester should have it too, and he intended to ask the captain to see if he could— Well, what could he do, really? Maybe instead of asking the captain, he just needed to corner Edfu.

Mother will know, Chester said. *I will ask her when . . .* He yawned hugely, sprawled out on the middle of the bed and fell asleep.

Jubal had a harder time sleeping. He wished he had brought something to read. By the time Edfu had arrived, it was almost dawn again and nobody seemed to be around during the day. Eventually, he curled himself around Chester and slept fitfully.

He woke up a few hours later to a knock on the door. Opening it, he was almost knocked backward by the heat. In the doorway was a small woman holding two pots, one full of fishy smelling bits, the other covered. "Your meal," she said.

"Thanks," he told her. "I can cook a little if you'll tell me where to find supplies."

But he said much of it to her back. He shrugged, refilled Chester's dish, and set his own on the table. It was some sort of rice dish with dried fruit of undetermined origin. It was hot but bland. He looked down at Chester, whose head bobbed up and down as he snapped up his food.

Don't suppose you could spare me some of your fish?

What fish? Chester asked innocently, looking up from his empty dish.

What did he expect? Chester might be his best friend, but he was a cat and he liked fish a lot.

Chester jumped up on the table and watched while Jubal finished his meal. *Maybe we should go fishing again*, the cat suggested.

It's really hot out there. How do these people live in this place anyway?

Chester didn't answer. Having eaten, he was ready for another nap.

Jubal decided that as soon as it cooled off enough, he would ask the captain if he could go back to the ship and get stuff—food, something to read, his pocket unit for music, games, and data, including a number of his favorite books Beulah had let him download from the ship's computer. Somehow he had thought it would be more interesting when they got here. That they'd have adventures. The fishing trip was the most adventurous thing they'd done so far. But going back to the ship was a good idea. He'd bring their communicators too. How could these people have spaceships for cats but no coms?

He must have fallen asleep again because when he woke up, Chester was gone. He filled Chester's water dish, then he left the house. The evening air was much cooler, and he turned away from the temple, toward the edge of town where most of the crew was supposed to be.

Tonight several other cats were out, lounging on the roofs or in the bead-decked open doorways of the houses. As he passed they looked at him expectantly, and he realized they were waiting for the treat that had come the previous two nights.

As he turned into the next street, he saw Bahiti scratching on a door, with Chessie and Edfu looking on. He was about to say hello to them when he heard a noise behind him. Every cat he had seen outside quivered with attention and looked back toward the temple. Chester called him. *Jubal, help! She's losing her kittens!*

Who? he asked, running back toward their house. Edfu and Bahiti outstripped him, the basket bouncing on Edfu's arm as he ran. The two other cat doctors, Heket and Hathor, streaked past him too, their attendants hot on their heels.

Her name is Romina, she says. She wants her Cat Person, Gordon. Help is coming, Chester. All of the cat docs are on their way.

Bes is here now, Chester said. *But Romina misses her human. I think we should have the human vet look at her, Jubal.*

Where are you?

Looking through the roof flap. I was just about to drop in for a visit when she started crying. Hurry! The room is getting crowded but nobody seems to be doing much to help.

Maybe there's nothing to be done, but I'll get Pinot just the same. He took off running, and immediately began streaming sweat again. As he reached the last street between the desert and the city, he started calling. People stood outside their doors, watching.

"Medic!" he yelled. "Pinot?"

Felicia Daily, smoothing her hair back, came from one of the houses farther down the street. Pinot, zipping his shipsuit, appeared behind her in the doorway.

"What?" the medic asked.

"You ever helped birth kittens before?" Jubal asked, waving his arm for them to follow.

"No, but humans—"

"One of the pregnant cats is miscarrying."

"Poor little thing," he said.

"I'll come too," Felicia said. "Should I get the captain?"

"He's closer to the temple. Probably heard the hullabaloo and is there already. Come *on,*" Jubal said, though they were right behind him.

The cats who had arrived earlier seemed to have lost interest, but there were a few people outside Bes's house. All of the feline physicians were inside when Jubal, Daily, and Pinot arrived.

The feline physicians sat around the cat whose dead kittens lay at her feet. There were four, very tiny, looking more like mice than cats. The physicians bathed the mother while she licked the nearest dead kitten, patting it with her paw, as if trying to wake it up.

Jubal glanced up and saw Chester, wide-eyed, staring at him through the roof flap.

When he looked back, one of the cat doctors had pinned the little mother's head and shoulders with her paws and was licking her face while Bes picked up one kitten after another and flipped it away from her. His human assistant scooped the little corpses into a bag.

Pinot frowned at the assistant.

"Examination of the remains may help determine why the mother lost them," Bes's flunky explained.

Romina mewed up at Pinot, and he stepped forward to caress her and speak to her. Jubal squatted beside him, with Felicia on the other side.

The cat doctors and their humans quietly departed.

"What happened to her?" Jubal asked them. "She was doing so well on the ship."

"Stress maybe," Pinot said, feeling her sides and checking her for any residue from the births that might cause her to bleed. The cats had already taken care of the placenta. "She seems okay now, though. Could be something happened to her in the lab in Galipolis that had a delayed effect."

She looked so pitiful. She needed cleaning and comforting. Chessie slid under Jubal's knee, lay down beside the bereaved mother and began to wash her. Jubal wanted to stay with them and protect them, but Chester told him, *Mother is going to stay with them tonight. She will alert me if there's any more trouble and I'll tell you right away.*

With that reassurance, they left. By then the sky was dark and full of stars, the moons hovering over the dunes.

It was too late to return to the ship now.

He walked with Daily and Pinot to the quarters assigned to the captain and Sosi to report what had happened.

The house they were staying in was very similar to his and Chester's. People on Sherwood didn't live in houses that looked alike—there were individual differences outside as well as inside. Here they seemed to be as standard as ships' cabins. Was it because the houses were considered to belong to the cats? That didn't make sense when you considered that cats were a very original kind of creature—they were each different from the other. But maybe because they carried those differences around inside their own fur coats they didn't need to express them or have their humans express them in furnishings or possessions?

CHESTER: FROM BES'S ROOF

It was a good thing I stayed behind to watch over everyone. I started to drop down into the room, once my boy left with the rest of the humans and all of the native cats, but my mother froze me with a look. "No males," she told me.

"I was just going to help keep her warm," I said, wounded by the rejection. When my brothers and sisters and I were born, there was one last kitten who hadn't made it out, and Mother had bled terribly. I couldn't see it then, but I could smell it, and the smell I remembered was still in the room below, even though the mess had been cleaned.

"Just run along, son. This is female business," Mother told me firmly.

I was on the edge of the roof, getting ready to spring to the adjacent roof, when a noise called me back to the flap.

Ninina, the other pregnant cat, gave a low yowl. "Not you too!" Mother said.

"My belly hurts," Ninina complained. "There it goes again— Yow! I think my kittens are coming too and it's not time yet. Not nearly time."

Her sides heaved up and down, up and down.

Better come back and bring help, I told Jubal, who promised to hurry. But despite the humans' and the cat doctors' best efforts, repeating the whole scene that had played out with Romina, it wasn't like they could push the kittens back inside the mother and let them grow until they were ready.

I thought Pshaw-Ra might show up. After all, he wanted kittens. He'd said so.

Of course, he did get what he wanted, as usual, but that came somewhat later.

Jubal and some of the crew went back to the ship to scavenge later that evening. I stood guard over Mother, Romina, and Ninina until Bes and his assistant returned. The cat doctor gave the two miscarried females something to help them sleep. They needed it because, as usual after the doctors made their rounds, it got very noisy outside. Maybe they missed the music that was played on shipboard sometimes, because my fellow cats, Barque and Mau alike, were singing love songs embellished with a border world warble and wail.

With the Bes household back under his paw, I took off across the rooftops, determined to wait at the edge of the city for Jubal and the crew to return.

Two streets down from the temple I saw more kittens, these the seven-week-old offspring of Flekica, a ginger. Her white kit was being carried by its mother in the usual manner, the scruff of its neck between her teeth, but it was so large its paws dragged the street. She waddled along purposefully, her gait impeded by the big kitten body bumping against her front legs. Three other kittens, two gray and a tortoiseshell, bounced along behind their mother and hapless sibling. They were truly kittens, small and still wearing fuzz rather than fluffy fur. They didn't even have proper tails yet, not fine and long and fully coated like mine.

I had been afraid that, although I wanted to be treated like an adult cat, everyone still thought of me as a kitten. Nope, compared to these youngsters I was a handsome, mature male. I wasn't sure if that was a bad thing or a good thing in current circumstances. Good, I decided, considering what had been happening to kittens lately, and what Flekica seemed to fear might be about to happen to hers. Moving the litter was a sign a mother was trying to take her brood out of harm's way.

*F*lekica didn't see me, and I stifled an impulse to call out to her. I was tired of getting yelled at and I had a feeling that if I made her drop the kitten to greet me, that was exactly what would happen.

I watched, trying to figure out what the heck she was doing as she suddenly, if clumsily, darted inside the open door of a house, the kittens trailing behind her. None of them came out again. I peeked into the roof flap to see her assuming the feeding position while the kittens crowded in for dinner. Nobody else was in the house, and as far as I could tell it looked the same as all the other houses, but she seemed to like it better. There was just no telling what was on the minds of some cats.

I resumed my explorations and was sitting there on the roof of the farthest house from the temple when my boy and his shipmates came lumbering up over the dune and slid down the other side and into town.

When Jubal returned he brought the little time-wasting machine most of the crew had for long hauls, a com device to keep in touch with the others, some ration packets for himself and—oh, he was my very favorite boy in the entire universe—the last bag of fishy treats for me!

Wouldn't you know that as soon as I lay down with the packet between my front paws, Pshaw-Ra would decide to put in an appearance.

"Ah, catling, there you are. I see your human has returned. I thought he had deserted you."

"No, but I was hoping you had."

"Those smell good. And familiar."

"Mine," I said, pulling them to my chest.

"Catling, you wound me. I come to share with you the secrets of my civilization and you cannot be bothered to share a few morsels with me, your benefactor, teacher, sponsor . . ."

I wasn't going to go into that either. "I imagined you'd come about the loss of the two litters of kittens."

"Tragic, naturally, but those were not the important kittens."

"Their mothers thought they were important," I said, growling through the fishy treat I was savoring.

"No doubt. Come now. You don't want to eat all of those."

"That's exactly what I want." I reached my paw in to pull out another treat, but he snatched the bag away.

"They will make excellent appetizers before the feast," he said.

"What feast?"

"A reception feast for you to meet the queen and her court properly."

"We sort of did already," I said. Once was plenty, as far as I was concerned.

"Not everyone."

"Am I supposed to be honored that an important queen's-sire cat such as yourself has come to fetch me to this personally when no doubt we'd all be receiving a summons, or did you just know Jubal had brought me fishy treats?"

"Of course you are honored. You're also going to be doing the summoning. I want every cat and kitten from the ship to attend. And naturally I keep myself informed of the really important events around me, such as the arrival of these treats." He looked inside the package. "Which seem to be gone. Now, let us alert the others."

The eating part of the feast didn't take very long. We nibbled or gobbled, each according to his appetite or custom, and then looked around to see what would come next. Would mice or birds be loosed for us to chase for entertainment, or would some of the humans be called upon to dangle strings for us? Or maybe we were supposed to have a communal nap?

Instead, it turned out that we were each literally supposed to kiss the queen's—tail. That was the reception portion of the evening.

I stayed near Jubal and the crew, who were eating with the locals, but most of the other Barque Cats seemed perfectly happy to mingle with their hosts. Except for Romina and Ninina, my shipmates looked relatively sleek and contented. When the queen passed them and presented her tail, each of the cats good-naturedly gave it a lick when it was understood that was what she wanted. My sire, Space Jockey, gave the entire tail a long swipe with his tongue, and the queen's guards had to crowd him into backing off.

She was sashaying my way, Pshaw-Ra mentally instructing me to greet her. Her eyes were fixed on me and all I could do was wonder how long it had taken for her to get her fur painted with that crown and necklace, when she lurched sideways.

A great thump had rocked the entire hall, and I found myself sitting on my rump, my ears ringing.

"What the . . . ?" the captain said, but before he could finish his question or I could pose one to Pshaw-Ra—like, maybe they were shooting off fireworks somewhere to cap off the evening?—the queen's supple body flipped so that she was facing the great golden statue. In two bounds she had disappeared into the open jaws of the cat idol. Right behind her was Pshaw-Ra, followed by two of her guards.

Then me, because although I had no idea what was going on, I intended to find out.

The statue's tongue and throat were the gateway to a long and winding ramp that descended into a level underground passage. Its ceiling was supported by lines of pillars carved with designs like the ones on Pshaw-Ra's ship. Connecting the tops of these pillars were catwalks running lengthways down the passage and width-wise from one side of the cavernous space to the other. Pshaw-Ra and Nefure, followed by the guards, leaped onto one of these and sprinted down the passage, totally sure of their footing. I like tall places as much as the next cat, but the floor looked like a better bet for my paws.

Running deeper into the passage, I soon saw that this was not just a big cave, it was some kind of workplace or factory. There were long tables or benches, and machinery and things that smelled like hot metal and oil, chemical smells that made my nostrils itch.

In other places there were beakers and tubes, and big metal structures that looked like the engines of spaceships. I couldn't put a name to any of it but I thought I might come back and investigate later. The tables were the right height for humans — so maybe this was where they made and repaired things? Why down here? To escape the heat?

I didn't have time to examine anything closely because the patter of crazy kitty paws overhead lured me onward.

Another floor-bouncing thump made the catwalks rattle above me and I heard a sharp, "Rowl!"

Then something flitted between the pillars. From the scent, I could tell it was a female cat, a particular fish-stealing female cat. I saw a flash of white behind her as the wretched handmaiden girl tried to keep up with Renpet. With a mighty leap I was among the shadows, face-to-face with the fish thief. With another leap I was upon her. I wasn't sure what she'd done to bounce the floor so noisily or why Pshaw-Ra and Nefure were in hot pursuit, but I wasn't going to let her get away with it.

"Gotcha!" I said. I hadn't forgotten what happened before, the part where her girl walloped me. I turned, snarled, and snared her with a paw full of claws. "Back off, you," I said, even though she couldn't understand me. "Don't clobber the cat who feeds you."

The girl hopped back, clutching her bleeding leg, and I returned my attention to Renpet. To my surprise she was paws up, showing her tummy in a submissive gesture. "Please do not slay me, mighty catcher of fish!" she said. "I mean no harm."

"Is that so?" I asked, hovering but not attacking. "It seems to me that whatever it was that made the temple shake and thump is probably your fault, since you seem to be running away from it."

"We only created a diversion while we took back what is mine by right. Nefure would have destroyed it. She is evil, Chester the Fisher. She assassinated my mother."

"Why? Was your mom in the habit of stealing *her* fish?"

"My mother was the greatest queen our race has seen since we came from the stars. She brought peace and prosperity."

"You must take after your sire. There's nothing peaceful about you."

"My sire is a traitor—I had hoped when he returned he would make Nefure pay for her treachery, but instead he has become her follower. Did you not see him join her in pursuing me, his own offspring?"

"You mean Pshaw-Ra is your sire?"

"None other," she said bitterly.

"And he's also the queen's sire? And you thought he was going to choose you over the sister with the power? You don't really know him very well, do you?"

"I fear not. He is something of a legend among us."

"I'm sure he started the legend himself," I said. "He thinks he's very impressive."

I noticed as I spoke that the girl had something strapped to her back. It smelled dead and musty. "Is that what you took? The thing she carries?"

"That is no thing. That is my mother. We are taking her to prop-

erly prepare her for the afterlife, something Nefure would have de-
nied her."

"Afterlife? There's something besides, well, no life at all?"

"Yes, of course. Royal cats are immortal and are granted nine in-
carnations on this plane. Of course, the trick is knowing which in-
carnation you happen to be on at the moment and how many
remain. For that we must clandestinely consult the former royal astrologer."

"And that would be?"

"A problem. She now serves Nefure. Before his departure, my
sire also served as royal astrologer, but the post was not evidently el-
evated enough to suit him."

No surprise there. "Complicated family you have," I told her. "I
had two mothers and two sets of littermates, and mine is much
simpler."

"You are not royalty," she said.

"Maybe not, but I am *very* well bred. Just ask my mother, or
even my father for that matter, he's here too."

"No time for that. We must spirit my mother away from here,
but we are going the wrong direction." She looked puzzled as she
said that and gave a small mew.

"Why?" I asked. Surely it would have been easier to go in the
right direction?

"The explosion we set accomplished its purpose, but it also collapsed the ceiling of the most convenient passage. There are other
ways but to reach them we must first pass through the temple,
where we will be taken by Nefure's guards. You must assist us,
Chester the Fisher."

Must I? There was absolutely no reason to favor this fish stealer
and her girl except that I wanted to see what they'd do next—that
and I thought it might really annoy Pshaw-Ra.

"I will, but only because I am a very heroic fellow," I told her. I
could feel my boy waiting anxiously for me above, and though I
hadn't been communicating directly with him since my descent,

I did now. *We have a bit of a situation down here,* I told him. *That pair we met at the river need to get out without being caught. Can you do something to distract everyone?*

Through his eyes I saw that the adult cats seemed to be getting extremely friendly with each other, the air thick with a hairy haze and a very musky scent that may or may not have been part of the cause of my sudden gallantry toward Renpet. I was not too young to respond to the scent with a quivering warmth in my stern.

All we have to worry about is the humans, I'm pretty sure, Jubal said, *and I think I can handle that.*

In perhaps five rapid heartbeats he said, *Okay, they're all watching me now, facing away from the statue. Tell Renpet to make a run for it.*

"Come on!" I told Renpet, a command relayed to the girl, and we sprinted back up the ramp and through the open mouth of the statue. The girl did not come the same way exactly, which made sense, as the hole was large for a cat but not nearly adequate for a human, even a young one.

We were just clear of the statue's mouth when I heard a cry and Renpet tried to turn back. "They've taken her! I thought you said your boy had detained the guards!"

"Where is she?"

"Humans use the servants' entrance, of course, under the Great Mau's tail. We must free her! Who else would care for me? Besides, she has my mother's remains!"

"Well, you can't help her if they have you too!" I said. *Jubal, we have to go back for the girl. There were guards at the statue's tail.*

I know. They're dragging her out now. Tell the princess to hide. And call the kittens. Maybe they can tangle the guards' feet and I can free her.

"Jubal and the kittens are going to try to free your friend," I told Renpet. "Meanwhile, we have to hide."

"Cover me!" she said.

CHAPTER 9

Surrounded by the feline revelers, I leaped on top of Renpet, giving her a well-deserved thump and a bite as I did so. To my surprise, she emitted a moaning sound as if I were doing her more of a favor than simply hiding her.

Behind me, back toward the statue, the captain shouted, "Jubal, catch the kittens!"

I rolled Renpet head over tail so we were facing the statue. Two human guards were holding Renpet's handmaiden, her head hanging down so her hair concealed her face. They stood by the statue's mouth, the guards no doubt awaiting orders from the absent queen. Flekica's kittens, led by my brothers Bat and Sol, chased each other through the maze of cats and tangled the guards' feet while Jubal, Captain Loloma, and Beulah tried to catch them, dodging and feinting around the guards. Simultaneously Jubal barreled after them and into one of the men holding Renpet's servant, knocking him off his feet. As the guard began to fall, he dragged the girl with him. Captain Loloma caught him by the arm holding the girl, and Jubal pretended to stagger back, knocking the other guard off balance too. The girl broke free and leaped over the cats as if she too were a particularly agile feline.

Renpet clawed me as she slid out from under me and bounded after the girl. In two more leaps she was balanced on top of the roughly cone-shaped basket the girl had strapped to her back.

A few of the guests stopped eating or woke up to stare at the departing renegades. Then six toms and five females of the native race broke from the party and sprinted after them in hot pursuit. I was right behind.

Chester, wait! Jubal cried.

Be right back, I said. I had no particular plan, but I wanted to see what would happen. Would those other cats or their humans hurt the fugitive princess and her friend, as she said, or was she exaggerating to make herself sound important? That they chased her really didn't mean much. She was running, after all, so of course they were chasing. Pretty soon so were many others, and the temple entrance and courtyard swarmed with cats, first the Mauans and then, curious like me, my fellow Barque Cats.

I hopped atop a wall and spotted the escapees disappearing into one of the houses. No one was paying any attention to me so I jumped down and then up toward the nearest roof, and then the next, and the one after that. Renpet's scent, the girl's, and the dead smell of the late queen told me when I'd reached the right house. Their other pursuers had covered those telltale scents with their own as they poured out, one leaping over the other, racing in the wrong direction.

I streaked inside the house just as a slab of flooring that had been raised to show a gap beneath it was lowered once more. My ears brushed the underside of the trapdoor as I scooted into the gap before it closed. I pulled myself in and jumped to avoid being crushed by the door.

But my paws touched—nothing. I rotored wildly, trying to find a place to hook claws, but I fell and fell and fell until I landed hard—but on my paws—at the bottom.

"Renpet?" I called. My eyes adjusted to the dimness, even darker than the night outside. Just in time I saw the sandaled foot raised to kick me and flung myself sideways.

Chione, no! Renpet cried. The foot withdrew. *It is Chester the Fisher, who saved us.*

Chione, the handmaiden, uttered an exclamation, then turned and hurried away. I rose from my crouch, stretched, and pattered after them as if it didn't matter to me whether I did or not. We were in another tunnel, and at least down here it was cool.

"Where does this go?" I asked Renpet. "Won't the others think to look here?"

"This is one of the secret entrances to the underground city. It is far vaster and more labyrinthine than the upper city. From it we can access the secret passage Mother showed me, and only me. She never trusted Nefure."

"Oh. That's good," I said. "Passage to where?"

"To our place of concealment and the royal place of preparation for the afterlife. We must help my mother begin her journey properly."

"Oh, okay." I was still curious but starting to wonder what to tell Jubal about how to find me, and how to make it back to the ship. My curiosity was satisfied now. Renpet had matters well in paw, and Chione had failed to kill me a second time. I didn't want to wait around for the third.

Chester? Jubal called. *Chester, where are you? Are you okay, buddy?*

I'm fine. I don't know where I am. Underground somewhere. You?

Still in the temple. The cat queen and Pshaw-Ra came back from inside the statue, and boy are they mad. They think Renpet blew up the queen's ship.

She blew something up, I told him. *Or had Chione do it for her. Chione is the name of her girl, you know.* I knew he didn't know, but I was pulling his tail a little because I was the first one to learn something. Looked like I was going to find out all the secret stuff first.

The other kittens are all okay, Jubal told me. *I thought you'd want to know.*

I hadn't even thought about it, but it was good that they were.

Something tickled my right forepaw and I looked down to see

one of the keka beetles—the kefer-ka, as Pshaw-Ra called them—skittering over it. That beetle was only one in a string of them that went forward and back as far as I could see. They were crawling back the way we'd come. Good. It was about time they showed up. I could use a snack.

I didn't even have to chase them. They just kept in line, streaming toward me, practically asking to be eaten.

While I nibbled, Chione and Renpet continued on ahead, and when I looked up after one more beetle, I couldn't see them anymore. That was fine. I could still smell, and I ran zigzagging down the tunnel, messing up the beetles' formation as much as I could, just for fun.

But the farther I went, the less I smelled Renpet and her handmaiden and the more strongly I smelled the dead queen. Her scent overwhelmed all the others, even mine, or at least I thought it was her scent.

As I rounded a bend in the tunnel floor, I saw Renpet and Chione ahead, but I also saw that what I had been smelling was not just one dead queen, but tier on tier of stinky bundles wrapped, rosined, and waiting for all eternity, from the look of them. These had been cats. I could tell from their size and general shape and also because the ears had been specially wrapped into pointy cat ear shapes.

I tried to tread more softly. It wasn't so much that I thought the dead might waken as that I was a bit awed by their number and state.

The chamber seemed to go on and on, and kefer-ka poured from among the cat mummies in a steady stream.

"I presume this is where we are taking your mother?" I said to Renpet.

"Oh no, this is the common tomb of the ancestors. My mother belongs in the royal tomb."

Silly me. I just couldn't seem to get this royal thing right.

"There are an awfully lot of kefer-ka here," I remarked, changing the subject.

"This is the spawning place of their present form," Renpet replied. "They are born within death."

"That's very poetic. Does it mean they eat the mummies?"

"The kefer-ka contain the essence of the ancestors and are the instruments of their reincarnation," she replied. That did it. I started hacking and choking until I spit up the last snack, along with a giant hair ball.

I am not a fussy eater but I draw the line at devouring decomposing cats. At least I do unless I get a lot hungrier.

"You are common born and alien," Renpet said, picking up on my disgust. "You cannot be expected to understand these matters. Are the kefer-ka not tasty?"

Well, yes, they were.

"Are they not plentiful?"

Their numbers seemed infinite.

"And easy to catch?"

Very easy.

"You have no cause to revile them or complain of them. They are the gift of the ancestors."

"Pshaw-Ra says they're part of his plan for universal domination."

"He says many things, some of which may even be true," she said.

I did a little figuring. "Now you sound as if you know him well, and yet you are surely not much older than I am. The keka bugs—kefer-ka—were in the barn where I spent my earliest months, and according to Pshaw-Ra, their presence was his doing. So how could you know him all that well?"

"There are lots of stories about him," she replied. "Mother told some and others did as well. Everyone has been a bit in awe of him. I can't believe he's been taken in by Nefure!"

The tunnel widened into a great chamber whose walls rose into darkness high above us. The smells in here were so pungent they hurt my nose and almost overpowered the stench of death, which was fresher than it had been elsewhere. It was a good thing that it was not nearly as hot down here as on the surface. This room, in fact, was downright chilly.

"The common embalming chamber," Renpet told me. And then to her girl she said, *Now, Chione. We may not get another chance.*

Chione went to the side of the chamber and touched a button. A circle of light suspended itself over one of the tables, and from the shadows other tables rolled in quietly across the stone floor to flank it. Chione drew her arms from the straps that held the basket on her back and gently laid the contents onto the table. There was little left of the late queen. Her face and neck were unbearable to look at and her body seemed to have fallen in on itself, her fur stiff and spiky, all turned the wrong way, toward her head instead of her tail.

Renpet hopped up onto the table, gave a little cry, crept forward to lick a shredded ear, and hopped back down to the floor again. I don't think she even knew she was crying. I went to her and washed her face for her, then wrapped myself around her for warmth, and she curled shivering within the cup of my body. It was spooky down there, not so much because of the dead but because of what the living might do if they caught us here.

Chione was busy above us. A lot of whirring came from the moving tables, and I supposed they were giving her some sort of electronic assistance in the task she had undertaken concerning the queen. From the pyramid ships littering the lawns of this city, and also from what Pshaw-Ra said, this place had been, at one time anyway, very high-tech. It seemed odd that these remnants dedicated to preserving the dead were among the few things I'd seen that indicated the civilization here was anything but extremely rustic. I was really curious about what was happening with the embalming, but I was also quite comfortable where I was. My curiosity had been indulged plenty for one day and had gotten me into lots of trouble already.

Chester! Jubal interrupted my doze.

What? I was sleeping, I said.

Sleep later. Right now I need you to stay alert so I can find you.

But I got distracted then.

Chione backed away from the table and keka bugs began pouring off it, down the legs, onto the floor. Renpet sprang into action, catching and eating them as fast as she could. Like a cat possessed, she pounced and gobbled, batted, caught, devoured whole. If these bugs held the essence of her mother, was she trying to eat her legacy? Only a few bugs escaped her, skittering, then forming a single column that marched back the way we'd come, as the ones I'd seen earlier had done. I ran to the entrance of the big room and headed them off. They moved fast but their legs, though many, were short.

Then I charged them, breaking up their line with pounces and zigzags, sending them scurrying for the shadows. Even knowing where they'd had their last meal, I still found their smell delicious.

Renpet cried, "Eat them, Chester. Don't torment them." Which was a really odd thing to say. It was all the encouragement I needed, however. I gobbled too. Then Chione got into the act, grabbing handfuls of them and dumping them in the basket with the freshly wrapped form of Renpet's mother.

Renpet sank to the floor and licked her paws, then the rest of her. *Leave them, Chione,* she said. *Perhaps some of her former subjects will partake of them and recall why they were once loyal to my mother as queen.*

Would eating bugs do that? I had just eaten a gob of them and I didn't feel loyal to anyone from this place, though Renpet was growing on me.

Abruptly she cocked her ear. "Listen!" she said.

I heard then what had been concealed by our own activity: the sound of heavy footsteps and the padding of paws on the packed earth floor.

I bristled and growled until there was a whiff of a beloved scent among all the dead smells. "*Chester!*" Jubal cried aloud, and ran toward me. In his wake were eight of the sleek Mauan cats.

I looked back over my shoulder to warn Renpet. She and Chione had vanished! Nor was there any sign of Renpet's mother's remains.

"I tried to catch them for you but I wasn't fast enough!" I lied to the Mauan cats, though I could have spared myself the effort.

The Mauans ran past me, snuffling at the table, the air, the ground, barely slowing down as they snapped their jaws around the occasional beetle. They did not speak to me, but that might have been because Jubal was scooping me up and holding me close to his chest.

"Are you okay, boy?" he asked me, still aloud.

Three kilted attendants and Captain Loloma appeared there next. "How'd he get down here, Jubal?" the captain asked.

I mewed and rubbed my boy's red and sweating face with mine. I had a fur coat and I was cool enough. But then, he'd been running, I could tell from his breathing.

"He's not sure," Jubal told the captain. "He was chasing them, then they came down here and he got lost."

One of the kilted attendants said something, and the captain asked, "He wants to know why Chester growled at us."

I mewed pitifully.

"He was afraid," Jubal said, petting me reassuringly. "This is all very new. Come on, boy. We're going home now."

I snuggled against him and let him carry me into the narrow corridor, Captain Loloma with us.

A familiar pair of eyes glowed back at us from the darkened far end of the corridor.

"So, catling, you make friends quickly," Pshaw-Ra said.

CHAPTER 10

We exited the underground passages by a different door than the one I'd used to enter. It was very near the temple.

Aboveground, the fur was flying. The streets were full of people rattling rattles and holding out hands full of food. Beulah rushed up to us, cradling Flekica, who was crying in a heartbroken way.

"They ran away, Captain," Beulah said.

"Who ran away?"

"The kittens. They're missing at any rate."

Pshaw-Ra had done a disappearing act when Beulah appeared and suddenly he was back. "The tracker cats have hitched up their humans and are following the scent," he told me. "We'll have them back soon."

Two humans emerged from the temple, each harnessed to a pair of the larger tawny Mau, long strands of leather connecting the humans to the cats, who also deigned to wear harnesses. They all looked big and fierce and scary, lovers no longer.

"They're just going to scare the kittens away!" I told Pshaw-Ra. "Call them off. The boy and I can find them much faster."

"Viti-amun and Vala-ra are excellent hunters."

My boy picked up on what passed between Pshaw-Ra and me. "Let Chester and me go find them, Captain."

The captain put his hand on the elbow of one of the harnessed human hunters. "If you could just loan us a flitter so we can see them from the air, I think we can get them back."

The man stared at his hand and I think he wanted to claw the captain, but the locals were supposed to be nice to us.

The queen's attendant answered in heavily accented but understandable Standard. "We regret that there are no flitters of a size to fit you," she said. "Such devices were designed only for the sacred ones, and even so, are now devoid of fuel."

I left them standing talking and began my own search. "Sol? Bat?" I cried. My brothers and I were still considered kittens, however mistakenly, and I figured if I could find them first, they could help me look for the others—or maybe I'd find them all together.

I poked around doorways and under awnings. Jubal followed calling, "Kittykittykitty" and "Fishfishfishfishfish" until the word sounded like "fush." This city was so tidy there were very few hiding places apart from the houses.

Maybe that was because these people kept everything important belowground? Belowground (except for the part that had all the cat mummies) had felt right, smelled right, more lived in. Like the barn on the farm where I was born had smelled right, full of the scents of life; plants, cats, people, other animals. Up here it felt kind of—well, like on shipboard. Something people had made up, that had nothing to do with anything natural. Which was strange since the houses seemed to be made of stone and mud.

My brothers came running, trailing my sire, Space Jockey. "We were searching too but couldn't find them anywhere," Bat told me.

"They're not very big. They can't have gone far," Flekica cried, struggling away from Beulah.

"We will keep searching the town," Pshaw-Ra said.

"I'll follow the riverbank," my father said. "If they did manage to leave town, I hope they'll have sense enough to stay near the water."

"Beware of predators," Pshaw-Ra told him.

Space Jockey puffed up. "It's predators who should beware of *me*," he said.

The queen's voice rang out in a raucous *rowwwwl* above all of the others.

"I saw the kittens following the renegade Renpet when she escaped the temple. She has taken them!"

"No she didn't!" I said.

The shine of her eyes narrowed to slits, and everyone else grew silent. "You dare to contradict me?"

"Uh—no, it's just, I was following and I didn't see any kittens."

"Obviously she hid them before you caught up with her," the queen said dismissively, and then broadcast in her piercing voice. "The renegade Renpet has stolen the kittens of our guest! Find her, interrogate her, and recover or avenge the unfortunate young."

I saw the mother moving them last night, I told Jubal. *Maybe she forgot where she left them.*

No, because they were at the temple.

He was right, of course, but that didn't help. I wondered what danger Flekica had feared, to make her move her kittens in the first place. It couldn't have been Renpet!

"She didn't do it," I told Pshaw-Ra, whose search of the town seemed to involve watching everyone else search. I thought he knew me well enough to believe me without asking too many questions, and he had influence with the queen. He said nothing but looked suspiciously shifty. Even more so than usual.

As soon as nobody was looking, I exchanged glances with Jubal. *They've hidden the kittens underground,* I said. *I can tell by the way Pshaw-Ra acted. Let's go find them.*

Pshaw-Ra was off someplace else acting important, and the crew had dispersed to search. My mother had taken Flekica to stay with

Romina and Ninina, and the woman Beulah stayed with them at Bes's house.

The point was, nobody was paying any attention to us at all. We had to return to the temple for me to get my bearings, but when I did, I saw the house with the secret entrance and we made for it. Ha! No one was even on the same street when we slipped in and Jubal lifted the secret door in the floor. He switched on the pocket torch he'd brought from the ship and it showed some stairs we promptly used, pulling the door shut after us.

I should have brought string or bread crumbs or something, he said as we started into the nearest passage.

Why?

So we can find our way back, he said. *That's what they do in all the fairy stories. Explorers use balls of twine.*

I could try to shed my white hairs on the floor, I offered.

I think you've done that already, he said, pointing the beam down at a spray of black and white hairs probably loosened from my previous fall from above.

It's okay. I know my way around down here now, I told him. *This way.*

I absolutely knew my way, could smell Renpet, Chione, and the dead queen. We walked confidently down the hall and through the twists and turns, all the time expecting to see the kefer-ka streaming toward us and smell the cloying scent of the mummies. *Any time now,* I reassured Jubal. *Won't be long now. We're almost there.*

Of course, it was funny down here with no natural light to judge the time of day or night, but it did seem to me it was taking a bit longer to reach the mummies than before. I didn't remember there being so many places where the tunnel made sharp turns either. Hadn't it been fairly straight?

Where are we? Jubal asked at last.

Here, I replied. *But I have no idea where here is.*

Maybe we'd better go back.

"Mew."

"Aw, Chester, don't cry, boy. It'll be okay," Jubal whispered.

I didn't cry.

"Meh-mew?"

That sounds too small to be you. Do you think it's one of the lost kittens?

"Yow," I said.

How did it get here?

I didn't answer because I wasn't sure it was here. The sound was coming from slightly above us. I put my paws on a rough place in the wall and tried to jump higher, but it didn't work and I slid back. Then the *mew* came again and I realized it wasn't directly overhead but down the passage by a few tail lengths.

"Meh-mew. Mew, Mee?"

More than one kitten voice.

I tried mewing back. They stopped crying. They were frightened. "It's okay, it's just me, Chester. The boy and I are here to take you back to your mother," I told them.

I didn't get an answer, or even any sense of a kitten brain at work anywhere nearby. All my life I've been able to thought-talk with other cats as well as with Jubal, as well as using the usual vocabulary of variations on *me* and *ow* and extensive body ballet to express myself. But I was getting zip from the kittens.

We stood still, linked and listening. The air was cool and not stale, although this portion of the tunnel did not seem to be used a lot. I got no clear scents of any humans other than Jubal. Nor did I detect the recent presence of any of the Mau cats. The walls were rough, and the height just cleared Jubal's head. I didn't know where I was but I knew that I was not anywhere I had been before. I hunkered down and watched the floor, hoping to see a kefer-ka or several hundred come crawling up to be my breakfast but was disappointed.

"Mew," the kitten cried from the darkness beyond the beam of Jubal's pocket torch. We advanced.

This time I heard something different, a scraping noise, stone on stone. I looked back over my shoulder in time to see the passage closing behind us.

Jubal turned, shining his light on the stone disk rolling between us and retreat.

"Crud," he said.

We didn't really want to go back there anyway, did we? I asked.

I don't like having our options limited, and besides, you know, this explains a lot. I think we're lost because somebody wants us to be lost.

That would explain a lot, I agreed. For instance, it would explain why my nose and memory had seemingly failed to put us on the right track. *There are secrets down here we're not supposed to find out.*

Or maybe, Jubal said, *maybe we're being herded toward the kittens. Maybe someone knows where they are and wants us to find them.*

It seems like an extremely roundabout way of doing it, I argued.

That "mew" business started up again, and I listened and meowed back and tried thought-talk too, all to no avail. I heard no sounds I hadn't heard before. More and more I felt we were deliberately being led astray.

"There's only one direction we can go," Jubal said aloud. And it was true, at the time.

The repetitive mewing continued and we walked forward until a circle of light from the ceiling illuminated the floor of the cave. The ceiling was higher in this passage, about two cat lengths taller than my boy.

"Skylight?" Jubal wondered.

I scrabbled up the wall, but Jubal had a better idea. He lifted me over his head so I could see into the light above us. I expected to see the city street or the desert, but instead I saw the all too familiar interior of a vessel somewhat smaller but otherwise identical, as far as I could tell, to Pshaw-Ra's. High atop it, the nose cone had been removed, and the hatches were open so the light from the sky beyond shone through onto the floor of the tunnel.

Pretty elaborate, using a recycled spaceship as a skylight, Jubal said, picking up my impressions.

As we continued onward, we ran into these skylights at regular intervals for a long while, and Jubal said, *Looks to me like this network runs right underneath the city streets.*

Other things were in this section too. Disused machinery and storage containers, some empty, others tightly sealed. They had no signs, not even the picture writing, to say what they were for.

Then the tunnel curved and we had to make a sharp right down a steep incline into another level.

What neither of us saw was any sign of the kittens.

CHAPTER 11

Chester, deprived of one of his favorite pastimes, eating, grew quickly bored with their search and fell back on his other favorite thing to do, sleeping. At least in the caves it was cool enough for Jubal to carry the cat slung around his neck. That left his hands free for feeling walls and holding the torch. Then he stopped and searched his pockets again. Pulling out a packet, he unfastened it and extracted a headlamp, which he put on. Not only was this more convenient, but it would save what remained of the charge in the pocket torch for later. Jubal had a feeling there might be quite a lot of "later."

He came to a place where the passage narrowed, but on either side of it there were openings. Entering the first of these, he saw that he was in a good-sized room, with arches and columns connecting the central room to others. This whole place might look like a collection of intertwangled root cellars but seemed to have been underground houses or maybe offices.

They were pretty thoroughly stripped of any hint of occupation, human or feline, and he wondered who had lived there. Maybe the people and cats who eventually were removed to updated worlds, leaving behind only the hardcore cat worshippers now living on Mau?

It wasn't surprising to him that they might have lived down here to escape the heat on the surface, but why had anyone ever built the houses exposed to the elements? Maybe because cats were so fond of the sun. The Mauan cats, being short-furred, wouldn't mind it the way the Barque Cats did. And from what he'd read, this whole culture was not only catcentric but solarcentric, so some of their time would be spent on the surface, even if the real work took place down below. He had to admit, they'd made the houses pretty cool considering the outside temperatures.

What he found odder was that the farther he went, the better constructed the tunnels seemed to be, as if the rustic ones on the upper levels had been practice for making the more sophisticated ones lower down. The people who first came here, according to what Pshaw-Ra told Chester, had advanced technology for the time. Maybe the root cellar houses had been a kind of base camp for their community while they made everything else, like the fancy hall beneath the cat idol in the temple?

After taking a wide ramp down and finding it led to a broad hall with lights that came on when he entered, he thought, *This is more like it.*

Just when Jubal began wondering where everybody worked, because so far he hadn't seen another soul, a loud *blaaat* filled the air. Claws dug into him and Chester levitated to the ceiling, then hit the ground running ten feet in front of Jubal, who was hard on his furry heels.

A voice said something in a calm even tone, with words so garbled Jubal couldn't tell if it was in a foreign language or only heavily accented. He got the gist of it, though. It doubtlessly meant "intruder alert." He pounded after Chester, hoping they were stampeding in the right direction.

Down they ran through corridors and caverns, each passage taking them lower. Jubal's breath rasped so loudly and his heart pounded in his ears so hard that he didn't realize that the alarm had stopped until Chester halted abruptly in front of him and sat down in his path.

Keep going! Jubal told him. *We should find cover, at least, before we stop.*

We're covered, Chester said, though his ears were still flat and the black fur of his back, ruff, and tail spiked to make him look twice his size. *Listen.*

A hail of footsteps and rumble of indistinct voices seemed to seep through the walls to their right.

At any time those footsteps could come through another doorway, another arch, and straight toward them. Jubal edged to the left-hand wall, thinking that if they were found, he could just tell the truth, that they'd been hunting for the kittens and become lost.

The voices ebbed, the footsteps pattered away, and he gulped to pull some moisture into his dry mouth and throat. He had never been so thirsty, and after the long sprint down first one corridor then another, he was no longer cool either. All of the water in his body was pouring out of it, soaking his skin and clothing.

Chester rose, his fur back down to normal again, and padded forward as if he were out for a stroll in a park. Jubal thought he must have run the equivalent of the length of Galipolis at least.

I smell water, Chester said, speeding to a trot.

Jubal wondered if it would be fit to drink. He hadn't brought a purification kit—well, he couldn't think of everything, and when he picked items from the ship to bring with him, he hadn't counted on a prolonged spelunking trip through the city's innards.

Then he too smelled the water and heard the rush and slap of it.

A wall opened on the left and the girl Chione stepped out. "Unless you want to go swimming again, come with me," she said.

"Is the underground river the same one that runs through the desert?" Jubal asked her later, in her hiding place, when he and Chester had enjoyed a long drink and what seemed to be dried fruit.

"Mmmm, this is good," Jubal said, biting into the fruit, which had a bit of a crunch to it. "What is it?"

Chester answered. *Keka bugs all squashed together. Smells yummy!*

Jubal dropped the morsel on the floor, and Chester and Renpet shared it with surprising daintiness for a pair who had been feuding less than a week before.

"No," Chione said to Jubal. "Not the same. But from the same source, I think."

"And where are we exactly?" He looked around the cavernous room, its stone walls painted with picture writing, furnishings carved from the same stone.

"On the west bank," she said. "We won't be followed here."

"Why? Can't they swim?"

"This is the official place of death. The royal catacombs are here."

"I thought those were on the other side, where we found Chester?"

"No, those were for the common cats, those who died before the Leavetaking, when there were many, and the ones who have died since. Here all of the royals are wrapped and waiting for their next lives."

"How long do they have to wait, generally speaking?" Jubal asked. He knew it probably wasn't a very bright question, but he wanted to keep the conversation going.

"It depends," she said. "They live longer these days—much longer than ever before—but there are so few kittens. Renpet and Nefure were the last born here, and as you see, they are nearly grown. But soon perhaps their mother the queen will return with the kittens of Renpet and your master."

"My what?"

She indicated Chester.

"He's not my master. He's my friend."

She shrugged. It made no difference to her. She had accepted, the shrug said, the human's place compared to the divine feline in the scheme of life.

"And what kittens? Chester's just a kitten himself."

She nodded to the two cats now curled together for a nap. "In your heart, perhaps. But Renpet is in estrus and soon there will be kittens."

Chester, a dad?

Chester looked up at him with slitted eyes, his head still resting on Renpet's golden belly, and yawned. *Why not? We'll make beautiful kittens, and you like kittens.*

Jubal felt an unreasonable pang of jealousy. Chester was *his* friend. He had always felt that Chester was his own age. And now he was talking about having kids of his own?

Chione was prattling on. When she wasn't on the run, she was quite a chatterbox. "They will be wonderful kittens, the kittens of Renpet and Chester the Fisher."

"Well, she shouldn't get too attached to him. I don't think we're going to stay. This place isn't real healthy for kittens."

"Yes," she said sadly. "As I said, Renpet and Nefure were the last to be born."

"Our two pregnant cats lost their litters—all of them born too early—and the half-grown kittens of one of the other cats have disappeared. The queen claimed you had them, but Chester and I both knew that was hogwash."

"She probably took them herself," Chione said.

"Why?"

"I don't know! She is not quite sane, that cat." She added quickly, "Of course, she is to be loved and respected, being of the superior species, but how she came to have the nature she has is a mystery. The late queen was wonderful, kind and wise, and—well, you know Pshaw-Ra. Perhaps he is not, as everyone thinks, Nefure's sire. Perhaps some lesser, common tom caught the queen before she had those final two kittens and his unscrupulous opportunism accounts for Nefure's behavior. Certainly Renpet is much more like the queen."

"That's nice," Jubal said, "but it doesn't seem to be doing her a lot of good." He shook his head and looked around at the painted and carved stone room, deep underground, in a place where a cat was queen and her sister a princess, in something like a catty version of a Dumas swashbuckler, though without the sword fighting, and people just helped the cats!

Chione caught his look, although the light from the wall sconces was not bright. "What troubles you, Chester's boy?"

"I don't get this place. I don't understand why the humans are ruled by a cat queen or why the cats are considered divine or why everything is underground and some of it is really modern and some looks ancient. I don't get how the walls slid around as we passed through it, and I don't get why you could send a cat into space and have all of these other cat spaceships laying around your yards and serving as skylights for the next layer of tunnels. This is a weird place. I love cats a lot but I just don't get it."

Chione shrugged. "I don't understand how you can live among the stars either, or what the cats did there. I wish I did. Renpet's distant ancestors traveled through space long before they settled among our earthly ancestors and taught them so much that is part of our culture even today, though many of their ancient teachings have been lost. When first we came to this planet, we brought with us the mummies of the original divine cats. Our society is a remnant of one that once revered them above all other deities. Many of the mummies of sacred cats were stolen and destroyed by foreigners, but many of those were the mummies of less nobly born cats, sacrificed by unscrupulous priests in the long ago. We have preserved the original remains lo these many millennia and brought them with us when we migrated. Our royalty claim descent from these starfarers and teachers."

"Is Pshaw-Ra royalty?"

"He is of the royal line, yes, though the power passes from

mother to daughter. But my father, who was once the servant of Pshaw-Ra, said that he bore the closest resemblance of any cat he knew to those described in the sacred texts."

"Did the cats write those?"

"They dictated them to the ancestors. They had great powers of thought transference through which they imparted their advanced ideas."

"Like what happens between Chester and me or you and Renpet?"

"Yes, only much more potent."

Jubal chewed the corner of his lower lip thoughtfully. "One other thing I don't get, then—from what I've read, back in the early days when the new worlds were being settled, there wasn't much of a luggage allowance—how did your people get to bring a bunch of cat mummies?"

"We would not leave them behind! We had to leave many of the sacred implements as it was . . ."

"The sacred scratching post, that kind of thing?" he asked. He was a little put off by all the "sacred" this, that, and the other thing. He loved Chester and thought he was very smart, but he didn't revere his cat particularly.

She smiled at him as if he'd said something very bright, and he felt bad for being sarcastic. "Yes, all of those things. The sarcophagi of the mummies were small, and I suppose were easily disguised as other things those in charge might have considered more useful. The sacred cats were thought to be mere pets, rather than our leaders."

"So the whole thought transference thing continued up until the time your people left Earth?"

"Only occasionally, among certain individuals with a special affinity, an important ingredient in a bond even now. But those cats who coupled their minds with the minds of human interpreters directed us."

Jubal wondered how much it was the word of the cat passing

through the interpreter that did the directing, and how much it would have been the interpreter making up edicts that would suit his own purposes and saying they were from the divine kitty.

Chester looked up at him through slitted eyes. *You don't think a mere cat could come up with that on his own? Is that it?*

No, no, that's not what I mean. I know you're smart and everything, but wouldn't inventing space travel interfere with your napping, hunting, eating, and the other stuff you seem to need to do every day to be happy?

Inventing feline space travel would be a lot like hunting . . . and we are natural-born explorers with a lot of what you humans call scientific curiosity.

Jubal was stung to suddenly be lumped with "you humans." *Of course you are, buddy. You're brilliant. I didn't mean you.*

Or Renpet? Chester asked, having evidently forgiven the little female for stealing his fish.

Jubal reached down and petted both of them between their ears. *Sure. Renpet too.*

Both of them purred up at him. He was evidently forgiven.

Chione gave him a startled look. "She tolerated your touch!"

"Any friend of Chester's is a friend of mine. Evidently your princess feels the same way about me."

"Walk with me," the girl said, rising to her sandaled feet and straightening her skirt. "Our friends wish to commune with each other, I think."

Chester? Jubal asked.

See you later, boy. Some things a tom has to do by himself, you know what I mean?

Jubal and Chione left the entire huge cavern room to the two cats, walking along the ledge that formed a bank for the vigorous and noisy underground river.

"What happened to the bridge that was here when we crossed from the other side?" he asked her.

"I retracted it," she said.

"I didn't see you do that."

"You didn't see a lot of things."

"You can say that again. You talk a lot about dead ancestors. Is this place haunted or something?"

"What would make you think that?"

"Well, back on the other side, we kept getting lost. Chester was looking for that mummy place you showed him before, and he said the tunnel had been fairly straight, but we couldn't seem to escape all sorts of twists and turns that led us up and down, just under the surface and to these sort of primitive houses. Just about the time we figured out where to go, the passage that seemed to be there wasn't anymore, as if someone was changing the layout of the tunnels."

"Someone was, at least on this end. When we heard the alarm, Renpet had me route you away from your pursuers and toward us."

She took a small device from inside her skirt and waggled it in one hand.

"You control the tunnel walls?"

"Not really, just a series of doors and sliding walls that block off some passages and open others. Mine only works within a certain radius. There is a control room on the other end where they can monitor activity in the critical passages and control traffic within them. This only has a little light that comes on if someone unauthorized enters the area."

"We still haven't located the kittens. I know you didn't take them, but do you suppose they might have somehow come to this side of the river—maybe someone brought them? Or do you think they've been killed?"

She shook her head and the tiny braids into which all of her hair was plaited bounced. "I do not think so. You are honored guests, and it has been so long since we had kittens here, I cannot think that anyone would harm them."

"We thought we heard them close to the surface on the other side, but Chester said that even though it sounded like kittens, he wasn't getting any mental response from them. I'd like to keep looking, even if he is otherwise occupied."

"I will clear the passages on this side for you, or those within my range. The west is reserved for the dead, and the living rarely visit here. It would be a good place to hide someone. Like me, like Renpet. There are doorways to the world above concealed beneath the sand."

"Thanks," he said. "Uh—is there another way back through them without disturbing Their Catships?" It came out a little sarcastic. After all he'd gone through to find Chester, the cat had gone and got his head turned by a kitty face.

"Oh, yes," she said. "There are many ways. This one will do," and she led him to another entrance that wasn't even cavelike. It had a doorway, with lintels and carvings, but until they got right up on it with his headlamp and her torch, the opening hadn't been evident.

"Thanks," he said, and stalked off into the tunnel.

He had barely started, however, when he heard the skitter of paws behind him. *Wait! You are my boy. How can you go away without me? Wait for me! I love you. I am lost without you,* Chester's voice pleaded inside his head. And in another moment claws dug into his shoulders and neck before the familiar furry weight settled against the back of his head. Chester licked his ears and his jaw and his hair, purring like a small machine.

I thought you had better things to do, Jubal said.

She clawed me! he said. *I did what she wanted and then she turned around and almost knocked my nose off my face. I'm sorry. Am I getting blood on you?*

Jubal sort of wanted to teach Chester a lesson and be a little standoffish, but it was hard to do that under the circumstances. He raised his hand back to pet his friend, and his fingers did come away sticky. *She nailed you a good one, didn't she?*

Yes, and I did exactly as she asked.

My pop would probably say that's females for you.

My mother's not like that! Git wasn't either, and I doubt if Silvesta is, even though I haven't seen her for a long time. Maybe it's that royal blood thing again.

Maybe. When we get back, you should ask your mother.

At some point while they'd been communicating, another set of noises beyond the gurgling of the underground river and the sandy crunch of Jubal's footsteps began.

A dry rustle and slide, and then — and this was what got through to them — high-pitched feline cries of fear and dread. At the same time, a nauseatingly pungent smell filled the corridor.

I think we've found the kittens, Chester said.

Somehow, Jubal didn't think this was a good thing.

CHAPTER 12

Pshaw-Ra had been running his tail off ever since he and the Barque Cats landed. Once his master plan was complete and the universe conquered, he would have a nice long nap.

Perhaps it would have helped if he had a dedicated two-legged assistant, but that seemed to defeat his purpose. True, humans here on Mau knew their place, but if cats were to be independent of humans, exercise their superiority over them, then he, the engineer of this metamorphosis, must lead by example. Besides, he didn't know of any human who could keep up with him. His former servant was much too old now—not to mention politically inconvenient, as the father of the outcast princess's handmaiden.

So Pshaw-Ra knew he had to convince the queen, house the Barque Cats, arrange for their feeding and for the proper medications to be administered to them and to the resident feline populace as well, so the breeding could commence. Sadly, this medication also made sure that no more inconvenient full-Barque kittens would be born, so that the mothers would be available to mate again and bear the superior sort of hybrid kitten he had in mind. Meanwhile he had to ensure that the polydactyl gene common among the Barque Cats got spread as widely as possible. And then there was the problem with the half-grown kittens and what to do with them so their mother would be ready to mate again.

Chester and his boy were in some ways an asset, but in other ways they were a pain, since they understood far too quickly what was on his agenda. He had not given Chester the drug, because he had something special in mind for Chester, the first specimen to respond as he had hoped as a result of his experiment with the kefer-ka. Chester seemed to have figured out the special destiny for himself. But now the reckless pair had gone after the blasted Barque kittens. How inconsiderate! If only they had stayed put until he was ready to deploy them for their role in his scheme.

Now he had to track them through the tunnels and reroute them to keep them away from secrets he wasn't yet ready to share, including the whereabouts of the kittens. He had thought he was being clever using a voice sim of the kitten cries to lure them into the right passages, but somehow they hadn't continued following it. And then, to his astonishment, the minute his back was turned, he lost them! He couldn't find them on the locator screens at all, so to be on the safe side, as if he didn't have enough to do, he snatched up the kittens again and transported them to a more secure location.

The area was disused, but he left them food and water, told them not to wander off, and stuck up a force field to seal off the tunnel.

He checked the underworld scanners one more time before returning to his lab, and located Chione and Renpet, who were where he expected them to be, along with, to his relief, Chester and the boy.

But then everyone had to start moving about, and soon the cat had reclaimed his boy and Chione returned to Renpet.

The males were headed for the kittens. They were moving very fast.

Watching them, Pshaw-Ra became aware that something else was moving fast, though less perceptibly, as it was roughly the same size and circumference as the tunnels.

But how could it be that? It was supposed to be dormant, inactive, trapped in the underworld. His force field was not going to protect the kittens from it, nor would it protect Chester and his boy.

He lightened his gravity and bounded down the corridors, praying to—well, to himself, since he was the wisest and most powerful entity he knew—that he would be in time. Otherwise, it would mean starting all over again with the kittens, which would be a great deal of bother.

CHESTER IN THE TUNNEL ON THE WEST BANK

This time the mewing was coming from real kittens, I could tell. When I sent a mental search party toward them, they latched onto it with all of their paws and teeth as well. *Get us out of here*, they said. Well, one of them did. Another one said, *Something's coming. Something big and stinky.* And the other two wondered if I'd brought anything for them to eat.

I know where you are now, I told them. *So shut up. Probably not a good idea to attract the scary thing, whatever it is. The boy and I are coming.*

But of course they were really young and kind of stupid. I'm sure I was much brighter at that age.

That cat who brought us here said we had to stay here, one of them said, making noises even while he thought-talked to me.

I said to be still, I reminded him. Now the stench was worse, and it wasn't the dead cats this time. It smelled like something had digested a meadow full of really rancid grass and horked it back up. I couldn't see the kittens in the tunnel ahead of us, and their voices seemed to be coming from the side—there were probably more rooms cut out along the way here, as there had been in some places on the other side of the river.

All I heard was the kitten voices in my head and, unfortunately, in my ears at times, and the dry scratching, scraping, and sliding sound. Now I felt a sort of a hump and thump once in a while, as if something was crawling forward on its belly.

I don't like this, Jubal told me. *I don't like this at all.*

Nevertheless, we continued forward, me in a low crawl slink and Jubal creeping on tippy toes. The kitten voices grew louder, but so did the other sound, and the smell was so nasty I paused to hork up my own last meal.

Jubal's headlamp picked up the opening in the wall marking a room, and I knew that was where the kittens were, but all of a sudden my nose banged up against some kind of barrier and no matter how I scratched and clawed it wouldn't give way. Jubal pushed too until he stopped. "Hoooooolysmoke, Chester. Stop. L-Look." He pointed.

At first I couldn't see what he was carrying on about because there was still just a big long tunnel, as there had been. Then I noticed the differences—the fangs at the top of it and the other teeth at top and bottom, plus big fiery eyes staring at us over a scaly snout.

What is that thing? I asked Jubal.

The most ginormous snake in the entire galaxy is my guess, he said. *Coming straight for us. Do you suppose this barrier keeps it in as well as us out?*

Meanwhile the kittens are going "Mew mew mew" even louder, and I keep shushing them but they are so terror-stricken they can't even hear me. The snake draws close to the opening in the wall and the head turns slightly so we can see its profile. Yuck. A tongue like forked lightning turned into a slimy slab of meat flicked in and out, searching for the kittens.

"Meeyew!" Poor little beggars. They wouldn't stand a chance with that thing. I didn't really see why it was going to bother with them. They wouldn't even make a good bite for a monster that big.

Jubal pressed against the force field, kicked it, hit it with his fist. It drew the attention of the serpent momentarily. The thing blinked its fiery eye then pointed its snout into the hole in the wall.

Cram yourselves into a corner or a crack, I advised the snake kibble even as they continued squeaking their terror. *That thing is huge. It might not be able to suck you out of there if you get wedged in good.*

Save us! the most optimistic one cried. What did it think I was going to be able to do against that thing?

"Chester, what are you thinking?" Renpet's voice cut into the kitten pleas. She sounded awfully close, and no wonder—she was right behind me. Her voice was high and shrill. "The great serpent Apep has come back to life! He will destroy us all!"

Jubal said, "Chione, what is that thing?"

Chione whispered, "I had heard his lair and prison were down here but never did I guess that the Apep was active. He is lord of the underworld, eater of suns."

"I thought the cats were in charge?" Jubal asked, sounding doubtful. That thing was enormous.

"They are—but, oh, how can we save those poor kittens?"

The humans couldn't, of course. And for some reason I didn't understand, I couldn't look away from what I was sure would be a terrible massacre, even worse than when Buttercup, my litter sister, and our foster mother Git had been slaughtered by a canine predator.

But Renpet, striking faster than any serpent, knocked the controller from Chione's hand and stepped on it. I had been leaning with my forepaws against the invisible barrier between us and the snake. Abruptly, I was through that barrier, on all four paws.

Renpet was ready for battle. "Attack its eyes, Chester. Ready?"

It was a foolish plan, a desperate plan, and a plan any right-thinking cat would have yowled at and taken off in the opposite direction. Instead I took the serpent's right eye, she the left, and we leapt much mightier leaps than I had ever leapt before, straight to the top of the ugly scaly head. It was slippery but that's what claws are for. I landed high up on the eye ridge, clinging with my other three sets of hooks, and lowered myself to attack the eye that blazed with such an unnatural light I feared at first to burn my back paws. I clawed with all my might. The head thrashed wildly, whipping back and forth, trying to scrape us off on the walls, but we clung tight and dug at those eye sockets with all our might. The eye went bloody, then dark, and finally dull and flat as I clawed and clawed and hoped that Renpet was doing the same.

The snake's body was so huge it filled the tunnel to the walls, preventing it from thrashing even harder since there was so little room for it to move. Nevertheless, faster than I could swat a fly from the sky, it had scraped me off the eye ridge and sent me scrabbling its scales until one front paw and one back paw latched into a nostril, dangling me above that toothy lower jaw.

Now it was backing away, hissing like all of the angry cats in the universe, back through the tunnels faster than an express tram. I unhooked and flung myself backward, tail over nose, onto the stone floor. My back right leg hit first, hard, and pain shot up my hindquarters.

Just as I was trying to rise, something heavy and soft landed on me, sending agony through my back and legs again.

I cried out but could not rise.

Chester! Did it bite you, boy? Jubal, suddenly at my side, patted and stroked me.

No, I said, and I confess I actually tried to bite him when his hand passed over the injured leg. *But I hurt. A lot.*

CHAPTER 13

CHESTER: CONVALESCENCE

Much to my surprise, I lived, and after some expert attention, stopped hurting as much.

I don't remember being carried back to the cavern, or that Renpet had to be carried too, or that kittens clung to Jubal's and Chione's shoulders as they beat a retreat back along the water and to the larger cavern.

I don't know exactly when Pshaw-Ra arrived, but he had brought the expert attention, and it wasn't any of those so-called cat doctors either. This was a human vet, very skilled and with good tools and medicine I didn't even have a chance of fighting. I heard Chione call him "Father," and Pshaw-Ra whispered to me, "This is Balthazar, my own man, father of Renpet's handmaiden. He will heal you. I wish it."

Sure enough, sometime later the leg hurt less, but I heard voices drifting around me.

". . . be put down, released from this life . . ." someone was saying. Male but not Jubal, so I thought it had to be the new human vet.

"No!" Jubal said. Of course he did. "He's better already, Balthazar. He'll recover. You'll see."

"He has partaken of the late queen's kefer-ka," Chione said. "He is brave as a lion and just as strong. You'll see, Father. He will recover yet to rule beside the Princess Renpet."

"Renpet rules nothing," Balthazar said sternly.

And then everything got as fuzzy as—well, as a warm kitten, four of which were packed around me most of the time. In some of my waking moments I would feel the dab of a sheathed paw against my sides or face, as if I were being tested to see if I still lived.

My leg was bound and restrained, and the rest of me didn't feel very well either. Jubal said that I had cushioned Renpet's fall and probably saved her life as well as the kittens'. I was a hero. I was glad everyone was okay, of course, but wished I were too.

Renpet licked my face every once in a while, but that was it. It was her idea to jump the snake, and I had been injured and she had not and all she could do was lick my face?

It took a long time before I realized why—she was very large and very round.

"Not more kittens!" I cried.

These ones are yours, Chester, Jubal told me. *Yours and Renpet's.*

I'm too young to be a father and I'm hurt. How can I take care of kittens?

"We'll help you, Chester," said the largest of Flekica's kittens, the one called Shahori, listening to our thought-talk. "We will tell them all about how you killed the snake."

"I didn't kill it," I said. "Though I am pretty sure we blinded it."

"The snake is immortal," Pshaw-Ra said. "Life begins and ends and begins again with it. It can only be defeated, never slain. The injury you dealt it will not last. It is unfortunate that so few saw your heroic deed. Soon it will be as if the battle never took place."

"But we'll still be saved," Shahori said.

No one mentioned returning to the surface. Pshaw-Ra came and went but Balthazar remained with me, under Chione's and Jubal's supervision.

The day came when he removed the bandage and I hobbled around the cave floor. It was good. The leg held my weight without pain.

"Oh good, now we can return to the surface and take Flekica her kittens," Jubal said to the other humans.

Pshaw-Ra was there then. Since I read the boy's thoughts and Pshaw-Ra read mine, he understood what Jubal said.

"That is not an entirely correct assessment of the situation," he said delicately.

"You surely don't mean for us to remain down here?" I asked.

"For a little while longer, yes, I believe it would be prudent," Pshaw-Ra said with his irritating air of mystery.

"At least let the kittens return to Flekica. She is so worried."

"You have been out of touch for some time, catling. She is no longer worried and has in fact adjusted."

"What do you mean adjusted?" Shahori asked, picking up on our conversation.

"I mean that when a mother loses one lot of kittens, the smart thing is to have more kittens to replace them, and that she is about to do. The sire of that litter would not look with favor upon the offspring of his mate's previous mate. He might kill you," he said to Shahori.

"Chester and Renpet fought that big snake for trying to kill us. They could handle some tom friend of Mother's. She wouldn't let any old male hurt us."

"Renpet dare not show herself above on pain of death, and Chester and his boy should remain here until her kittens are born, to protect them. You are all but grown now. Give yourselves a few more weeks and you will be adults in your own right. No tom will attempt to destroy you then."

"If he does he will be sorry!" Shahori said stoutly.

I was alert enough now that I began to see a pattern. "How *many* of the queens are pregnant, Pshaw-Ra?"

"Not *your* mother, catling. Don't worry."

"Of course not my mother. She is unable. How many of the others?"

"This is a very friendly place and our race are most attractive and passionate, so of course . . ." The old cat danced around my question.

"How many?"

"Er—almost all. But that is fortunate! I knew when first I saw you that our kinds would blend well, had characteristics of mutual benefit to us. The first litters will be born quite soon. They promise to be amazing young cats—with our superior intelligence and breeding, knowledge of how to exercise control over humans, and your large feet with that adaptable toe that is sure to develop into something like the human thumb, your work ethic and knowledge of the current condition of the galaxy and the inner workings of ships. Do you not see, catling, there is little this new breed will be unable to accomplish?"

"Including achieve universal domination?" I asked, having heard the old short-hair say that this was his ultimate goal.

"Perhaps not immediately, but within a couple of generations, why, yes, I think it entirely feasible."

Ask him how so many of the cats got pregnant so fast, Jubal said. He'd been privy to the entire conversation.

But Pshaw-Ra chose that moment to clean his claws and pretend he didn't understand the question. I was not fooled. The old cat had told me long ago he intended that I would help breed new kittens. Not much surprise that all of our feline shipmates were doing the same.

"What about us?" Shahori asked. "We are amazing young cats already. We survived getting gobbled by a giant snake."

"What you need to learn is to keep your mouths shut when a giant snake is searching for you," Renpet told him.

"If we had, we might not have been rescued."

"If you had, the snake might never have presented a danger and crawled back into his hole, and Chester would not have been injured."

"Shoulda woulda coulda," I said, bravely dismissing my injuries with a phrase I had heard the boy's father utter on occasion when chided about some of his less wise moves. "What do we do while I'm healing and Renpet and the other females are having kittens?"

"Prepare for the rest of our mission, of course," Pshaw-Ra said. "For instance, Chester, you should stay off that leg as much as possible. Therefore, you should learn to levitate."

"I should?"

"Oh yes. You kittens should pay attention too. All cats are capable of manipulating their personal gravity field. I have known how to do this since I was younger than any of you. It is one of the most useful things you can learn, and I am the only remaining cat on this world or any other who can teach you how."

Jubal sent a message to the captain with Balthazar, telling him not to worry, that they were safe, just on another really important mission. Chione's father was persona non catta, but as Pshaw-Ra's former handler, he still had a certain amount of clout and friends who were willing to carry messages for him. Just to be sure not to give away too much information, Jubal wrote the message in pig latin. Sosi could always translate if her father didn't get it.

The underground river held fish as plentiful and tasty as in the one on the surface. But unlike the surface river, the subterranean one had a dangerously swift current and ended in a bottomless black whirlpool many miles away, so Chester's fishing technique would have been far too dangerous. Jubal was very careful to avoid falling in himself. He would be swept out of sight and hearing of any possible rescuers before anyone noticed he was no longer standing on the bank. Balthazar brought him a dip net, advising that this was the best method for fishing the river whose name, like that of the snake, was Apep.

Farther down on the west bank, where the transition from land to water was less steep, Jubal was amazed to see a large garden and orchard.

"How can you grow things down here without sunlight?" he asked.

Chione had left Renpet with Chester and Pshaw-Ra for once. In response to his question she pressed her control, and shutters hissed away from the eyes of the tunnel, many lenses set to catch the angles of many more lenses on many more levels until they reached those embedded in the surface.

"Are there more of the cat ships up there, making the skylights like the ones throughout the town?" he asked.

"Better," she told him. "The monuments to the ancestors are engineered to serve just this purpose. The light collects into a very small lens in the pinnacle and is amplified as it travels down to us. This, Renpet's mother confided to her long ago, but not, I think, to Nefure."

"So we could hold out down here for quite a while if we need to, right?" Jubal asked.

"At least until Chester heals and the kittens are born," Chione said.

"And until you can gather enough fuel to refuel the vizier's craft and go forth once more into space," said Balthazar.

"And leave the others behind?"

"Only temporarily. Ideally, we will find enough fuel to take the human craft beyond Mau's orbit, so it can be rescued without disturbing life as we know it here."

Jubal had trouble hiding his surprise. "I thought his nibs and that nasty queen of yours wanted to keep us all prisoners or something."

"Nefure's plans and the vizier's are not necessarily the same,"

Balthazar said, just as evasive and aggravating as the cat he had once served and seemed to be serving again. Chione handed Jubal a piece of fruit that resembled a cross between a peach and a fig, and when he looked up from taking a bite, Balthazar was gone.

Renpet's litter arrived four weeks later. There were only two kittens, but she was young and it was her first litter. One kitten looked almost white, with very faint apricot-colored markings; the other was black and white like Chester. Both kittens were very fuzzy, once they were dry, and had six toes on each paw.

"He looks just like you when you were a baby, Chester," Jubal told him. Since both kittens in Chester's litter were polydactyls, Jubal hadn't seen anything unusual about him having the mitten-shaped paws, though he did note that the paws looked very large for such a small cat.

What are their names, Chester? he asked.

Chester nuzzled Renpet, who accepted his attention with a brief lick to the nose before returning to nursing her kittens.

No names yet, he said, *Renpet says they will be "him" and "her" until they find their true names. Mother will want to call them something related to her lineage I imagine.*

I hope so, Jubal said.

You don't think she's going to be mad that the kittens aren't all Barque Cat do you? Chester asked. *The crew and Janina put a lot of emphasis on our being purebred.*

Renpet hissed. Through Chester, Jubal heard her say, *Who cares what she thinks? Our kittens are better than those who are all Barque Cat. They have the benefit of my royal blood.*

Although he had looked forward to the birth of the kittens, Jubal found that the event achieved something he didn't think anything but distance could do—drive a wedge between him and Chester. Renpet and Chione made it clear that his help was not required, that as females they were automatically more skilled at meeting the needs of the babies, and he supposed that was true, at least of Renpet. His mom hadn't been any help with Chessie's or Git's litters; he himself had handled what caregiving was done for them, but then, they were not *royal* kittens.

Chester paced around, or slept beside Renpet, allowing the kittens to climb over him. Jubal started calling the black and white baby "Chester Junior" or just "Junior," and he thought of the tabby as Buttercup, like Chester's lost sister, though he didn't say it aloud and feared it might be bad luck.

Jubal noticed that they matured a lot faster than Chester's brothers and sisters had, or Git's kittens, and he told Chester how smart they were and marveled at how fast their senses developed. But Renpet told Chione she was afraid he would step on them, and hissed at him when he tried to handle them.

Finally, he started exploring the tunnels on his own, or sometimes with a little assist from Balthazar, though the old man was too ancient and crippled to participate in much exploration. Jubal tried to draw him out, thinking he must have some good stories about Pshaw-Ra growing up, but apparently the kittenhood antics of the Grand Vizier as observed by his handler were classified.

He did get a handbook on how to read the hieroglyphs from Balthazar, and he passed the time when he wasn't fishing or gathering other food reading the walls and carvings deeper in the tunnel leading to the cavern where the cat family was. He wasn't too worried about getting lost, since Chester always knew where he was, even if he didn't particularly seem to care.

One day he was surprised to find Balthazar and Pshaw-Ra beside him as he studied the walls.

"We have something to show you," Balthazar told him.

They led him farther within the tunnel system than he had ever been, through walls with cubbyholes carved into them. In most of the cubbyholes there were boxes or bandage-wrapped bundles shaped roughly like cats. Farther on, the bundles were stacked in elaborate designs, and farther still, there were fewer bundles and more naked bones, tiny and delicate, arranged in patterns and pictures similar to the symbols on the walls. Little skulls punctuated the designs, their round knobbiness breaking up the matchstick quality of the long bones. Every now and then he saw side chambers where human-sized bundles and human bones were arranged, but only a few showed the same detailed placement into sacred symbols—such as the ankh for life, the eye for protection, flowers, zigzags, and diamond shapes.

Jubal and Balthazar's steps raised clouds of dust that spiraled and whirled in the eerie light of their lanterns, but Pshaw-Ra glided over it. Jubal coughed nervously, feeling he was breathing in dust that was all that remained of the flesh once surrounding the bones. At first the smell got to him, but he grew accustomed to it, or maybe it had dissipated from the older bones a long time ago, since the farther they walked, the older the bones were.

Balthazar explained the dynasty or origin of some of the crypts and ossuary collections, and said that some of the oldest bones had been preserved since before the pyramids of Earth were constructed.

By the timer on Jubal's com, they walked for a whole day before they stopped. He recalled that they had only walked forty-five minutes from the ship to the city, so he reckoned they must be way out under the desert somewhere. When he looked up, grains of sand occasionally sifted through from above, just two or three at a time, as if they were in the bottom of an hourglass.

"Where are we now?" he asked, pointing overhead. "I mean, relative to the temple?"

"Come, I will show you," the old man said. He led the way up a side passage that turned off onto a steep ramp leading upward for what felt like four or five stories. "Push there," he said, pointing to a handprint on the wall at the top of the ramp.

Jubal did so, and more sand showered in through the door as it opened onto a clear star-filled night. To his surprise, it was actually chilly. A brisk wind blew the sand in whirls and eddies between the huge dunes surrounding them.

He could smell the river on the wind. "What's all this, then?" he asked Balthazar.

"This is the City of the Noble Dead. And these," he said, sweeping his arm toward the dunes to the south of them, "are the great burial pyramids, buried beneath the sands. Those humps there are the covered remains of mortuary palaces, temples, and shrines. These are replicas of original structures from Earth, dedicated by our ancestors to the glory of our extraordinary felines who have guided us and led the Mau from time before antiquity."

"Why do you need these buildings if all the mummies and bones and such are down below?"

"These were intended to stir the memory, not simply cover the remains. Alas, since the Leavetaking, there have been too few of us to hold back the sands."

Jubal watched as the wind resculpted the sand, playing hide-and-seek with the structures beneath it. He could make out the top cone of the closest pyramid, then the side, before the sand settled back around it and another side was uncovered before it too was shrouded.

As he looked around, he saw a glint of light. "What's that?" he asked, pointing.

"Probably just a hunting party, but it could be searchers. They are far away, across the river, but still, we must not be spotted. Always best to travel the catacombs."

Jubal didn't much want to go back down underground. He sighed when the door closed behind them. "It seems to me like you have a lot more dead here than you have living," he said.

"That is so, especially since the Leavetaking," Balthazar admitted.

"Isn't it kind of, you know, morbid?" Jubal asked.

"In the ancient culture, it was thought that as long as the body was preserved, so was the soul, the ka. When we had been here long enough for the kefer-ka to mutate from the union of a native alien species and the dung beetles that accompanied us from Earth, our scientists presented a vindication of our beliefs. So long as we have the physical DNA of our kinds preserved, the kefer-ka will revivify it, circulating it through their strange interaction with the food chain to link the dead and the living, one species to another."

Jubal was about to say it still sounded creepy. On the other hand, he thought, it was why he and Chester had become so close, and that was actually wonderful, so instead he asked another question that was on his mind. "From what Chester said, I thought I might see a lot of the beetles—the kefer-ka?"

"Not here," Balthazar told him. "Not now. The beetles from the oldest burials have long ago been consumed. Those that remained, the Grand Vizier took with him on his journey to infest the rest of the galaxy—in a good way, of course."

"I hope so," Jubal said. "Pshaw-Ra told Chester eating the beetles is what created the link between new kittens and people, but I don't think very many links got established before the cats were all quarantined and ended up here. It makes me wonder where the other bugs went."

Balthazar had brought water and dried fish cakes, and that served as supper. Pshaw-Ra joined them, and dined first, of course. He washed his face while Jubal and Balthazar sat cross-legged on the sandy stone floor and shared their meal. Pshaw-Ra had already gotten the best part of the dried fish. He lay down afterward as if about to take a nap, but watched them over crossed front paws. Jubal didn't trust him and felt uneasy dealing with the tricky old feline without having Chester around to interpret.

Balthazar chewed his fish. He was so thin that every muscle in his jaws and throat gave a visible demonstration of its function as he ate, working within his dry brown face and throat. Despite his age, his teeth were very white and seemed in excellent working order. "The kefer-ka will find hosts," he said, "though the great affinity is of course only between cats and men. Before the linking power of the beetles is exhausted, the cats must return to the galaxy to play their role."

"Masters of the universe?" Jubal asked, joking, because he thought the whole universal domination thing was just some daft plan of Pshaw-Ra's. Surely nobody else seriously believed it was going to happen.

"Even so," Balthazar said with a sober nod. "That and other things. For this reason, we must refuel the Grand Vizier's ship. That is why we have come."

"I don't understand. There are all those ships all over town. Surely you have some kind of a port, some way of manufacturing fuel?"

"Indeed we do not. When the great corporation came and removed many of us to what they assured us would be a better place during the Leavetaking, they took with them industrial resources as well. We hid the ships of the cats from the corporate overlords, but they took most of the extra fuel. The vizier used what was readily available for his first journey."

"So now what? Is there someplace here to call a taxi or what?"

"No, but our ancient royal ones were buried with their worldly goods, including their ships—and with all of the fuel that they contained. It is of course sacrilege to disturb their tombs and remove anything within them."

"Because of the extraordinary circumstances, you don't think anyone will mind?" Jubal asked, but he had a sneaking suspicion that was not the case.

"Oh no, such desecration is punishable by slow and painful death—at least for us. You are an outsider and may be presumed to know no better, if you get caught."

"How am I supposed to transport all of this fuel?"

"The elements are contained in small light packets, not bulky or heavy, but designed so a cat can easily transport them in his mouth and install them. However, many of the elements will be partially spent already, so you will need to take all you can glean from the royal tombs. We will then guide you through the underworld back to the tunnels beneath the desert upon which the vizier's ship rests."

Jubal nodded but said nothing. Why did he get this feeling that the wily old cat was simply using him because he was handy? Maybe because that's what was going on. It sounded, at least, as though Pshaw-Ra's plan included getting both cats and humans off Mau and back into space, so he and Chester wouldn't be separated again—unless Chester wanted it that way.

"You'll have to show me what I'm looking for," Jubal said.

CHAPTER 14

Balthazar, holding an electric torch, led Jubal and Pshaw-Ra farther through the tunnels until they reached a door in the side of the wall. Hieroglyphs, most made up of cats, pyramids, lightning bolts, birds, and sun disks, marched down a central panel carved into the door. This room contained only one cat mummy, encased in a box carved to look like a cat with jeweled eyes and gilded fur. The mummy case lay at the top of a pyramid ship that was a smaller replica of Pshaw-Ra's.

"How come if this cat was so important his ship is so much smaller than Pshaw-Ra's?" Jubal asked.

"The vizier needed a cargo bay for the large and clumsy vessels of your humans to dock within his ship. Our ancestors had no need of such a large space."

Pshaw-Ra placed a paw on the ship's hull and the hatch swung open. He marched inside, tail curled high over his back.

Below the entrance to the nose cone containing the cat-sized bridge, he pressed a paw to a round symbol split by a lightning symbol. Another hatch opened. Pshaw-Ra inserted half his body, looked up, then pulled himself out and stepped back.

"The vizier says the packet is intact. You should pluck it free."

"I can't get in there!" Jubal told him.

"Reach up with your hand," Balthazar told him. "There is a tab on the outer side where the feline navigator manipulates the packets with his teeth. Your hands are still small. Your fingers should reach it readily enough."

Jubal reached inside and up, half afraid something might bite him, but it felt familiar, like pulling an egg out from under a sitting hen, without the hen or the straw. The little tab was just about the right size to grasp with his forefinger and thumb, and when he pulled it into the beam shed by Balthazar's torch, he saw a tiny clear packet somewhat smaller than the hen's egg he'd compared it to. "This is enough to fuel a spaceship?" he asked incredulously.

Balthazar took it from him and held it to the light. Jubal could see that the contents did not fill the packet all the way to the top. "Alas, only for a few months. But there will be more, in other chambers like this, in other ships and—" He looked at where Pshaw-Ra was sitting, atop a metal box engraved with the lightning in a circle symbol Jubal had seen on the bulkhead inside the mummy's ship. "Aha! In storage containers such as this one."

His point made, Pshaw-Ra jumped down, and Balthazar opened the box to find two more full packets and another implement, scalloped and rounded at the bottom of a short rod. Retaining the fuel packets, he handed Jubal the implement.

Jubal turned it over in his hand and saw that it was shaped like a cat's paw.

"This you may use to gain entrance to the ships," Balthazar told him.

"Uh—thanks," he said.

He followed Balthazar and Pshaw-Ra back through the maze of tunnels to reach the ones that opened almost directly beneath where the ships were docked, so he'd know the way.

Then all he had to do was continue searching a Galipolis-sized underground city of sepulchers for the distinctive and hard-to-conceal pyramid ships. After he acquired each cache of elements, he'd been instructed to take them back through the subterranean passages to Pshaw-Ra's ship. There, he had to wait for nightfall, deliver his goods to the old cat, then return to the Valley of the Royal Dead and search for more.

On his first solo mission, he was spooked by the deadness all around him as he worked. Vague rustlings came from behind the cat mummies and the bones of mummies that had fallen out of their wrappings long ago. He thought the other bones must belong to less noble cats. Nobody had admitted it, but maybe all cats weren't mummy material? His lantern glinted off eyes smaller than those of cats but too large to be those of the kefer-ka. In one side chamber he thought might belong to another royal navigator cat mummy, he found instead human mummies in a seated position to form lap beds for the cat mummies. He wondered if the ancients had killed royal servants like Chione when a royal cat died, just to keep the nobility from getting lonesome.

Then came a long trip through the tunnels beneath the desert, and he was scared it wouldn't lead to the ship as he'd been told, that the whole mission was an excuse to lose him in the tunnels, maybe as bait for the great, though now blind, snake. On the last leg of the trip, though, when he stopped for a rest that turned into a nap, he felt a familiar warm weight settle against him and a familiar purr vibrate against his side. Chester had come to help him.

Thought I'd lost you, Jubal told him, stroking his back and tail.

I was just trying to be a good father, Chester said. *But Renpet doesn't want me. Pshaw-Ra says what I have to teach the kittens will come later, so I thought I might as well help you.* He rubbed his head against Jubal's face, tickling his nose with whiskers. *Besides, I missed you.*

Yeah, me too.

They lost track of time in the tunnels, finding tombs and ships, extracting fuel modules, hauling them back to Pshaw-Ra's ship and waiting for the old cat to install them, then starting all over again.

Sometimes Balthazar showed up, and he would tell Jubal what more of the symbols meant and some more of the history of the Mau. More often Pshaw-Ra himself would pop in, using some mysterious route known only to him, and use the old ships as show-and-tell to explain to Chester how cleverly he had modified their functions in his own ship. Chester followed him as intently as if he were a fish, watching his paws as they pretended to work the controls.

"I wondered how he made it work, but he never showed me be-fore!" Chester told Jubal when the old cat had gone.

Once, they came upon a stretch of tunnel where the wall went on and on for what seemed miles without an opening into a side chamber or ossuary. Chester was uneasy the whole time, sniffing along the bottom of the wall. It was unusually dirty and seemed to have been scraped, but Jubal began to make out a few drawings on it too—they seemed to be astrological or even astronomical in nature, the sun, moons, and stars growing larger as he walked down the length of the wall. The artist had begun a second line of drawings below the ones higher on the wall. These showed a long wavy

line that he took to be a river, a cat, an eye, a dagger, and a wavy line chopped into little pieces. The symbol Balthazar had told him stood for wind appeared next, and the wavy lines ascended to the upper drawing, heading toward a sun disk, then appeared to encircle it.

In the next panel, the boat symbol appeared with a cat symbol beside it and a sword symbol beside that. There, the swirl resolved itself into a snake biting its own tail, surrounding an unoccluded sun. Then, below it, a long serpentine shape plummeted back into the long wavy line that stood for the river.

When he looked down, Chester was sitting at his feet looking up at him quizzically. *What do you suppose it means?* he asked the cat, but other than a brief hiss, Chester had nothing to add.

From time to time they returned to the river for fresh provisions and to visit Chester's kittens, who were sleek young cats now. The fluff in their fur frilled around their faces, draped their tails, and softened the mittens on their feet, but they were not quite as heavily coated as Flekica's kittens, which seemed huge compared to the younger litter but were still playful enough to enjoy games of chase with the smaller ones. The faces of Renpet's kittens were somewhat sharper and more triangular, and their tufted ears larger and more pointed. They ran all over the cave, as well as Chione and Renpet, greeted Chester with extravagant purrs and rubbings, and treated Jubal as if he was Chester's extra paw. But although Chester sometimes interpreted the kittens' thoughts for him, Jubal had no more special knowledge of them than he did of any other cat. He had hoped that his connection with Chester might extend to his family, but that wasn't happening.

On his last visit, Renpet had seemed more nervous than before. Chione told him, "She has smelled the great snake again, and felt his body thudding through the passages."

"But he's blind now," Jubal said. "He won't be able to find any of us if we hide."

"He smells with his long forked tongue," Chione answered. "And nothing down here would smell as sweet to the eater of souls and killer of light as the new lives we nurture."

If Pshaw-Ra had paid any attention to the nature of others rather than what use he could make of them, he would have realized that Nefure was not exactly the maternal type. She had in fact inherited his lack of interest in others, but was sadly lacking his intelligence or curiosity.

Being the queen, she had not nursed her own kittens. She had not seen them for more than a few moments before the nurse took them away to clean them, let them pull nourishment from *her* body, and presumably teach them something about being cats. Nefure would wait until they developed manners before she herself undertook to instruct them, however perfunctorily, in being royalty.

She rested for a time after the onerous task of giving birth, and though she missed the ministrations of her usual servants, who were caring for new kittens, she got a great deal of extra attention from the toms among her courtiers, including the new tom from the star cats, the one she supposed had sired her latest litter.

At some point she recalled that these kittens were supposed to assist her in dominating the universe, so she thought perhaps she should have a look at them. Only two moon cycles had passed. She expected they would still be as adorable as kittens were supposed to be—as everyone swore she had been—and yet old enough to be presentable.

Viti-amun, her principal maid and captain of her guard, fetched them and brought them to her.

They had stripes and spots in gray and black. One had an unruly reddish ruff around her neck and black striped legs and tail, and another was totally white. They scratched their longish fur often with their monstrously huge feet; their grotesquely, monstrously, appallingly huge feet. She'd been told they were "polydactyl," but Pshaw-Ra had made it sound as if that were a good thing. The extra toes didn't deform the paws of the male she had taken—what was his name? Jockey? "There must be some mistake, Viti-amun. You have the wrong kittens. These cannot be mine."

Viti-amun looked trapped. She knew better than to contradict her queen and yet she didn't wish to seem derelict in her duty. "I found these kittens where I was told to look for yours, Majesty," she said.

The kittens looked confused and rather stupid. They seemed to expect something of her. "Well, they won't do. That one is hideous." She indicated the little female with the red ruff and striped legs. "Their feet are much too large. Have the doctors remove some of those toes, or better yet, dispose of them and I'll start all over when I get in the mood again. And fetch my father, the Grand Vizier. He has some explaining to do. Am I correct in surmising that my city is now filled with this sort of ill-bred offspring?"

"Most of the kittens look similar to these, Majesty, yes. The Grand Vizier indicated they had turned out as he expected and wished."

"That is why I must speak to him. They are not as *I* expected or wished. The red-maned one is far too ugly to be from my elegant line. And all of their faces and tails are too fat, their body lines stocky, their eyes not set at the proper angle. Oh no, they will not do at all."

Nefure's tail swatted back and forth as she issued her edict, and the kittens, led by the red-ruffed one, decided she was playing and attacked the tail.

She swirled and swiped, but the kittens rolled under her swings, and the minute she righted herself attacked again. "Get the little monsters off me!" she cried. "And bring me Pshaw-Ra *now*!"

———————

Viti-amun's brother and first lieutenant, Vala-ra, deployed the guard to find the Grand Vizier while Viti-amun made the kittens scarce. She had hoped her mistress's pride in herself would spill over into pride in her kittens, that the old vizier's promises that the kittens were the key to universal domination and absolute power would be enough to endear them, however superficially, to the queen. But she had underestimated the depth of Nefure's super-ficiality.

Viti-amun's own darling kittens by the handsome Barque tom Bat, with their beautiful big ears and clever many-toed paws, were waiting when she and the young princes and princesses returned to her house. Essentially a security officer, she had selected a home with access to the tunnels of the underworld, though she had not had occasion to use it for anything other than checking on the status of some project or fetching the queen a serving of kefer-ka. Now she wished she had force-fed the kefer-ka from the wisest and oldest of the ancestors to Nefure. Perhaps it would have helped suit her to the throne. Why Renpet had allowed her sister to run her off was a subject of great speculation.

There was no time now to consider what might have been or should have been. It was not beyond the realm of possibility that, having decided her own kittens were not worthy to be in her pres-ence, Nefure might wish to rid her realm of all of the kittens mothered or sired by the Barque Cats—and right now, there *were* no other kind of kittens. Viti-amun was quite fond of them, both her own and the little princes and princesses, for all that they might someday take after their mother.

Opening the trapdoor in her floor, she told the children they were all going to play a hiding game. She shushed their questions and pushed them onto the stairs, closing the trapdoor behind her. Now she knew she must put as much distance between the kittens and her own house as possible, lest the queen send the guard—

Viti-amun's own troops—to ensure that the kittens were dispatched.

Vala-ra could not understand what the fuss was about or why it was necessary to act as though the vizier needed to be apprehended. All he had to do was put out a call on his com and Pshaw-Ra answered immediately. He explained that the queen wished to see him, but did not say how displeased she was.

"I am at the city's outskirts now," Pshaw-Ra said.

"Stay there," Vala-ra said. "I will meet you."

Minutes later the two tawny sleek-furred cats met in the middle of the road farthest from the temple.

"Got her tail in a twist over something, does she?" Pshaw-Ra asked when he saw Vala-ra's face.

"I'm afraid you must come with me, Grandsire," Vala-ra told the vizier, who was in fact his oldest living ancestor. Pshaw-Ra had cut quite a swath among the ladies. "She doesn't care for the looks of the new kittens."

"Looks? Who cares about looks? Didn't she see those amazing paws? Does she fail to—excuse me—grasp that with those paws and the superior intelligence of our race, our progeny will be able to do without humans altogether?"

"She doesn't like the paws. Viti said she might settle for cutting off the extra toes of the kittens instead of killing them, but she finds the kittens ugly. Even her own."

"You think she'll listen to me?"

"I think from what Viti said about the mood she's in, she might have you skinned and thrown into the desert to die."

"Why in the name of Bast did you let that fur-brained female take control of the throne? Renpet was supposed to be crown princess."

"Was she? That is not what Nefure told everyone. She had a circle of toms to do her bidding when she made her move, and they

and their servants pursued Renpet and Chione with weapons.
They would have killed them if they'd caught them. By the time
the guard found out, Renpet was gone, Nefure had assumed the
throne, and when you returned and deferred to her, that validated
her rule."

Pshaw-Ra snorted. "I wish everyone would stop trying to interpret my moves or divine my motives. I am highly mysterious for a
good reason. I don't want others to know what I'm doing."

Vala-ra knew that this was precisely the problem with trusting the
vizier to exercise any sort of leadership, even by inference, and his
ears flattened with irritation. "Look," he said, "if you get away, I can
always claim you escaped. You could disappear. You do that well."

"Is that censure in your voice, grandson? Never fear. I have a
plan. I always have a plan. Right now this is my plan. I will keep
Nefure busy, and you evacuate the new kittens—I have a feeling
you had better evacuate the Barque Cats as well. Take them underground and lead them to the River Apep."

"Then what? Drown them?"

"Certainly not! Do I have to think of everything? You will see
my apprentice Chester. Tell him all is in readiness and if I am not
there when it is necessary to contact the outer worlds, he should
start without me."

Vala-ra passed the message on to Viti-amun when he and the
Barque Cats, kittens, and those of the Mau who wished to join
them, caught up with Viti and the kittens. "I will return to assist
Grandsire," he told his sister.

She inclined her head, and like the warrior she was, headed the
column of cats and led them through the maze of tunnels, halls,
caverns, and corridors, always west, toward the Apep underriver
and the Valley of the Royal Dead.

Pshaw-Ra could not believe he had sired such a stupid daughter.

"They are an abomination," she declared. "I cannot believe you talked me into defiling myself with one of those creatures—polluted the purity of our race by having us mate with the outsiders to produce such ugly kittens."

"Majesty, I—" he began, but even he could not talk fast enough to stem the great sandstorm of Nefure's rage.

"I want those kittens destroyed. I want the outsiders destroyed. I want them *all* expunged from our genealogy for good."

"May I remind Your Majesty that our genealogy is at an end without the contributions of the Barque Cats?"

"That is your fault. If we can have kittens with them, we can have kittens among ourselves if you'll only apply yourself to the task and stop running off to conquer the universe all the time. After all, the late queen and you produced *me*."

He badly wanted to say that she was proving his point about the decline of their race but merely purred assent and bowed with his tail curled over his back. "As you wish, Majesty. I will return to my laboratories at once."

"I will see to it that you do. Phylla!"

A grizzled black queen stalked toward them from the shadows of the temple. "Majesty?"

"Escort the Grand Vizier to his laboratory. Post a guard to stay there with him. Do you understand?"

"I do, Majesty. It shall be done."

CHAPTER 15

CHESTER: THE WORM RE-TURNS

I didn't have to wait for the fugitive cats to arrive to know what I had to do. Pshaw-Ra came to me while I was having a nap and instructed me to go to the pyramid ship, which he said was fully fueled, and take it into space to try to find someone to help us leave the planet.

I rose and found Jubal, who was fishing at the underground river. He pulled out his net full of fish and hauled them onto the bank, saying, *Okay, but I'm coming with you.*

Carrying the net with him, he returned to the nest Renpet and Chione had made for the kittens. "More cats are coming," I told Renpet. "Your sister has rejected her own kittens and ordered the deaths of them and all of the others, and she is not very fond of my kind either."

Renpet spat. "She would! Do you think the exiles would help me mount a revolt against her?"

"Why bother? The boy and I go now to bring help to evacuate us all—no need for you and the youngsters to stay here among cats so stupid they put up with your sister as queen. Frankly, my dear, we're all too good for them."

Renpet froze suddenly, her ears back and her fur as puffed out as it would go.

"Chester, I am afraid . . ."

"Of her? Pffft! By the time she finds you, if she does, the kittens would be able to send her hiding under a bunk. She's a bully-girl, Renpet. You're worth ten of—"

"I'm not talking about her. I—I hear the great snake."

"You said you thought you had but—"

"Not *had*. I hear it *now*. Listen."

She was laying down, and when I lay still beside her, I felt it too—the same ominous *thump-bump thump-bump* I remembered from our first encounter with the worm.

"Can Chione block him from us with her wall-controlling thing?" I asked.

Renpet consulted with her handmaiden. "She tried."

Jubal questioned Chione a little more, and told me, *She felt the snake break through the last barrier she put in front of it. We'd better get out of here. We can't go too far, though, because those other cats are on their way. We don't want them to walk right into the snake.*

Can it cross the river?

I don't see the river giving it any major obstacle, but I think it's a good idea to get the river between us and it.

The kittens were now too big to make carrying them in our mouths any kind of an advantage, but Jubal and Chione scooped them up. Jubal lifted Shahori and one of his sisters onto his shoulders, where I usually rode, and Chione extruded the bridge, using her little device, then scooped the last two kittens into her skirt and crossed the burbling water. Jubal was right behind her, and Renpet and I were on their heels.

But something else was right behind us.

The fresh smell of the water had masked the snake's musk until it was upon us. Renpet shrieked and I spun and leaped at the same time, sounding my own battle yowl and landing on the snake's long forked meaty tongue, knocking my mate off it.

Chester! Jubal cried behind me.

I stared, for a split second transfixed by the bobbing head and dripping fangs, and back down the stinking grinder that was the snake's inner musculature, good for swallowing me whole and crushing me inside it.

I was too young to die! As the snake tried to flick me back into its throat, I pulled backward with my front claws, raking the sensitive tongue. The snake spasmed, shrinking from the damage dealt it by my built-in rapiers, and I jumped off, twisting in midair to land on my feet.

The serpent had pulled itself into a huge coil inside our cave, filling it halfway to the ceiling.

Hearing a strange cry, I saw Renpet was trapped between the serpent's lower jaw and a cave wall. She raked at its hide with all of her claws but the serpent didn't notice her or the scratches.

I ran toward her but Chione was ahead of me. Jubal picked me up and flung me backward, onto the riverbank beyond the cave. I slid just short of the edge and scrambled back up again. He jumped around hollering and made jabbering noises at the snake, drawing its attention from Chione, who hugged the wall as she reached for Renpet.

I leaped back into the fray, but even as I did I heard the kittens making a terrible racket behind us and hoped they would not return to "help."

I watched the flickering tongue searching for my mate, her handmaiden, my boy, and each time it flicked out, I darted forward and slashed it, then darted back before the great head could descend and drip venom on me.

Dancing sideways, I slashed and slashed. Snake blood slimed the floor, already moist with mist from the water. Jubal had found some sort of stake to jab at the snake.

I heard Renpet scream to the kittens, "Run!" We could hold the serpent at bay only a little longer before it devoured us all. Chione dove in and grabbed Renpet while the snake tried to strike Jubal.

A louder yowl sounded behind me. I lost focus long enough to listen, to turn my ears back, and the snake struck.

Chione was almost to the bridge, Renpet in her arms, when the snake arched over us and came down upon her, its right fang striking her to the ground. Renpet flew from her grasp, her back legs writhing against the slippery stone. The snake had uncoiled enough in its strike that its body now blocked Jubal from attacking its head. I skimmed the slick stone on my belly to reach Renpet.

But even before I reached her, doom fell upon the snake as the snake had fallen on Chione. The queen's warrior cat and a delegation of the guard, my mother, my sire, Sol, Bat, Beulah, and a great multitude of battle-ready Barque Cats, closed on the snake. Balthazar was there too, not doddering now but using his walking stick to strike the snake's snout over and over.

Beulah settled it by taking out a weapon and sending a bolt of light into the snake, which writhed and hissed and then dropped its head while all of the cats clambered onto it and worked on its hide with their claws, flaying it. The laser pistol hadn't killed the snake but we cats did. Renpet kept clawing the tongue long after the long body stopped twitching. Bits of it littered the floor.

Then Balthazar knelt over his fallen daughter, shaking his head slowly. Renpet cried and would have licked at the blood on Chione's shoulder, but Balthazar held her back. The blood would be mixed with venom. Jubal picked her up and petted her over and over again, trying to comfort her as she cried for the girl she had loved as deeply as I love Jubal. "Can you help Chione?" he asked Balthazar.

The girl's sire looked up at him and shook his head. "Her spirit has flown."

The cavern would be no haven for the new fugitives, full of unmoving and immovable reptile as it was.

Balthazar tried to carry Chione by himself, but he was old and the fight had taken most of his strength. The rest was sapped by loss. Jubal let Renpet down and took the girl from her father, carrying her over his shoulders as I had once seen him do a sheep, taking her to the fruit grove. Beulah helped him lower the girl to the ground and then she and Balthazar began washing the body, cleaning away the venom with strips of cloth.

Pshaw-Ra chose that moment to check in. Did the refugees arrive safely?

Yes, but all is not well, I told him, and related what had happened.

I suppose Balthazar won't be much use to you then. You'd better get going. I'm not sure how long it will take Nefure to understand that the kittens, and many others, have truly disappeared as she wished them to. Go!

But—

There are many of them to tend to the burials and defense of the kittens. They have Renpet to lead them. There is only one of you. You must take that boy of yours and find help. Only then can we implement our reentry into the galaxy at large.

From the way he put it, I knew he was much less interested in the welfare of any of us, including the kittens, than he was in pressing forward with his master plan. Stupid she might be, but the selfish Nefure was his daughter all the way.

When we reached the ships, Jubal took his former seat in the landing bay portion of the pyramid vessel and Pshaw-Ra guided me through the takeoff procedure. By now I was much more familiar with the picture writing. *If you touch the bird, the sun, and the pyramid, you will reverse our original course,* Pshaw-Ra's dream self told me. *If you are not intercepted, you will eventually end up where we first met, drifting.*

I did what he said because our escape was also the beginning of us rescuing everyone else. But once the ship had broken Mau's atmosphere and Pshaw-Ra's thought-voice could no longer reach me, and after I had set the course as he directed, I began to shiver and quake. Everything that had happened and that might yet happen swept through me, and I was suddenly very frightened. Having done all I could at the helm, I ran back down the gangway leading from the nose cone to the outer, human-sized portion of the ship, swam free-falling to the bay where Jubal sat lashed to his seat, and anchored myself to him with all of my claws, aching to be petted, to be told that we would be fine, that someone would save us.

I don't suppose you preloaded any food, did you? Jubal asked.

This was not what I wanted to hear.

CHAPTER 16

By Jubal's reckoning, he and Chester wandered and drifted the best part of a month before they made contact. They went through different scenarios about what would happen, what they should say. They were still fugitives, so they knew it would be a mistake to invite rescue and risk bringing an extermination team down on themselves and all of the other survivors. They couldn't just board any passing ship that might take an interest in them. They needed to find someone they could trust to return with them to Mau and rescue the others.

Fortunately, food wasn't as desperate a problem as they'd feared at first. Pshaw-Ra had provided a good swarm of kefer-ka, and someone, most likely Balthazar, had stocked dried fish, fruit, and water.

Nevertheless they had to be on short rations. Chester dreamed about food so much he was amazed when all of a sudden he found himself dreaming about his milk brother Doc instead.

Checking the charts on the bridge, he showed Jubal that they were approaching a space station. They had crossed two star systems close to Mau already but were not yet back in the main space lanes. This station would be an outpost of some kind, if not a derelict.

Does it say which one it is, or if it's still working? Jubal asked.

Not that I can tell, Chester said.

Jubal hadn't seen a space station on the trip to Mau, but then he wasn't thinking about the scenery on their flight from the pursuing Galactic Government ships. If this were a human ship, like the *Ranzo*, he could find out soon enough, but the cats of Mau—at least Pshaw-Ra—did not seem to find the same details relevant that humans did. That kind of thing apparently bored them.

I'm tired, Chester said, yawning, emerging from the bridge to climb onto Jubal's crossed legs and settle down for a nap.

CHESTER: ON THE PYRAMID SHIP AND, SIMULTANEOUSLY, ALEXANDRA STATION

It's true I was a little sleepy, but mostly I was curious. While I was with Pshaw-Ra on the pyramid ship before Jubal came for me, the old cat showed me how to dream-travel and to use dreams—mine and those of other cats—to board passing ships, get answers to my questions, even to plant messages.

When I closed my eyes this time and relaxed into Jubal's lap, I let my mind wander, searching for another cat mind. Honestly, I didn't expect to find one. I thought most of the surviving space cats would be those we'd left behind on Mau. But to my surprise, I locked dreams with a very familiar fellow dreamer, one who had shared my very earliest dreams. My milk brother, Doc, brother of Bat, was on that space station. My littermates and I had been cared for by his mother, Git, while our mother recovered from a birthing gone wrong. And when Git was killed while protecting us on a hunt, my mother took over care of Doc, Bat, and their brother Wyatt. Doc, apparently not a good judge of character, had bonded with Jubal's father, a wily old human called Ponty.

I felt around in the bond with Doc, and sure enough, Ponty was there too.

Jubal had dozed off, and I reached out and grabbed him by the dream to pull him in with me as I made the mental leap through space, as easily as if I were jumping onto a bunk, through the view port of a battered old ship that could have been a derelict but contained Doc and Ponty. Here, surely, was the help we needed. I needed to be careful not to sound too desperate, however. Ponty, unlike Jubal, was not entirely trustworthy.

My dream self found Doc and Ponty on the man's bunk, Doc curled up sleeping on the man's chest. The man's eyes were closed too, but when I jumped up, he opened them and looked straight at me. I thought he must be looking through me, but no. He spoke to me.

"Did you know it was okay to come back now, boy?" he asked softly, waking Doc. He repeated to Doc, *Did he know?*

That was too much for me. I didn't want to deal with Jubal's crooked sire head-on, even in my dream form. I had to up the "cat of mystery" illusion here—which was hard to do with a man who had been there practically at my birth.

I jumped down and trotted away, beckoning Doc to follow me, which he obligingly did.

Jubal's old man was still talking to my tail, knowing who I was if not what I was, and evidently glad to see whatever part of me he was seeing. *Yeah, everything is fine and everybody really misses all you cats and wishes you'd come back. Jubal's mother and I miss him too. Is he okay? Doc, dammit, can't you talk to him?*

Doc was following my lead, however, and I led him to the bridge. I projected my message onto the com screen. I could not yet type at that time, but it was my dream and I was in control of what was in it. Even the parts others saw. Thank Bast for spell check. I jumped up to the chair and put my paws on the keyboard, moving them as if I were typing.

The com screen filled with words, glowing green on a black background.

Some of us are ready to negotiate, the screen said. *The planet of Pshaw-Ra is all that he said it was, more or less, but it is also hot.* I proceeded to list our complaints about Mau, with the general idea that while it had sounded like a nice idea to live on a planet where we were worshipped as deities, it wasn't all it was cracked up to be.

How is Jubal? Ponty tried asking me mentally, but I wasn't about to turn around. Instead I segued from "It's okay but we're ready to go" into my list of demands.

Some like it here very much, but some are ready to negotiate. Kibble should come, and Weeks. And the doctor.

Come where? Are you and Jubal ready to come back, Chester boy?

That was my cue to disappear, letting the last few letters remain on the screen like the smile of that cat in the fairy tale Jubal once read to me. I wrote, *Some are willing to negotiate.* Then, as I had seemed to, they disappeared.

"You're giving him too much credit, Chester," Doc told me. "He's a human. You're going to have to show him where to go."

I let him see me again, sitting beside the navigation screen. Doc joined me, saying, "See, there's us at Alex Station." I told him the boy reckoned we were two solar systems away, and he helped me find Mau. I made it blink.

Ponty was rather amusing, moving in slow motion as though he thought he was still dreaming. With a click of a button he saved the chart.

Good man! Smart man!

I touched noses with Doc, thanking him for the help, then rubbed my dream self against Ponty's arm, suggesting that he could feel my fur.

Sending one last message to the com screen, I leaped through the view port and back through space and the hull of the pyramid ship, safely back in my body on Jubal's lap. I hoped Ponty got my last message about the fishy treats.

Carlton Pontius, aka Carl Poindexter, known as Ponty to his shipmates, had just the tiniest little conflict of interest when it came to rescuing the cat and his son aboard the derelict ship, and ultimately from the Planet of the Pussycats, as he thought of the place where they'd gone.

His current berth was on the *Grania*, which was just a crossed bone short of a pirate ship. On the plus side, the captain, Mavis, did like cats, and officially Chester's milk brother Doc was hers. Doc saw things differently and considered Ponty his. Ponty walked on thin ice all the time trying to keep Mavis from getting jealous, when she noticed the cat at all. She probably would have liked it if Doc had ridden on her shoulder like a parrot, but Doc disliked the incense sticks she sometimes tucked lit into her dreadlocks.

On the minus side, since the Barque Cats had been MIA and the other cats pretty much exterminated by the wisdom of the Galactic Government, the vermin problem had reached disastrous proportions and any cat was worth tons of money, which made this whole rescue thing an important business opportunity for Mavis.

Ponty was still trying to come up with cat clones, but he'd forgotten a couple of ingredients at their previous port, and Alex Station didn't offer much but booze, drugs, and extra-large rats, both four- and two-legged.

Still, his kid was involved.

So he got busy on the com. "*Molly Daise*, this is Poindexter at Alex Station. Did you copy my transmission about the pyramid ship? . . . What do you mean, am I sure it's them? You'd better get here before someone hijacks it. The local populace are inclined to see anything not nailed down as salvage. Which sorta reminds me, did I mention you should bring weapons?"

Then he commed the vet, Dr. Vlast, and Janina Mauer, Chessie's girl, the *Molly Daise*'s Cat Person. He told them briefly what was going on and asked if they could pass word on to his almost ex-wife, Dorice, that Jubal was okay and coming home.

He was glad when they promised to pass on the message because he much preferred to deal with Dorice indirectly. She was a bit high-strung, but if he didn't let her know he'd heard news of the kid, he would be looking over his shoulder for the rest of his life, which might be cut tragically short once she got hold of him.

He had come to a mutual respect with the vet and Janina, from whom he'd "borrowed" Chester's mother, Chessie, to begin his short-lived career as a Barque Cat breeder, while teaming up with them to try to save the Barque Cats from the idiocy of the galactic politicians. There didn't seem to be any hard feelings on that end. He wasn't so sure about the crew of the *Molly Daise*, but he guessed he'd find out for sure when they reached Alex Station.

Meanwhile, how to keep kid and cat in good health until reinforcements arrived? Of course, the cat hadn't actually said the kid was with him, but since the boy had crossed the galaxy (and in an even gutsier move, defied his mother), Ponty figured that where the cat was, his boy was too. He would need to take them some supplies.

He set about gathering up protein bars, water (which was not in great demand on Alex Station—if he'd tried to stockpile booze, someone would have noticed right away), and cat food.

Boss, not my food! Doc complained, dogging—well, catting— his footsteps. He didn't have to worry too much about being disturbed on the *Grania* while she was docked here because Mavis and most of the crew preferred the bars to shipboard for doing their business. Occasionally someone returned to sleep, but he was pretty much left alone, supposedly working on his cat cloning project. Ponty picked up the kitten—cat now, and a pretty big one at that—and scrubbed his ears, stroked his soft gray back, and tweaked the fluffy end of his plumed tail. *It's for Chester, Doc.*

Doc indicated that family feeling and philanthropy stopped at the rim of his food bin. *I'll tell Mavis*, he threatened. *You'll get in trouble, boss.*

Ponty knew Doc couldn't actually talk to Mavis—this telepathy thing seemed to be one to a customer—but he could maybe draw her attention to the fact that he and some parts of the cargo were not where they were supposed to be. It was a little hard to get Mavis's attention these days, but she did have that weakness for cats.

Tell you what, Ponty said. *Why don't you come with me? Maybe they have some ultradelicious cat food they're keeping to themselves on that ship. Besides, it's from a planet where cats are worshipped. Don't you want to see a ship from someplace like that?*

It can't be too great or they wouldn't be back now, looking for us to pull them out, Doc said shrewdly.

Okay. Have it your way. I may have to just stay with them and go back to that place too. I hope you'll be real happy here.

That's not going to work, Doc said, but he jumped into the hatch of the *Grania's* shuttle before Ponty loaded the last of the food and water, enough for two people and two cats, and took a seat himself. He hoped nobody would sober up in the next few hours.

Touching reunions were not the order of the day, but Jubal told his old man thanks for bringing the provisions, and Doc was interested to see how a cat could fly a space vessel without human help.

Jubal asked after his mom, and Ponty asked a lot of questions about where they'd been and what they'd been doing, but all Jubal said was, "It's a long story. You'll see soon enough if you're coming. Meanwhile, hadn't you best get back to the space station before they miss you?"

"Here's the thing, son," Ponty told him. "I don't think they're likely to miss me right now, but it might not be so easy to get away next time. Especially since I have their shuttle and Doc with me. So what I'm thinking is, Doc and me should sign on with you and Chester and we get our tails out of here before Mavis finds out I'm missing. I have the coordinates for the route the *Molly Daise* will take to get here. How about we meet them halfway? You got enough fuel and oxygen and that kinda thing? I brought provisions to see us through."

Jubal consulted with Chester, who was having a hissing contest with Doc, seemingly just for old times' sake.

It's not like he can steal this ship, Chester pointed out.

Jubal knew that was true enough, since the old man was no

more able to fit into the pyramid ship's nose cone than he was. Still, he had been ready for a nice quiet rescue mission with Chester, not having to listen to his dad's BS for the duration of the journey.

But if his dad's boss was going to make trouble for them, then he had to agree that the best thing was to leave the area, meet the *Molly Daise*, and fly back in with reinforcements.

Actually, catching the old man up on what had happened since they last met turned out to be easy compared to what came next.

Chester pawed and pawed at the pictures on the control panel but could not figure out how to make the mouse hole work. He sat in front of the panel for hours at a time watching it in case it tried anything tricky that would give him a hint to its secrets. It didn't help that Doc kept making helpful suggestions, touching the controls with paw pats or sticking his nose against them and asking, "What does this do?"

At least with Doc there, the old man could also see what the bridge looked like.

Come on, boy, Jubal told Chester finally. *Pop checked our course and he says we should be back in Galactic space soon enough. The mouse hole could lose us permanently if we don't know how to work it.*

Chester growled with frustration and whipped his tail back and forth twice before following Doc's example and abandoning the bridge for a snack and a nap.

However, in warp drive, the ship entered Galactic space inside two more weeks. By then the old man had caught Jubal up on what had been happening in the galaxy, as far as he could tell from com traffic at Alex Station, and Jubal and Chester caught him and Doc up on what it was like on Mau.

Jubal's mom, along with Janina Mauer and Dr. Vlast, were waiting outside the *Molly Daise*'s docking bay when the pyramid ship landed inside Chester's old ship.

Jubal's mom hugged him so hard she almost crushed Chester, who was cuddled in his boy's arms. Then she stepped back, scanning him, walking around him, looking scarily fierce.

"Hi, Mom," he said.

Behind her back he saw the old man take Captain Vesey, who was giving him a flinty-eyed look, to one side, before the captain signaled for Janina and Dr. Vlast to join them in a walk up the corridor, leaving Jubal alone with his mom and Chester.

"You're taller," she said accusingly.

"Am I?" he asked. It wasn't like there'd been a lot of mirrors down in the tunnels. She nodded. He swallowed and asked, "So how are you, Mom? How's the farm?"

"I lost it," she said, and even though she didn't put a lot of emotion in her voice, Jubal knew how upset that made her. The farm had been her family's before she married Pop. "I'm sorry, I tried. I went to work for Mr. Varley, but when Dr. Vlast got your call, he and the girl came after me. Mr. Varley paid my way." Her voice softened a little. "It's good to see you again, baby."

Jubal took a deep breath, stepped forward, and hugged his mother again. Though always strong and sturdy, she'd never been a large woman, and now it felt like she was all bones. Whether it was losing the farm, losing track of him, or a combination, he could tell how hard all of this had been on her. "It's okay, Mom. I'm okay. Chester's okay. Pop's okay."

She snorted at the last but didn't make any overt threats, which was a hopeful sign, Jubal thought.

Dr. Vlast examined the cats and pronounced them fit for duty.

"In that case," Captain Vesey said when the vet had made his report, "we'd appreciate it if Chester and his friend would take care of some of the rats and other pests infesting the ship."

Chester and Doc needed no persuading. They headed for the ventilation ducts and other hunting grounds even before Jubal and his dad relayed the message. There was no need to ask a cat to hunt. Chester, who already knew the *Molly Daise* from kittenhood training with his mother, led the way.

Jubal, his parents, Janina, and the vet sat down in the galley for a real cooked meal.

"Jubal Poindexter, don't bolt your food," his mom said.

"I can't help it, Mom," he said through a mouthful. "This tastes so good. I haven't had much but fish for months. This tastes as good as what you used to cook."

His mother looked pleased. "That's because I cooked it. The cook they had knew how to use a replicator but he had no idea at all how to prepare the food properly once he got it out of the machine."

Jubal nodded and looked down at his almost empty plate. "What kind of meat is this?"

"It's not meat," Janina said. "It's a bean-based substitute. Most of the animals that are left since the epidemic are too valuable to slaughter. They're being used to rebuild breeding stock. But Mrs. Poindexter has done a wonderful job of making this taste like chicken."

"Pop was telling me while we were on the way here that you and him and Dr. Vlast got that big shot in the government to admit that the epidemic was all a hoax. Too bad all the animals got killed first."

"Yes," Janina said. "And I feel awful that we couldn't do it before Chessie and the others left. Is she well, Jubal? How are they all doing?"

He began relating some of the adventures he'd had with Chester on Mau, and ended by saying, "There are a lot of kittens now." Janina smiled, showing dimples, and Dr. Vlast squeezed her hand.

The hull and bulkheads and the deck under their feet rattled and thumped and occasionally squeaked.

After quite a ferocious yowl, Jubal anxiously called out, *Chester? Later, I'm hunting.*

CHESTER: RATTING

I remembered the *Molly Daise* as a very clean place with the worst infestation being the kefer-ka. Now the keka bugs were nowhere to be seen, and instead squeaks and skitters, rattling and banging, came from the inner hull, the ventilation ducts, the overheads, and from beneath the decks. We had not been on deck two seconds when a rat sauntered across the corridor in front of us.

Doc and I had a little discussion about the new breed of vermin while still aboard the pyramid ship en route to the rendezvous with the larger ship. "They're super smart and extra mean," he said. "They'll strip a ship or a man down to the bones. There was one old cat at Alex Station, mostly slept all day, and they killed him too."

"That's just wrong!" I said, my skin twitching with horror.

"The bugs are bad too, but the rats are the worst," Doc said. "They eat the insulation from the walls and from around the electrical wires and start fires. One reason Mavis let me stay onboard with Ponty was that I kept the rats down. I am only one cat, though, and Alex Station was full of the boogers, so as soon as I cleared out one, two came in to replace him."

Needless to say, the rat who sauntered across our path didn't live to saunter anywhere else. Doc was all over him before I could lift a whisker or the rodent could utter a squeak.

Not that I was any slouch. I was, after all, a cat who had fought the great snake—twice. Rats were no big deal, at least not one at a time. Or even in twos and threes—but there were dozens in the ship, maybe hundreds. I lost count. We cleaned out the biggest nests in the first few days, stopping only to eat—other stuff, that is—and sleep. It was a terrible time. In my sleep I heard them crying, "Mother!" and "Head for the outer hull! I'll try to hold the monsters off."

In the ducts, one of us would go in and start luring them out, and the other one would pounce them as each one emerged. If two came, we both pounced. Sometimes we were surrounded by rats. They tried a pincer movement on us but we were bigger, smarter, and seasoned warriors against vermin like them, whereas they had had it easy—I doubt any of them had even seen a cat before.

Tackling the ones in the wiring got tricky. The rats didn't care if they got electrocuted or not. Doc and I were not so reckless.

We surprised four of them gnawing on the electrical system that fed power to the engine room.

"Avast there, ratty," Doc said. He didn't expect them to understand him. "Belay that chewing now!" Doc had picked up a few piratical phrases at Alex Station.

Not on your life, catty, the biggest of the rats responded—thought-talk, the first time we realized they could use it just like us. It had been kind of creepy hearing their dying squeals and interpreting them as last words, but I thought I'd been imagining things. But it figured that if eating the kefer-ka could let cats share thoughts with humans, the same might be true of cats and rats. I didn't like it, but it seemed to be the case. *You may kill our families but we are going to go down gnawing.*

Go down is right, Doc said. *But you won't be alone.*

Oh yeah?

The. Ship. Is. Under way. Rat-brain. If. You. Destroy. The. Wiring. It. Cannot. Fly. And. How. Long. Do. You. Think. Anyone. Will. Last? He spoke slowly and used simple words, mostly. The rat thoughtfully chewed the plastic it already had in its mouth.

Huh. You might *be right about that. But we'd take you with us, aha!*

Nah, we'd just get into our special cat ship with our humans and fly away, Doc said. *You and your families would be* wishing *we killed you, though, as you die from lack of oxygen or sudden decompression that will flatten you like someone stepped on you.*

We'd be just as dead, the rat said.

How about if we make a deal with you? I asked. *We're tired of killing you rats, but we can't let you wreck the ship either. Our job is to protect it. If you stop doing damage, we'll make sure you get enough to eat and drink during the rest of the trip, but as soon as we land—off you go. No more ship rats.*

You're going to offload us someplace where there's no oxygen, is that it? he asked. *You cats are sly.*

We were. But it had nothing to do with oxygen.

Nope, there's plenty of oxygen. But once we land there will be a lot more cats coming aboard too. I don't think you're going to want to stick around when we teach our kittens how to hunt.

You'll let us go free? You won't chase us to kill us? There's something to eat there?

Sure. Lots.

We'll think about it and get back to you, he said, and he and the others started chewing again.

I trotted off and Doc followed. But behind us the chewing noise stopped.

The truce took. The rats kept the noise down and got out of the wiring, and we, after making token rounds, enjoyed the rest of the trip in the company of our humans, although listening to my boy's parents "not speaking" to each other made the atmosphere tense.

When we landed on Mau, as soon as the hatch opened, rats, unseen by the humans, streamed out into the desert. We didn't have the heart to tell them that this planet was ruled by cats.

CHAPTER 17

The *Molly Daise* landed unchallenged on Mau, docking beside the *Reuben Ranzo* in order to refuel the stranded ship.

No sooner had they landed than cats began boiling out of the desert floor, or at least it looked that way. By now Jubal knew they were using one of the doorways concealed beneath the sand, the same one he had used to bring the fuel to Pshaw-Ra.

The human crew, although sweating profusely and complaining of the heat, disembarked from their ship to welcome their new passengers. One of the first cats to greet them was Chessie, with Chester and Renpet's kittens behind her. Chester ran out to meet them, then kept looking and sniffing, searching for Renpet. As he ran forward, the other Barque Cats and kittens and a few of the Mau cats as well swarmed out of the hole in the desert.

But though Chester searched every new surge of cats, Renpet wasn't with them. *I'm going in after her,* Chester told Jubal, wriggling his way through cats pushing in the opposite direction until he disappeared down the hole.

Jubal suddenly understood that he and Chester had abandoned poor Renpet during a terrible time for her, when she'd just lost Chione. He could imagine how she must feel. When he'd been separated from Chester for the first time, they both suffered something awful from the loss, but at least they had the hope of seeing each other again. There was no such hope for Renpet.

Janina scooped Chessie up, kissing and petting her while Chessie purred and purred. Then the girl had to pass Chessie around to the other crew members, who petted her, called her a pretty girl, and told her how much they'd missed her.

Jubal was about to go down the hole after Chester when he reappeared, followed by Beulah, holding Renpet. Chester's mate didn't look as if she'd been doing much leading of her subjects. She was thin and listless, her fur greasy looking and spiky, like that of a very old cat. Her eyes were half filmed over with the nictating membrane—a cat's third eyelid that extended from the inside corner of the eye toward the center and showed itself when a cat was unwell. Jubal had a bad feeling about Renpet.

The kittens, oblivious, climbed Beulah's legs and chased Chester's tail until Jubal picked them up and showed them to Janina.

"Very cute. They're both polydactyls!" As if to confirm her observation, Junior grabbed her finger with his toes and held on.

"Take a closer look at all of these kittens," Jubal suggested. "Just about every Barque queen had a litter and every Barque tom sired one. Cute, huh?"

"Their fur isn't as long as Chester's or Chessie's," Janina observed.

"That's the Mau part of them. Heavy coats are too hot for this climate," Jubal said, waving Beulah over. "Janina, this is Princess Renpet, Chester's mate and the mom of his kittens."

Janina smiled but looked a little dubious at Renpet's condition. "I hope the kittens will be good ships' cats too. We really need them now. The rats have been ruling the galaxy since the cats left."

Unlike the *Ranzo*, whose rescue of the cats had been sudden and unplanned, the *Molly Daise* had an opportunity to prepare for their new cargo. Crew members were delighted to share their quarters with the cats. Since so many of the passengers were little kittens who required monitoring, some crew members made new berths for themselves in the cargo hold, so the kittens could be closer to the humans who knew how to care for them. Janina had her old berth, with Jared's one door down. Chessie, Sol, and Bat and their kittens occupied Janina's quarters. Renpet, although she had grown attached to Beulah, was placed in Jared's quarters, along with the two families of the newest kittens, those born to the mothers who had lost their Barque Cat babies earlier. The new kittens seemed healthy but were still quite young.

Chester wanted to be near Renpet too, though Jubal was nervous about having him remain on the *Molly Daise*. "They could still claim that Chester belonged to them," he said.

Beulah told him, "Renpet needs to be near the vet, but I think she should be near Chester too. She just seemed lost and confused after Chione died. She had no interest in feeding or grooming her kittens. It was a good thing some of the other mother cats came down when they did. She sleeps, won't eat, and cries all the time. I hope having Chester nearby will perk her up."

The purser, Mr. Yawman, overheard them. "You and Chester and the kittens can share my quarters, young man. Looks like Chester has done a lot of growing since he was last aboard."

Beulah cast a guilty glance at Renpet. "I'll feel better with you and Chester near her, Jubal. I have to get back to work on the *Ranzo*. I've taken care of Flekica ever since her first litter disappeared and was there when her second litter was born. I can hardly abandon her now, but poor Renpet . . . every time she cries I want to cry with her."

She and Flekica and the two litters of kittens did return to her duty station after Captain Vesey and Captain Loloma informed her that since the ships would be traveling together, she and the com officer on the *Molly Daise* should set up their systems so there was a tight link between the bridges of the two ships. They reconfigured each ship's view port and security screens into an array, with a central display surrounded by feeds from the crew stations and officers' quarters. Each ship could show the instrument readings or the view of surrounding space from either bridge.

While refueling the *Ranzo*, the crew of the *Molly Daise* also helped the *Ranzo* crew outfit their ship properly for the remaining cats, with bedding, food, water containers, and feline waste disposal units.

It wasn't easy for either crew, with the heat of the desert sun beating down on them as they slogged back and forth from ship to ship, sometimes carrying several warm, fluffy, wiggly cats and kittens, as well as the provisions for them. But even Sosi pitched in, carrying cats and bags of food from the *Molly Daise* to her own ship. "At least this time Hadley won't have to worry about sharing his food," she told Jubal. "And they brought more for him."

Once the *Ranzo* was com-linked, fueled, and had the cooling system back online, and the cats, kittens, and quarters sorted out, they were ready to go.

Before either ship could begin countdown, however, the closest doorway to the underworld reopened and Pshaw-Ra popped out. The *Molly Daise* hadn't unloaded the pyramid ship, and in fact Jubal's pop, keeping a low profile, was there now, in the shuttle bay, studying the parts of the ship he could reach.

Pshaw-Ra looked panicked when he saw his ship was not where he expected it to be, then ran to the *Molly Daise*.

He was immediately followed by a hastily hobbling Balthazar, who wore a shipsuit and a large backpack that almost bent him double.

Before the old man reached the ship, pursuers were hot on his heels. Jubal reckoned they must have been trailing the others through the tunnels.

What seemed like hundreds of cats and humans from the city—including the queen's golden guards, one of them the female who had brought the Barque Cats and their kittens to hide in the underworld—sprang from the hole in the desert.

Right behind them was Nefure herself, and she was not happy. She bristled to twice her normal size, her ears flat against her skull, fangs as fierce-looking as the great snake's. Her painted crown and collar vanished into the fluffed uproar of her fur.

She yowled a battle cry, challenging him.

Pshaw-Ra, who was surrounded, assumed his best "Who me?" expression.

Jubal, Chester, and Chester's kittens watched from the bridge of the *Molly Daise*. Jubal's old man, who evidently had shown up to see what the fuss was about, put his hand on his son's shoulder and squeezed reassuringly.

Captain Vesey pointed in the direction of the weapons locker and someone rushed to obey. The humans with the cat posse were brandishing guns, but of a much earlier technology than the ones standard on contemporary ships. The spears and arrows and such, which were the only weapons Jubal had seen, were evidently as ceremonial as the kilts, because these humans wore lightweight white pants and loose shirts, somewhat grubby from the underground. None of them seemed happy as they watched their queen.

Pshaw-Ra didn't bother to bristle. He put himself between the queen and Balthazar. Nefure yowled again, and the guard advanced. Captain Vesey had positioned newly armed crew members there, and the hatch abruptly opened to admit Chione's father. Pshaw-Ra flicked his tail twice and turned to sprint for the hatch himself, but the queen sprang at him and fell upon him. The two of them rolled over and over in the sand, creating their own dust devil as they snarled and yowled their fury.

It happened so quickly no one could intervene, and then, to make matters worse, the three closest guard cats jumped into the fray.

The queen yowled louder, and when Pshaw-Ra's bloody form detached itself from the dust devil and streaked into the open hatch, they understood why.

The guard cats had flattened their queen into the sand. One had his teeth in her neck, another lay across her, and a third pinned her paws with his own. Then two humans stepped forward bearing a cage, and the queen—former queen, from the look of it—was bitten and clawed and shoved toward it.

But suddenly she exploded in a whirl of claws and tail, straight up, away from restraining hands and paws, and flew across the desert, away from her subjects, toward the river.

I wish Renpet could enjoy this! Chester said.

I wonder why they didn't do that sooner, Jubal said as the cats and people backed away from the ship, looking up at it wistfully. The mothers and sires of the kittens had big sad eyes, and their humans stroked them reassuringly.

Pshaw-Ra popped back out of the ship, now that the lay of the land had a different topography, so to speak, and addressed the Mauans. *My friends—and I see by your actions that you are still my friends, and believe in me—I know you are loath to part with your kittens and new mates among the Barque Cats, but their destiny lies among the stars. Their dual lineage will enable them to do great deeds that will elevate us all to our proper place as rulers of the universe. Meanwhile, each kitten must seek his own human to do his bidding and assist him in his path to greatness, to the glory of Mau. Fear not, your mates may return soon to beget other young and your kittens return to you with their own litters. For now, though, we must part. Your families are safely aboard, bedded down and being cared for. The universe will be theirs for the taking!*

Viti-amun pawed the air in the direction of the ship. *Keep them safe, Grandsire. And when they are ready to learn of their heritage, lead them back to us.*

He pawed the air back at her and returned to the ship, tail waving, muttering to himself, *But don't hold your breath.*

CHAPTER 18

PIRATES: CHESTER

From the bridge, we watched the Mau cats and their humans trudge overland back to the city, a more direct route than the underground labyrinth.

The captains continued their countdowns. Darkness crept over us before they got down to double digits.

Jubal and I returned to our quarters. I had forgotten about his mother. Originally a passenger on the *Molly Daise*, she had now signed on as an assistant steward in order to stay near Jubal. She glared at me when Jubal wasn't looking, though she didn't kick me or anything. I couldn't imagine someone actually disliking cats, but *I* was not about to try to win *her* over. Jubal was mine now more than ever, and she was just going to have to get used to it.

While the two of them talked, I sat on what I had decided was my perch, though the purser thought it was his desk, where I could look out the porthole. The night was dark but the moons were up, casting shadows across the dunes. At first I thought there was wind too, but as I hunkered down and watched more carefully, the sand that had seemed to blow up out of the ground off toward the river appeared to gather itself together and settle back down into the long curves and humps of gray and black landscape. It seemed to me that its lines traced those of the underground passages — and I had never noticed sand behaving that way before.

The movement traveled through the desert until it disappeared under the ship. I relaxed, yawned and stretched, shaking off a vague, uneasy feeling that was much less interesting than what was in my food dish. I said nothing to Jubal, who was arguing with his mother. It probably wouldn't have changed anything; who could have known what it meant even if it was clearly visible then?

The trip from Mau was a happy one. The cats were chowing down on familiar food, Pshaw-Ra slept when he wasn't trotting around seeming to inspect everything, and the crews were busy planning how to make some kind of profit out of their good deed of rescuing the cats, or at least pay for the trip.

"After all, we ditched cargo to load cats," Captain Vesey said, speaking to Captain Loloma and Beulah via com screen during the conference between the ships in flight. "It was the right thing to do, but meanwhile we spent fuel and time and maybe alienated clients. Now the ships are going to expect us to return the cats and kittens to them for free, since the cats belonged to them to begin with."

"Yes, and we'll be lucky if we don't get charged with cat-napping," Captain Loloma agreed. "Never mind that we saved the cats they surrendered to the government from being destroyed."

Ponty was delighted to speak up, offering them his expert opinions and advice. "The thing to do, sirs, is return the Barque Cats to their original owners okay, but charge a finder's fee for bringing them back. And clearly, Cap'n Loloma, your ship was hijacked by that alien cat who brought you all here, right? He incited the Barque Cats to riot, scared as they were, and they just plain overran you."

"They're not going to believe that! They chased us."

"Yes, sir, but you were under duress—besides, if you tell the truth, it brings up stuff they don't want to talk about. This story lets you off the hook, and lets them save face because they were dumb enough to try to kill off highly valuable and perfectly healthy animals on bogus evidence. *They* know it, *you* know it, but if you don't say so out loud, they will probably appreciate it enough to pretend to believe you."

"Why should we listen to you? You're crooked as a dog's hind leg," Captain Vesey said disgustedly. Ponty glanced over at him uneasily. The *Molly Daise* skipper had no actual evidence that he'd stolen Chessie, but Vesey was very suspicious of him and made it clear he didn't like him even a little bit.

"No, wait, he might be right," Captain Loloma said from the screen. "It makes sense to me. That might get us out of trouble, and we could say we contacted you as soon as we were able so we could get unhijacked, which could earn us some of that finder's fee for the cats too."

Ponty beamed into the screen at Loloma and, more cautiously, at Vesey as if they were really bright students. "Okay, so that's our stay-out-of-jail card and reimbursement for some of our losses. That's good but the really good thing is the kittens. Those little buggers are going to be worth their weight in gold now."

"Maybe so, if they were purebred Barque Cats with papers, like our kittens would have been," the *Molly Daise* first mate said. "But these kittens, cute as they are with their big floppy paws, are clearly not purebred Barque Cats."

"Good point, friend," Ponty said, pointing to the mate. "But—"

"But any cat is better than no cat at all, with the vermin problem being so bad now," argued the pretty brown-haired second mate, Soine, according to her name tag.

"No kidding," the *Molly Daise* purser, Yawman, agreed. "There are not only more of them since the cats have been gone, but they seem to have become a lot smarter."

"Supply and demand, my friends, supply and demand," Ponty

said, rocking on his heels a little. "And we have the supply to fill the demand."

Jubal and Chester had been quiet up till now, and Ponty thought Jubal seemed amazed at how everybody listened to him as if he wasn't just full of bull pucky. Now the kid spoke.

"These kittens may not have papers on both sides of the family, but Chester can find out who their Mau parent was, most of the time, and some of the babies—like his—have royal blood on the Mau side. The reason they're all crossbred is because their—uh—chief scientist believes they will be even better space cats because of it. So if they're properly cared for and allowed to train with their Barque Cat parent, they may be the best space cats ever."

"See there?" Ponty asked proudly. "We're going to come out on top of this, ladies and gentlemen, reuniting most of the original cats with their crews and having all of these extraordinary—did you hear the boy say 'royal'?—kittens to sell as well. It's going to be smooth sailing for us from now on."

But before they finished planning how much to charge per kitten or how they were going to spend all their money, they were intercepted by the *Grania*. The *Grania*'s captain, in full battle array including lighted incense twined in the red dreadlocks that went so incongruously with her Asian features, appeared on the linked com screens.

"Prepare to be boarded," Mavis O'Malley said.

Captain Loloma was the first to reply to her challenge. "Mavis, haven't you got anything better to do than attack a couple of poor trading ships?" he asked her. "We don't even have any cargo this run."

"Maybe you do and maybe you don't," Mavis said, "but I got friends in low places tell me that thief and cat rustler Ponty was seen boarding the *Molly Daise*. He took off with my shuttle and my cat, and I want them back and his guts for my garters."

She hoisted a leg into view of the com screen. It still bore some semblance of shapeliness above its black and dirty white striped sock, but where it wasn't tattooed, it showed varicose veins from a lifetime of variable gravity. She pursed her lips in a parody of a kiss as she snapped an imaginary garter on her skinny thigh.

"Yuck," Jubal said. He lay beside his bunk, concealing Chester and the kittens, as fascinated by the image on Purser Yawman's cabin com screen as if it were the great snake getting ready to strike.

"We have your shuttle on the *Molly Daise*, Captain O'Malley," Captain Vesey said politely. "And will be glad to leave it for you at the next regulation space station."

"Screw that," Mavis snapped, her mouth thin and pointy like a turtle's. "I want my cat back and I want Ponty in irons. We drink slop and eat bugs while he runs around in our shuttle with my cat!"

"Mr. Poindexter had a family emergency . . ." Captain Vesey began.

Jubal could hear his mother's voice scolding, ". . . got us into this, so get your scabby behind out there and pretend to be a man!" That was good. His parents were talking again.

His father's face appeared on the screen from one of the crew quarter's feeds, which was quickly switched to the main screen. "Why, Mavis, to what do we owe the honor?"

"You know damn good and well—" she began.

"Look, I hated to run off like that without saying anything," he began, oozing apology and sincerity, "and I knew you'd worry about Doc, but you were otherwise engaged, so I took him with me. See, I was busy trying to clone cats when lo and behold who should float by, marooned and all, but my boy and *his* cat. Jubal's cat and Doc were raised together, so I thought having the little guy along would calm Chester down."

"Shut it, Ponty. Nobody steals from me and lives to set a bad example."

"Of course not, Mavis. I was just borrowing."

"I said shut it. To my way of thinking, the *Ranzo* and the *Molly Daise* are harboring a thief—namely you. They must pay interest on what you owe me."

"You're a tad outnumbered, don't you think?" he asked.

"Small job like this, I still got friends," she said.

"So you do," Captain Loloma's voice replied. The feed that had displayed his bridge zoomed out to include a view of the *Grania* and the two ships that suddenly appeared right behind her. Like her, they had a less than legal look about them.

The last words they heard Mavis say before they felt the jolt were "Tractor beams."

Aboard the *Molly Daise*, the kitten her father, Space Jockey, called Spike—but who privately thought of herself as the Fury—watched the com screen more intently than she had ever watched prey. The exciting-looking female on the screen awakened something warm and gleefully wild in her that she had never felt before. Not when meeting her stupid royal mother, nor from the patient teachings of Viti-amun, nor from her sire's casual neglect. Helping to claw the great snake to death had come close, but while the experience was satisfying, it was not as sweet as the mere vision of the woman.

According to the conversation that passed between her and the man, the woman already belonged to a cat named Doc—which was unfortunate for Doc, the Fury thought to herself. She would kill him if she had to in order to claim that woman for her own.

They can't come here, Chester cried to Jubal. *They'll take the kittens.*

Yes, they will, and you too probably, and all of the other cats. Pop said that woman likes cats, but I don't think she wants to keep you all to play with.

Will the crews fight for us? Chester asked. *Like they were going to fight Nefure?*

Small arms against cannons? Probably not. I figure with the kind of business those ships are in, they must have some big guns. The Ranzo *doesn't, and I'm pretty sure the* Molly Daise *doesn't.*

Out in the corridor, footsteps thundered by and orders were barked. When Jubal heard the last order, he pulled down the protective cover on the kittens' bed and strapped himself in with Chester, ready for a bumpy ride.

The purser's com screen showed the pirate vessels extruding their boarding tubes, reminding him of Apep again. Chester shivered against him, and Jubal felt the kittens crowding as close as they could to the back of his legs. He dangled his fingers down to the mesh and made vague petting motions through it to try to soothe them. One of them sank tiny needle teeth into his index finger.

"Ouch!"

But he forgot his pain, letting the blood drip down his hand as he watched the screen. When Pop had spoken of this Mavis before, she sounded comical, maybe not as bad as she tried to seem. But now he saw the businesslike tube coming toward them and the first boarder at its front, weapons of all descriptions strapped all over him. The ships shouldn't have sat there and let her talk at them until she had them in her tractor beams, he realized. They should have flown out of range. Maybe Pshaw-Ra, who had been awfully quiet lately, should have made a mouse hole and flown them all through it.

It was an idea. *Chester, can Pshaw-Ra load all the* Molly Daise *cats into the pyramid ship and break out of here?*

How does that save us?

It doesn't, I guess—but maybe if they decide to chase the pyramid ship and he mouse-holes it like he did when we escaped the Government Guard ships, the big ships could get loose and escape?

"Pshaw-Ra?" Chester asked, and told him Jubal's idea.

"Better if the other felines remain here, Chester. If I am going to risk my tail to save everyone, I should not carry the kittens with me. Your help, however, would be welcome."

"Jubal too?"

"Your boy should instruct the bridge in mouse-hole protocol. It will be enough simply to instruct Captain Loloma's ship what is required. That flamboyant floozie who is attacking us will have no idea what the mouse hole is."

Jubal, hearing the whole thing through Chester, didn't like it. What if Pshaw-Ra simply decided to take off and leave the ship to the pirates? What if Chester and Pshaw-Ra were killed? On the other hand, if they just sat around and waited for the pirates to board, he and Chester would be separated for sure.

"Okay," he said, and while Chester hightailed it for the shuttle bay, he made his way to the bridge.

He had a hard time getting Captain Vesey's attention, and when he did, the captain glowered at him. He made his face as innocent and helpful and childlike as he hadn't felt in a long time, and drew the captain away from com screen range to explain the plan to him.

"You say the cats thought this one up?" Captain Vesey demanded, lowering his voice slightly as Jubal gave him an urgent palms-down signal to lower his voice.

"It worked before, sir, when Pshaw-Ra led the *Ranzo* through the mouse hole, away from pursuers."

"As I recall reports of the incident, the *Ranzo* was not at that time attached to the pursuers by tractor beam."

"No, sir, but the pyramid ship is highly maneuverable. We're thinking Pshaw-Ra can make them release the tractor beam, lead them away from you, then flip back, open the mouse hole, and lead our ships through while the pirates are still turning to try to overtake it."

"Why should they chase the pyramid ship anyway?" he asked.

Jubal hadn't actually thought of that. "Uh—they'll want the alien technology?"

"Not as bad as they want your old man. How about he chases the pyramid ship in the pirate shuttle. If the *Grania* thinks he's getting away, they'll be sure to pursue."

The captain turned to gesture to Jubal's pop to join them so he could explain the plan.

But then Jubal heard Chester say, *Whaaaat?*

Looking up, he saw the feed from the shuttle bay that showed the outer hatch opening. The pyramid ship whirled through it and knifed out into space. Since the pirate's shuttle the old man had hijacked wasn't in the bay, it must have still been inside the pyramid ship.

"So here's how the mouse hole works, sir . . ." Jubal began, following the captain's gaze first to the screen with the disappearing pyramid ship, and then to the other screen, where a boarding tube was attaching to their hull.

CHAPTER 19

CHESTER: REVENGE OF THE SERPENT

"Sometimes I get so tired of being the only hero to save the day," Pshaw-Ra complained, or pretended to, as we sped away from the *Molly Daise*. His paws were flying all over the picture symbols, but now I understood what he was doing—except that I didn't know how to activate the mouse hole.

"We have to get the pirates to let go of our ships first," I reminded him. "Get them to chase us."

"A game of cat and mouse hole, maybe?" he asked.

He dived our pointy nose right into the nose of the pirate ship, so close we could see incense smoking in the old pirate woman's dreadlocks. Then he zipped away again. The pirates did not react as we'd hoped.

"Hmmm, they might mistake us for a drone," Pshaw-Ra said.

The tractor beam apparently stayed in place. The boarding tube began wiggling with the movements of the people inside it. I felt an almost irresistible impulse to pounce on the bouncing thing and bite and claw it.

We tried the same maneuver with the ship that had the *Ranzo* trapped in its tractor beam, darting in closely. There was a flash and a concussion, and we ricocheted off the picture symbols from one wall to the other before the pyramid ship righted itself.

"They fired on us!" Pshaw-Ra cried triumphantly, giving a couple of stiff-legged hops from side to side as a victory dance.

"That's a good thing?" I asked.

"You watch."

We zoomed back in more closely, but this time when we veered off, the pirate ship followed course while the *Ranzo* slipped away.

"Mouse-hole time!" Pshaw-Ra exclaimed.

The symbols I had seen once before appeared—the great snake, whom I now recognized, opening its mouth to swallow our tiny ship. The pirate ship followed close on our tail. Before the hole could close, Pshaw-Ra steered our craft back toward the opening, skimming the belly of the pursuing craft now headed the wrong way, and we flew back into the sector where the pirate woman still held our friends in thrall. The hole closed behind us—and the second pirate ship was somewhere else. I didn't know where that was, but they wouldn't know either. They would be lost, lost, lost, and it served them right!

Now we were free to help the *Molly Daise*, and so was the *Ranzo*—if we were not too late.

Jubal hoped Chester's plan would work, because he didn't think this was something Pop was going to talk his way out of.

The *Molly Daise* was a peaceful trading ship and had even fewer arms than the *Ranzo*. Captain Vesey ordered the passengers and crew, including Jubal, to lock themselves in their cabins.

Pop handed a protesting Doc to him as he left the bridge. "Take care of him, son, and yourself," Pop said with a seriousness that was scary. "Mavis doesn't exactly take rejection well. I'm afraid she might hurt Doc if she finds him. And she might not draw the line at hurting you, even though you're a kid, since you're my kid."

"I'll take care of him, Pop," Jubal promised.

As Jubal locked the door to the purser's cabin behind him, he heard Mr. Yawman say, "I'm ex-Guard, Cap'n. If we organize, we can take 'em."

He sounded excited, not at all like the careful records keeper who figured every credit the ship and her personnel earned or spent.

Over the cabin's screen now displaying the bridge, he saw Pop saying to the captain and purser, "No need for anyone to get hurt. Mavis is a businesswoman. She'll rob you blind, true, but as far as killing anybody goes, she might kill me, but probably not . . ."

To his surprise, Jubal saw his mom enter the bridge with a laser rifle she held as comfortably as she did the shotgun she'd used to run Pop off the farm. "Killing Carlton is still my privilege," she said, "and that old harpy will have to go through me to get him."

"Now, Mrs. Poindexter—" Yawman began, but she froze him with a look. She was good at that.

"May I remind you that in addition to this sorry excuse for a husband, I have a boy on this vessel, and I do not intend that he be harmed or sold into slavery or any such piratical nonsense."

Then the screen switched to the feed from the security camera positioned near the maintenance hatch, the one the pirates' boarding tube had clamped onto. The hatch blew and the boarding party crowded in.

Huddled on the floor in front of Chester's kittens, Jubal heard the ring of booted footsteps on metal as the armed crewmen ran down the corridor, toward the hatch in the aft section of the ship.

Looking up at the screen again, he saw the pyramid ship pop back into view. *Chester?* he asked.

Here, mission accomplished!

The pirates have boarded. They're in the maintenance air lock.

But Chester didn't respond this time and moments later Jubal heard the patter of paws running down the hall. He knew it couldn't possibly be Chester so soon, but it might be some other cat following the running crewmen.

Jubal opened the door and slithered out, closing it behind him, then slunk along the wall calling, "Kitty kitty," softly.

There was an excited cat noise from farther astern, and he hurried after it. All the fighting would be at the docking bay lock, so if he could just intercept the cat first, at least he could keep him safe.

It didn't help that the lights had been dimmed throughout the ship, which made it difficult for him to see where he was going, but then it would have the same effect on the pirates. And by now he at least had some idea of the layout of the decks.

"Kitty?" he called, and for a moment the kitten ahead of him stopped and turned to fix its big eyes on him. They were glowing through the gloom, and he got a distinct impression of annoyance and impatience.

He didn't recognize the kitten at first, but whoever it was, it shouldn't be in the midst of a pitched battle.

He had a few loose pieces of Chester's favorite treat in his pocket and he pulled one out to lure the cat, hunkering down to proffer it gently. "Here, kitty. This is no place for you now."

The cat ignored him and ran on. Three doors down the darkened corridor the noise from the direction of the lock was growing increasingly distinct—reverberating blasts at the door, shouts, cursing, his mother's distinctive snarl, his father trying to BS his way through the barriers and out of trouble. The kitten turned suddenly and trotted back to him.

He knew who she was now. One of Nefure's daughters, the funny looking one with the spiky red lion's mane and the black-and-white-striped legs and tail. Chester said Space Jockey had named her Spike. It fit. "Hey, Spike, hi there girl, want a fishy treat? You remember me? Come on now, a people fight is no place for a kitten."

She bit his finger as she snatched the treat, then dashed down the corridor toward the fray.

Jubal started after her, sparing one backward look for Chester's kittens, still hidden in the purser's quarters.

We are here. Chester's thought-voice broke through his concentration on the kitten. *We took the second pirate ship into the mouse hole and left her. The Ranzo now has the pirate ship in her spaceship-pulling thing.*

That's good, Jubal said.

There is something funny happening out here, Chester told him. *There's a kind of long skinny dust trail winding all around the pirate's tube, like a great serpent trying to mate with it. I'm not sure whether I should enjoy watching it or hide from it.*

Let me see, Jubal said, and he saw through Chester's eyes, looking out into space, where there was indeed a dark twisting column wound around the boarding tube he had seen on the *Molly Daise* com screen. It looked like dust. The gleam of distant stars was visible through its particles, but it was oblivious to the tractor beam, neither dispersed nor controlled by it, and it was squeezing the boarding tube, which had to be made of pretty strong stuff, and pulling it away from both ships. If there were any pirates still inside it, they were about to go for a swim in deep space. The boarding tube collapsed, detached, and floated away from the ship.

But the thing was already attached to the pirate vessel. Now it fanned out across the ship's hull, making it look like it had just been for a drive down a dirt road.

Huh. Unfortunately this meant the pirates who boarded the *Molly Daise* had no mother ship to return to.

He drew back from Chester and shook his head hard to regain his bearings. He was still standing in the middle of the corridor, and the sounds of fighting were louder. The kitten had skedaddled while he conferred with Chester. Should he follow orders and go back and lock himself in with Chester's family?

He heard a kitten scream, and that settled it. He could no more help running toward the sound than he could help loving Chester.

The fighting had spilled into the aft corridor, where the crew had taken cover behind barricades of heavy cargo crates, and the pirates, having breached the air lock, slashed at the barricade with big whopping knives. Nobody was actually shooting at that time. Laser rifles were known to damage hulls.

In the midst of all of this, the spike-maned kitten screamed and screamed, though nobody was hurting it. In fact, Jubal's old man had caught it and tucked it into the pocket where Doc used to ride when he was a baby.

Mavis, the pirate captain, held up her hand, ordering her crew to stop hacking while she listened to the bawling kitten. "Let her go, Ponty," she told him, pointing to his pocket.

"You got no claim on this cat, Mavis," Pop responded, but Jubal thought he could hear the beginnings of the-old-man-starting-to-negotiate in his tone.

"That not what she say," she told him.

"This here is a royal kitten, Mavis," Pop told her. He had, of course, made a point of learning as much as he could about the genealogy and possible value of each of the feline passengers. It was the sort of thing he did. "Why, she's probably worth more than all three ships put together."

"Shut up, you. Let her talk. Let her out." And to everyone's surprise, Mavis hunkered down on her haunches, stuck her saber and pistols into a gaudy sash belted around the middle of her spacesuit, and rubbed her fingers together, saying, "Come, kitty. Come, my Fury."

Everybody was watching Mavis, so no one told Jubal to go back when he hunkered down beside Pop. The old man's eyes were narrowed and his hand went to his pocket flap like an old-time gunfighter about to draw.

A tiny black-and-white-striped paw whipped out and slashed his hand. "Ouch! Damn, kitty!"

Mavis laughed. "Let her go or she shred you same like government papers, Ponty."

"If we let you have this cat, instead of Doc, you gonna go back to your ship and fly away, all forgiven?"

"No no. Still take you guts for garters, but will have this kitten. Better kitten than phony one."

Jubal spoke up. "Do you know that you're cut off from your ship, and I'm pretty sure something may be eating it?"

"Huh?" she asked, and in some dialect Jubal didn't know directed one of the pirates to go look. He came back squawking and pointing back toward the air lock.

"Never mind. We just use this ship for a while."

"Not on my watch, lady," Mr. Yawman said, drawing a bead on her.

"Belay that," the captain said. "Nobody's been killed yet and we don't want to start if we don't have to."

"Yeah," Jubal said. "But just so everybody knows what the stakes are, I think you should know, Captain Mavis, that your backup ship mysteriously disappeared. Once the *Ranzo* was released from its tractor beam, it locked the *Grania* in its own beam."

"Who that?" Mavis searched the barricades, which were as dimly lit as was strategically feasible, to see who was talking.

"My boy," Pop said, putting a hand on Jubal's shoulder.

"Sure. I know that," Mavis said, and made an exasperated face, though her expressions were a little hard to read, what with the wrinkles, the tattoos, and the shiny things stuck into her skin, not to mention the general grime.

But when Pop moved his hand, the kitten in his pocket made a break for it and with a mighty leap cleared the heads of the crewmen and the barricade, and made a four-point landing on Mavis's shoulder. Fortunately for the pirate, she still had on the space suit, and the top was impervious to claws, among other things. The pirate queen reached up two jeweled fingers. Jubal expected her to lose them, but the kitten leaned against her cheek and purred loudly enough for him to hear it from behind the barricade.

Ponty shook his head. "Maybe there really is someone for everyone," he said, and winked at Jubal while nodding toward his heavily armed mother. Fortunately for Pop, she had her eyes trained on the pirates and didn't see, or he might have been the first casualty.

Chester's voice mewed in Jubal's mind, calling him.

Jubal called back, *Where are you, boy?*

We're docked in the Molly Daise *shuttle bay. Pshaw-Ra wants someone to get your sire's shuttle out of his ship. It's heavy and makes flying tricks harder.*

Obviously none of the adults still glowering at each other and rattling their weapons would be free to get away, so Jubal whispered to his dad, "Good luck. I have to go pee," and put up with hearing the pirates—and, he suspected, some of the crew—laugh at him as he walked quickly back toward the bow.

The shuttle bay was within sight of everyone so he had to keep going, even though he wanted to see Chester. He didn't know how to fly that shuttle anyway. Janina did, though! Or at least she could fly *a* shuttle. He knocked lightly on the door to her cabin and got no answer. "It's me, Jubal," he said in a loud whisper. "I need your help."

There was a security camera right outside her door, and he looked up at it and waved. The door opened a crack and he slid inside.

"Are the pirates gone?" she asked.

"No, but we're working on it."

"The captain said we should stay locked in our cabins and take care of the kittens."

"This will only take a little bit, and it may help evict the pirates. Chester and Pshaw-Ra need someone to move the pirate shuttle out of the pyramid ship's bay."

"Why can't the pirates go back the way they came?"

"It's kind of a long story. If the crew gives the pirates the shuttle to return to their ship in, the pyramid ship needs to be long gone first or I wouldn't be surprised if Mavis tried to take it too."

"Who's Mavis?" Janina looked scared and angry at the same time.

"She's the pirate captain Pop was working for. Like I said, a long story. Could you do it? Please?"

"The cats—" she began.

"It will only take a minute."

Chessie was not buying it. With a reproachful look at Jubal, she shot out into the corridor ahead of Janina, and fell in step with them as the girl and Jubal sprinted toward the shuttle bay.

CHAPTER 20

As soon as Janina piloted the hijacked pirate shuttle clear of the confines of the pyramid ship, the *Molly Daise*'s outer hatch opened and the pyramid ship whirled out into space.

Where's Pshaw-Ra going? Jubal asked Chester, who had climbed into the shuttle too.

Who knows with him? He took a look at those things attacking the boarding tube, said, "Uh-oh," and told me to call you. He doesn't want pirates looking too closely at his ship.

In which case he had left not a moment too soon. When the docking bay hatch closed and the O$_2$ gauge said it was safe to exit, Jubal, Chester, Janina, and Chessie stepped out onto the bay's deck in time to see the pirates being marched in. Mr. Yawman's jaw was tight and his eyes hard as he watched every move the captives made. Jubal thought the purser was disappointed he hadn't been allowed to shoot any of them. Mom looked like she was in a real bad mood too, but Pop was smiling, running his mouth the whole time, like he was leading the pirates on a tour of the ship.

Mavis stopped and Mr. Yawman's laser rifle dug into her back, which didn't bother her at all. "Ahhh," she said, eyeing Chessie and Chester, and reaching up to stroke Spike. "Cat shortage not so short now, eh?"

If only she knew! He hoped Spike wouldn't tell her about the other cats.

Chester caught his thought and exchanged glares with Spike. *No danger of that for now, I think. Spike doesn't want her new best friend to even see other cats. Look how she's bristling, just because that Mavis noticed Mother and me.*

But as the pirate queen climbed into her shuttle, she gave Jubal a nasty wink, as if to tell him this wasn't over.

Dad let his breath go at the same time the shuttle left the bay. "You're even with *her* now," Mom said.

He shook his head. "That was only round one."

But they returned to the bridge and the captain ordered that the all-clear signal be given. People, most of them cuddling at least one cat or kitten, poured into the corridors and headed to their duty stations, awaiting further orders.

The pyramid ship was nowhere to be seen, but the shuttle was fast approaching its mother ship, the outline of which was blurred by a layer of whatever had destroyed the boarding tube.

It looked so innocent somehow. They could see the shuttle bay hatch open and light try to spill out into the blackness of space, but it was swallowed at once by the stuff covering the ship. It all rushed toward the opening at the same time as the shuttle.

On the bridge of the *Molly Daise*, the cats who had accompanied crew members—Chester and Chessie included—lined up along the view port, hindquarters twitching and jaws chattering.

The shuttle did a 180 and the pirate queen's voice came through the com. "Change mind, we stay with you."

Captain Vesey declined to invite the pirates back on board. After all, just because Mavis reported that there was no response from the crew left aboard the pirate ship didn't mean that anything was wrong—or even that what she said was true.

"They've got their shuttle back," Mr. Yawman said. "Let them fly that for a while."

Jubal's mom growled worse than he'd ever heard from any of the cats, who had wandered off now or were under the consoles sleeping, preening, or grooming each other.

But the *Ranzo* had a different attitude. Captain Loloma said, "You confiscated their weapons, right?"

"Of course," Captain Vesey said.

"We'll toss them in our brig, then," Captain Loloma said. "You maybe aren't seeing from your side what we see from ours. Something has attached itself to the *Grania*'s hull. The spooky thing is, we saw it leaving *our* ship, creeping along the path of the tractor beam."

"We saw something of the sort, but the *Grania* had deployed a boarding tube on our side. All anyone reports seeing is a collection of wiggly things, like a cross between dust moats in a sunbeam and a herd of worms, but it was fast and powerful enough to swarm up the tube until it reached the *Grania*, leaving the tube crushed behind it."

"We weren't all that alarmed when our own running lights picked out the—like you said, a herd of worms—sort of flowing away from our hull, following the tractor beam. You can't see the beam, of course, but we saw these wiggly things writhing off toward the *Grania* and disappearing into the darkness between the ships. Then when they got in range of the *Grania*'s lights, the worms reappeared along the same path before they flowed across the *Grania*'s hull. They were glowing then with a light of their own. I suppose they might have picked up some kind of energy charge from the tractor beam? Some kind of parasitic thing? Because once they'd spread out across the *Grania*, her lights dimmed and then went dark. I hailed the *Grania*'s bridge—we'd already demanded surrender—but got no response. We cut our tractor beam damn quick, I can tell you. But what the heck can those things be, and why did they seem to come from us but didn't attack us?"

The bridge of the *Molly Daise* was full of noncommand personnel then, including Jubal and Balthazar, who looked very pensive. He had been quiet and sad since Chione's death, and Jubal thought he might have survived only because of his link with Pshaw-Ra. Now he cradled the listless Renpet, stroking her fur and rocking her a little now and then.

"You got any ideas about that, sir?" Jubal asked Balthazar, indicating the dark and drifting pirate ship.

"Perhaps it feared the ships guarded by so many of its foes," Balthazar said slowly. "It has always been said that the great serpent Apep cannot be destroyed."

"Apep? What has Apep got to do with it?" Jubal asked. "We killed him. And besides, this was a whole swarm of snakes, and Apep is just one big one!"

"Apep has many aspects. And although it is said that only the sacred cats can defeat Apep, even they cannot destroy the serpent utterly. After those fleeing the wrath of Nefure were safely moved to a new place of concealment, the vizier and I returned to the great snake's corpse, to dismember and remove it, only to find that neither it nor its remnants remained in the cavern. It is also said that Apep never dies, only transforms."

"But that's just a story. It was dead as dead—wasn't it?"

The old man shrugged. "So it appeared. But our oldest chronicles tell us that when Bast defeated the serpent in material form, it transcended that form by breaking into many parts and ascending to the sky, where it tried to eat the very sun."

"I saw a drawing about that—on this long wall back in the City of the Dead."

Balthazar looked stricken for a moment. "You saw that? Then you were outside the serpent's lair, built to contain it in dormancy when first it reemerged on this world as the monster you saw. Had Bast not flown to the rescue of Ra the sun, the world would have been ended."

"But why would you bring a thing like that with you when you came?"

"Perhaps it or one of its parts came as an ordinary serpent and

grew into the monster. The crossbreeding may have revivified it."
The old man shrugged again. "But it came, and once before the
vizier, in his cunning, contained it in the lair you found."

"This was—uh—recently? Before we came?"

Balthazar said, "It was before my time, and before my grandfather's time. The vizier is a very old cat."

Jubal gave a low whistle. "I guess he is. I'm still not clear how
that humongous dead snake turned into the worm herd."

"It is clear to me that Apep simply changed form, the large serpent breaking into many small ones fueled by its inner fire, so they
could take flight on the hulls of our vessels in order to ascend the
skies. When your friend fired her weapon at it, the power from the
weapon may have begun Apep's transformation into its space traveling form, a dispersion of its mass into energy-hungry particles
that may be carried on the wind—or on the hull of a departing
ship."

"Why didn't it eat us, then?"

Balthazar shrugged. "Perhaps it had not yet reached the stage in
its growth where it could do so. The serpent is no mere serpent,
any more than the vizier is a mere cat. It is cunning and even wise.
Even in its altered shape, it may have sensed the presence of you,
its foes—but the pirate ship had no such protection. And the
beams of attachment were natural conduits for its spawn."

"Spawn? It had babies?"

"Its more diffuse aspect," Balthazar corrected himself.

Jubal felt his eyes widen as he looked at what was left to be seen
of the pirate ship. "So these are like little snakelets that came from
the big snake, like the kefer-ka come from the cat mummies."

Balthazar shrugged and Renpet gave a little cry of distress and
buried her nose in his armpit. "It has not happened before," he
said. "Or not for a long time."

Jubal wanted to ask more but the old man turned abruptly and
left the bridge. His step faltered and the lines in his face seemed
deeper than before.

Captain Vesey was not nearly as interested in the snaky things as Jubal was. He was busy talking with Captain Loloma, and both of them agreed that if the things were going to attack something, the pirate ship was a good target. It sounded almost as if they wanted to think of the Apeplets as an ally. Bad idea.

CHESTER IN FLIGHT BACK TO THE NORMAL SPACEWAYS

I couldn't sit still. I paced, and prowled, and hunted. I almost wished I was back in the pyramid ship with Pshaw-Ra.

Even though Jubal and I were together now, often our link was broken, our shared experiences interrupted, by so many distractions.

Renpet was gaining strength, and Mother had taught the kittens all of the basic cat things, but now she too was unhappy. "So many cats and not one of the young ones is getting a proper education," she complained. But there wasn't room to move. When the ship was quiet, the kittens could charge up and down the corridors and expend some of their energy, but mostly they ate and slept.

Sleep. I could not seem to get a complete nap without someone interrupting my rest. The crew knew about my link with Jubal, so every time they needed to know something about us cats, Jubal and I had to act as interpreters.

One day I crawled deep into one of the ventilation ducts and curled up and slept for several hours. I was sorry that Jubal couldn't come and nap with me, but he was busy taking care of other cats and trying not to get between his mother and father, who fought every time they passed each other, as my mother and Jockey would have done if they weren't perfectly content to ignore each other. It wasn't fair. His attention should be for me, doing things with me, even if it was just sleeping or sharing something to eat. He wanted it that way and so did I. He was my boy. We were supposed to be together.

In my dream, I was back in the barn again, listening to Git, our first teacher, telling us to watch out for canines. Just then something swooped down from the rafters and picked her up. She had been silent when she was killed that day in the field, but in my dream she mewed like a tiny kitten, piteous and heartbreaking.

And then I realized that what I was actually hearing was a kitten. It was my kitten, crying to himself. *Lonely*, he was saying. *So lonely.*

This was the one Jubal called Junior, the kitten who looked like me, crying over and over again. I knew somehow that Kibble was sleeping beside him, along with his sister, Mother, Bat, and Sol, but still he cried as if he'd been abandoned.

That woke my daughter, who picked up his thought and echoed it. "Lonely."

It was infectious. Soon kittens cried all over the ship; my ventilation duct echoed with their mews. I put my paws and tail over my ears but it did no good.

Jubal, who had been kept busy as assistant Cat Person to Kibble, asked, *Chester, what's wrong with them?*

I don't know except that they're lonely.

How can they be lonely? There's a jillion other kittens here! Maybe they're just bored.

I jumped down from my hiding place, halfway up the inner hull, and padded back to our cabin. Jubal met me there.

The crew will be returning the Barque Cats to their original ships if they're willing to pay the finder's fee, Jubal told me. *But they want to keep the kittens for new homes in other places.*

Mother sat upright between us, looking up into Jubal's face and then over to me. She understood Standard very well from years of being a ship's cat. Kibble confided in her all the time.

"They are not ready for new homes," she said to me. "There are so many of them, and some of the poor mites, the ones whose mothers were left behind on Mau, have only their sires to instruct them, and you males are a total loss at kitten training."

We stood in the open doorway of the purser's cabin, while he was on the bridge. My sire trotted up to us, tail high, trailed by three kittens trying their best to imitate him. Their tails were not very long or bushy yet but they held them straight up and strutted behind their sire. Of course, they got a certain amount of strut from Nefure too.

"Says you, babe," Jockey told Mother. "Spike found herself a home already, and Duke, Prince, and Princessa here will be the first to find new ones."

"Oh? I thought our crew had taken care of the pirate problem in this sector," Mother said. "So where do you think raw, untrained kittens are going to find ships that want to take them on?"

"Haven't you heard about the rat problem?"

"Have you forgotten it takes training to learn to handle a rat? Have you been teaching your offspring to hunt, Jockey?"

"Well, not yet, of course . . ."

"Then I think it's time we start."

"Don't look at me. I'm needed back on my old bucket of bolts. And there's only room for one top tom there. I cannot wait to see the faces of my crew when they see me back again. The treats and pets are never going to stop." He sat down and preened his whiskers. The kittens did the same thing. "They will be lining up all the most gorgeous queens in the galaxy to partake of my services."

"You can start wooing them right away," Mother told him sharply. "Because quite a few of them are on the ship."

"I've already started," he told her.

"It's time for me to start too, then, if you'll excuse me," she said, and sauntered off down the corridor, stopping at each cabin to consult with the cats inside. Within a couple of hours she had a trail of six kittens behind her as she toured the ship, showing them all of our passages. There would be no place for me to hide now.

When she finished with one group, and whatever grooming,

sleeping, or eating she had to do, she began with more kittens. Sometimes their mothers came too, but more often the ladies enjoyed a little well-needed rest.

Jubal and I lay on our bunk while he stroked me, and my children too, since they wouldn't leave us alone. What was it with them and my tail anyway?

Chessie's started a kitten school, hasn't she? he asked me. *Your mom's quite a kitty.*

Better her than me, I said.

But I got antsy after a very short time because as infested with vermin as the ship had been before, once the kitten school started, there wasn't enough work left to keep any one cat occupied.

Even my sire decided to get into the act, making all of the kittens call him "sensei" and instructing them in the arts of feline battle. Some of the male kittens came away looking like they'd done something naughty, and I suspected he was telling them his seduction techniques after class.

Renpet was still too weak to be much of a mother to our two, so I ended up kitten-sitting them when they weren't with one or the other of their grandparents.

"Papa, what is all of that stuff in the room with the big piece of space in it?" Junior asked me one day.

It took me a whisker twitch to realize he meant the bridge—the view port held the largest piece of space he'd ever seen.

"That's where they run the ship," I told him.

"Why is it only humans doing it?"

"Well, I guess because the ship is their toy."

"Pa-Ra has a ship. Mother used to have one." Pa-Ra was what the kittens called Pshaw-Ra, who was their grandfather. He had never spent much time with them, but both Renpet and Balthazar had told them stories about him.

"Yes, but only Pa-Ra's ship works. And it's ·specially made for him. Humans wouldn't be able to work it at all."

We hopped up onto the platform with all of the consoles. There were two other cat families there already, sleeping or just resting beside their humans' feet. Shahori and Sheleg and their siblings were among them.

Indu was at her console, so we hopped up there so I could show the kids the controls. I wished Jubal were there so he could give them a guided tour, but he was off changing other cats' litter boxes again, probably. However, Indu reached over, gave me a nice pat and said, "Hi, Chester. Showing your kittens how things work, are you?"

Yow! Understanding cat must be catching. The crew was so used to Jubal doing it, they seemed to be getting the hang of it. "You know all about the gravity control," she said, pointing to the button I'd accidentally pushed when I was a baby. "I can't see demonstrating it with so many kittens and a sick mother on board, however. The kittens will just have to wait until they get their new assignments before they swim in free fall."

Shahori and Sheleg joined us, Shahori putting his paws lightly on Indu's thigh. "What's 'assignment' mean, Chester?"

"All that stuff my mother is teaching you to do? That's what you will do on your own when you get your new home—your new home is your assignment. You'll have your own Cat Person with nothing to do but take care of all of the human stuff for you so you can devote yourself to hunting and making the ship safe."

"Are we all going to ships?"

"Your mother already has a ship that will want her back," I told him. "So do most of the other adults. The crew is looking for other places for most of you kittens."

"Even us, Papa?" my daughter asked. "We can't stay with you?"

I didn't know how to put it. I was sure that it would be okay with Jubal if my kittens stayed with us forever, but his parents would probably sell them as they had with the rest of us.

"They're looking for better homes for you. Ones where you can be top cats instead of just one of a clowder. We are all a very special kind of cat, and they have to spread our specialness around."

"This," Indu said, "is the scanner array, where we can see other ships even when they are too far away to see through the view port. Over there where Charlotte is sitting is the com unit. You've all seen what it can do in your cabins, where it shows pictures of what's going on in other cabins and holds, on other ships, even dirtside."

"What's 'dirtside'?" Junior asked me.

"It's like Mau—a planet or maybe a moon," I explained. "Not a ship or space station."

When there's no big catastrophe happening on a space vessel, it can get pretty boring, so the rest of the crew enjoyed explaining to the kittens, not knowing they understood more than the humans could imagine, about the controls, the charts, the gauges.

By the end of our tour of the cabin, I was puffed up with pride at how bright my babies were. They understood everything and asked questions I wished I could ask the crew but would have to save for Jubal to interpret later.

One of the most repeated questions was what made the ship go, so our next stop was the engine room, Shahori and Sheleg trotting along beside us. The crew were perfectly willing to show us anything we pointed our noses at, but the kids were overawed by the large machines and their strong metallic scents. We retired for a bite to eat and a nap soon after.

The kittens were still sleeping when I awoke to the feeling of being stared at. The door of the cabin was open and filled with wide-eyed fluffy faces, every one of them focused on me.

"Mama says we can go to the bridge too if you'll take us, Chester." The speaker was one of Flekica's new litter. Their older half brothers probably had bragged that I'd shown them how to fly the ship. My guess was that Flekica and the other mothers wanted a little more rest and didn't mind me sacrificing my nap for them to get theirs.

It was only a game for us, though, or so I thought. Then Pshaw-Ra returned to dock inside the *Molly Daise* again and upped the ante.

CHAPTER 21

After the precipitous departure of the Barque Cats and the *Ranzo* during their escape from the lab in Galipolis, landing in Galport was out of the question, but the *Molly Daise* and the *Ranzo* needed some other central place to rendezvous with the ships whose cats they'd rescued. Ponty had argued for selling the kittens first, or offloading them somewhere, but Captain Vesey and Dr. Vlast argued that the vermin problem was so severe, lives might be lost if the cats weren't reinstated on their ships as soon as possible. Ponty hoped the ships saw it the same way and would be prepared to pay the hefty finder's fee for each cat as he had suggested—and of which he would get a cut, though he wasn't officially crew on either ship.

But he was nervous that the ships would try to claim the kittens too. Jubal helped him document the parentage of each litter on the Mau side—the more titles and provenance he could dig up for every little kitten, the better. He was sorry they'd let the queen's kitten go to Mavis, but there was no separating them. One of the crew had tried to take Spike away from the pirate and was clawed by both Mavis and the cat. He might as well have tried to take one of Mavis's tattoos.

There was a certain irony to the place finally chosen for the exchanges. The captain of the *Makarska*, Flekica's old ship, suggested it.

"You know that Klinger guy, the nephew of the ex-secretary?" Captain Arijana asked. She was elated to learn that the *Makarska's* beloved cat was returning to them, and eager to set up the rendezvous that would place the fluffy feline back in the loving arms of her crewmates. The *Ranzo* and the *Molly Daise* contacted the *Makarska* first because there were, they decided, extenuating circumstances regarding the kittens. Since Flekica had been pregnant with her litter when incarcerated, the crews decided that in her case, Sheleg, Shahori, Rizhic, and Masic still belonged to the *Makarska*, though the rescuers would ask a finder's fee for the kittens as well as Flekica. They also decided to offer at a discount to the crews of those ships the half-Mau kittens of the little mothers who had lost their litters.

"Yes, we know all about that," Captain Loloma said in the com conference among the ships.

"Well, when all of it came out about the lies Klinger and his uncle told, which took not only Remy Trudeau's horses, but our cats and many of the animals throughout the galaxy, Klinger seems to have developed a streak of remorse and generosity. He gave Trudeau half his land in reparation—no court proceedings, mind you—and relocated to one of the outer worlds. It is said that his uncle the disgraced councilor assisted him financially. Without animals to fill his new lands, Remy Trudeau has created a small private spaceport, not under the same kind of direct government scrutiny as most of them."

Captain Loloma and Captain Vesey agreed this would be a fitting place to dock and rendezvous with the ships of the displaced cats.

"I'm not sure we'll be able to afford the fees for a private port before we sell the kittens," Yawman the purser told the captain.

"We'll offer him a kitten," Ponty suggested. "He still has some farm, right? So he'll have a lot of vermin. He should be thrilled to have one of our royal kittens."

"They're not all royal," the captain pointed out.

Ponty just gave him a long look.

"Or maybe they are. I didn't quite understand the ins and outs of the social structure among the cats of that planet."

Ponty nodded wisely. The captain was catching on.

They landed beside the *Ranzo* at the small port called Trudeau's Landing. The *Makarska* landed a short time afterward, and Flekica was reunited with her crew, who exclaimed over the kittens and admired them with lots of pets and baby talk. Shahori, Sheleg, and their siblings were sorry to leave Chester's kittens, and there was a lot of face licking to be done before they finally allowed themselves to be carried away in the arms of the crew members.

Flekica's family was loaded and Mr. Yawman completed the financial arrangements with the *Makarska*'s purser. The day was a fine one, with a warm but not oppressive temperature, sunshine, high clouds, and the sweet scent of freshly planted crops wafting over from the farm portion of Trudeau's property.

Over the next few weeks most of the original Barque Cats were reunited with their ships. Romina was so glad to see her Cat Person Gordon she forgot all about her litter of half-Mau kittens, and Ninina had a similar reaction when her ship came for her. Neither ship quibbled about the finder's fee, although one crewman was overheard referring to it as "ransom." But they did not want the kittens.

"It's too bad about the first litter," Gordon said, inspecting the half-Mau kittens not unkindly, because he was a smart man and really liked cats. "But we can't buy these little guys from you. They'd make good pets but people don't pay that kind of money for pets."

"But the vermin problem . . ." Ponty reminded him.

"Our Romina and the others will sort them out soon enough

once they're back home," he said. "And I see you've plenty of intact toms to be returned yet, including some fine studs. We'll soon have proper Barque kittens to help their parents, and things will get back to normal. None too soon for me, I can tell you."

"Pets," Mr. Yawman said when Romina's ship departed. "We're going to be bankrupt on this trip, even with the finder's fees, if people think our kittens are only good for pets."

Ponty looked glum.

CHESTER ON THE MOLLY DAISE AND AT TRUDEAU'S LANDING

Pshaw-Ra had returned to the *Molly Daise* shortly before she docked at Trudeau's Landing. He'd of course had extremely critical business to attend to while away from the ships. He spent a long time inside his little ship with Balthazar and Renpet when he first arrived, and when they came out, Balthazar's expression was carefully impassive, that is to say, almost as sneaky as Pshaw-Ra's.

Balthazar explained to the crew members that the vizier, as he always called Pshaw-Ra, had been scouring the galaxy, mouseholing to the better traveled spaceways, always searching and remaining alert for good situations for cats in need of homes. After inspecting the mechanisms of the human society currently ruling the galaxy, he had discovered one major hitch in his plans and a brilliant idea for kitten placement.

"There are institutions for training the handlers of cats who travel space," Pshaw-Ra told me. "The ships should send many of the kittens there to find humans they can bend to their will. Tell your boy to tell them."

I yawned. "That is such old news. Tell your old man to tell them himself if you want, but they already know about the school. Mother's Kibble trained at the Galipolis school before Kibble was hired to serve her."

"Oh. Then they should have no difficulty carrying out my instructions," he said.

"Are we not going to wait and see what cats have connections with certain humans, like Jubal and I have?" I asked. "I thought that was part of your plan?"

"It was, but it may not be possible to do that quickly enough. Had we not developed such highly bred kittens, establishing links for each would have been essential. Fortunately, these kittens are so superior that even without that connection all is not yet lost."

"Lost how?" I demanded. "Why? Don't tell me it's because the humans aren't good enough—I know you don't like them, but—"

"That has nothing to do with it. It's just that opportunities for forging the bonds have become scarcer. The humans have not become as highly prepared as I anticipated, have not had the opportunity to ingest sufficient kefer-ka to heighten their link with similarly nurtured kittens."

"Why not?"

"Because with so many of the meat animals destroyed by the human government, the kefer-ka did not continue working their way into the human food chain and instead were ingested by the vermin."

"So none of the kittens will find their own human like Jubal and me?"

Pshaw-Ra changed the subject. "So, we must begin training the young now."

"Mrrr—I have news for you. We've *been* training them during the entire journey while you've been off thinking up new ways to make this even more difficult than it already is."

"Whatever do you mean by that, catling? I have dedicated myself to the welfare of these young ones. I have traveled far and spent a great deal of the fuel you procured. I do not suppose you hid some someplace for future use, did you?"

"If I did, I don't think I'd tell you right now," I said, miffed. My son and daughter both expected that they would have a relationship with a human like Jubal with me, or their mother's with Chione. Now the old cat was saying this was not likely to happen.

"Very well, I have no time to quarrel with you now. As I said, the education of the young must commence at once."

I might as well have saved my mental energy. I left him trying to demonstrate paw exercises to a kindle of kittens who were crying because they weren't allowed outside with their mothers. I could feel Jubal's heart going out to all of the newly abandoned children of mothers and fathers returning to their ships.

"It's just how it is with cats, Jubal," his father tried telling him. "They don't have the same kinds of feelings as us humans. They expect the kittens to go their own way while the parents go theirs."

"Like you going into space and leaving me behind?" Jubal asked resentfully as he tried to stroke the dozen or so half-grown cats who crowded around him, feeling his sympathy.

"Cats grow up faster than people. Just ask Chester here."

For a change Jubal's sire was speaking the truth.

But although the crying increased every time a new lot of ships arrived and the adult cat population decreased, at a certain point everything grew quiet again, almost eerily so.

I was pleased until I noticed Junior and Buttercup doing paw exercises in their basket at night, the ones Pshaw-Ra had been showing the other kittens. With his slender tawny feet, it looked kind of pointless. On my kittens with their oversize feet—like mine, shaped like lopsided hearts, thanks to extra toes—the exercises looked as ominous as anything a kitten does can look. They flexed their larger toes so they bent back into their paws and then they made the tips of the large toes and the tops of the small ones bend inward to meet.

Every time I caught one of the kittens making these moves, it sat on the paws that had been busy flexing and extending as I approached, and looked up at me with big innocent eyes.

I was not fooled for a moment.

Later, even before most of the adult cats had returned to their original ships, little things with no legs began moving around the ship. Mr. Yawman's reading glasses were the first prey to go missing, then the captain's favorite pen, and Janina's Cat Person badge mysteriously detached itself from her dress shipsuit.

I found these things in the ventilation ducts and hull linings and shoved them out where they could be found by the crew. None of them were large or bulky, nothing that couldn't have been whapped from a surface with a swipe of a paw and rolled or batted into the places where I found them. They could have been picked up and carried in the mouths of cats too. Yes, it could have happened that way.

Then came the day when my sire was to be returned to his ship. Nefure's remaining kittens, the ones who weren't pirates, cried and cried as our feisty father was put into the carrier because they knew by now, from the experiences of the other kittens, what that meant. He would not be coming back to his offspring.

But an hour later I heard Janina calling and calling him, and found him deep inside one of the ventilation ducts, curled up in his own fluffy tail, napping.

Jubal had been so busy with the other cats and kittens, I hadn't seen much of him, but when he saw me sitting outside of the duct he sat down beside me. *Have you seen Jock? Janina put him in a carrier but she says she must not have latched the door real well because when she came back it was wide open.*

He's asleep in the duct. I think if his people want him back, their Cat Person had better board and call him.

The crew doesn't really want the other crews to know how many kittens we have aboard.

You could try to hide them, then. But Nefure's kits don't want Jock to go. I think they sprang him.

Those little guys?

Humans! Even the best of them could be so taken in by an ingenuous little face. I yawned and gave him a pitying look, but he was getting to his feet.

Moments later hatches closed and soon a voice began calling my sire, who came ambling out of the duct, purring and looking around expectantly. "Jock!" his Cat Person, a young male, cried joyfully and knelt down rubbing his fingers together. My sire moseyed over to him, sniffed his fingers, and jumped into his arms.

As he carried my sire away, a door sprang open and the kittens burst out and scrambled down the hall, but Janina and Jubal scooped them up.

They cried and cried until Jubal crumpled a piece of paper and rolled it on the floor for them to chase.

Kittens! So difficult and yet so easy.

Aside from his cat duties, Jubal helped with routine dirtside maintenance on both ships. This included cleaning and checking the outer hulls, not that onerous a task since the weather was fine.

That's how he found the worm segments. However immortal the great snake might be, these were thoroughly dead—crushed and broken. He noticed the smell right away. Chester, who had been lying in the grass beside him, taking a break from the kittens, lifted his lip to show fang, slit his eyes and growled.

You think it smells like the snake too, huh?

There's no mistake. Is it really dead? Shall I kill it again?

No, but I'm going to show the captains. I don't like to think of these things growing inside that pirate ship.

Chester had no response to that, but sauntered, black feathery tail held high, back to the ship to watch the kittens. He'd been very attentive to the kittens lately but hadn't shared why exactly with Jubal, and Jubal hadn't asked. After all, he was a father now. Jubal sometimes feared he and Chester were growing apart, and he hoped the kittens would get their own homes with their own peo ple and maybe Renpet would too, so he and Chester could return to being a team.

Captain Vesey looked at the worm and said, "Well, good thing that one's dead now, at least. Would you ask Chester and Chessie to make sure none got aboard somehow and are living in the ducts?"

"Yes, sir."

"There's something else, Jubal."

"Sir?"

"You and your father are still part of Captain Loloma's crew by contract. Your mother has signed on with me and asked if I could get Captain Loloma to release you and sign you on with the *Molly Daise* instead. You're a good worker and your ability to communicate with Chester and through him with the other cats is very handy. I'd be glad to have you, though your father will be returning to the *Ranzo*. How do you feel about it?"

"How about Chester, sir?"

Captain Vesey actually looked embarrassed. "You know, most of us think of Chester as a short crewman now—we know he talks to you, and that he's concerned for the welfare of the ship, but he has no contract as such and you are his chosen partner. You and I both know, I think, that you have no legal right to him—"

Jubal opened his mouth to protest, and the captain made a "hold on" motion with the vertical palm of his hand before continuing.

"But we're not sure anybody does. His stud fees will be worthwhile, especially if the ships continue to feel that our kittens aren't as good as purebred Barques."

"I don't care about the stud fees, sir. Its kinda—embarrassing really."

"Well, you will, son. Your parents and the crew have discussed this and decided that the fair thing is for Chester to be considered your partner and an emancipated cat. Those who want him to make kittens with their queens can negotiate for the privilege, but since he was originally our kitten, how about half his fee reverts to *Molly Daise*'s crew?"

"That's okay with me, sir. And Chester doesn't care about that stuff as long as we're together and there's kibble in his bowl."

"Fair enough. Just one thing, son?"

"Sir?"

"I want you to handle the money. Your mother has been a big help and your father is a good horse-trader, but you seem to have gotten most of the integrity in the family. Do I have your word?"

"Yes, sir."

"So, are you staying with us or the *Ranzo*?"

"The ships are on different courses after we leave here, are they, sir?"

"It makes sense not to have all the kitten salesmen in the same area, don't you think?"

"Yes, sir. If we go with the *Ranzo*, can Chester's family come with him so he can approve the homes for his kittens?"

"I have no problem with that if we get our share of the sale."

"Then with all due respect, sir, and appreciation for the crew's consideration of us, the *Molly Daise* seems like a more—I dunno, official kind of ship than the *Ranzo*. Like you do what you're told more, and Captain Loloma and his crew risked their lives and their ship to help us, and—"

It was the wrong thing to say. Captain Vesey's face closed up. "I understand." Because what Jubal was trying to say, evidently not diplomatically enough, was that, however respectful the *Molly Daise* crew was to Chester now, when the government had ordered the impounding of cats, the ship left Chester drifting in space and gave Chessie up to the authorities. Captain Vesey trusted Jubal, but Jubal wasn't entirely sure he returned the favor. Besides, being with Mom wasn't nearly as interesting as being around Pop.

The *Ranzo* was no longer considered too dangerous for Jubal now that the pirates had been taken into custody by the local police, who almost shot Spike for resisting arrest. He wished there was a nice way to explain how he felt to Captain Vesey, but the captain had marched away.

He consulted Chester, of course, but already knew how the cat would respond.

Nice of them to admit I don't belong to them, Chester said, though not entirely graciously. He remembered very well that when he was a kitten there had been talk of destroying him for misbehavior. The *Molly Daise* had just now gotten around to acknowledging that he was not their property, whereas the *Ranzo* crew had from the first seemed to look to him and Jubal for leadership in cat matters.

To their surprise, though, Buttercup didn't want to change ships. She had discovered Jubal's mother.

CHAPTER 22

During the layover at Trudeau's Landing while the silly Barque Cats purringly returned to enslavement to their masters, Pshaw-Ra made himself and his instruction generously available to the next generation. In addition to their paw exercises, he taught them a thing or two about a cat's natural ability to increase or decrease gravity, thereby gaining advantage in fight, flight, and tromping heavily on others with pressure far greater than accounted for by a grown cat's weight.

While such skills came naturally to almost any cat, a Mauan mage of Pshaw-Ra's level could extend these powers until they seemed superfeline.

The time came when the ships were ready to depart with only Chessie aboard the *Molly Daise*, and Chester, Renpet, and the hapless Hadley on the *Ranzo* as adult cat crew. Pshaw-Ra hoped he had also taught the kittens to hone their powers of observation to a degree that would allow them to employ their strengthened paws to advantage. Meanwhile, he returned to his own cozy ship, once more docked in the *Ranzo*'s shuttle bay, where he stayed sequestered with Balthazar and Renpet when he wasn't—as Jubal's sire put it—subverting the kittens. Balthazar said the vizier had decided for a time to conserve his fuel by allowing the *Ranzo* to ferry him around the galaxy.

Meanwhile, the vizier's advice and leadership were available to all who wished to call upon it to help run the ship, the galaxy, and the universe more efficiently, and of course in the event of any emergency he would be handy to help out. Meanwhile he required a supply of the excellent cat treats the *Ranzo* had taken aboard at Trudeau's Landing and needed to catch up on his rest.

The older cats had taught the kittens the basics of vermin extermination, but the skills Pshaw-Ra taught would help this new breed become the best that they could be. Unfortunately, kittens were not the only rapidly evolving creatures in space.

"It's so peaceful here now," Beulah said, leaning back in her chair and stretching. "Mavis and her lot gone from the brig, the *Molly Daise* en route to Sherwood again so she can drop off Dr. Vlast and try to sell some of the kittens to the farmers. Your father says they'll pay top dollar regardless of breeding to have help with the rat problem."

Jubal didn't like the idea of the kittens going to farms, even if they needed them. Farmers were not always kind to cats, as he recalled, and while they might be okay with this generation, he thought subsequent generations would probably be treated like four-legged trash.

Besides, the kittens would have to develop some new tactics if they were going to beat the smart rats on Sherwood. Chester told him he and Doc controlled the worst of the rodent problem on shipboard by explaining to the kefer-ka-enhanced rats—who were highly intelligent to begin with—that if they chewed the insulation from the wiring on the ships, the ships would crash, life support would end, and rats would go down with the dying ship. The cats reading their thoughts probably spooked the rats worse than the idea of being spaced.

Most of them had deserted the ship back on Mau.

"Who could resist the little darlings?" Beulah went on, beaming at the kittens. "Look at them! They are so cute, hunkering on the console or sitting on shoulders, watching our hands when we manipulate the controls. They think it's some sort of a game. That little ginger-stripe puss looks like he's about to pounce on Felicia's hand when she moves it."

Of course, Misu was doing no such thing. He wasn't going to pounce on the mate's hand, but he might nudge it gently, to correct her course, perhaps. He was carefully studying her every move and what prompted her to perform certain actions at certain times. Jubal knew that was what Misu and the rest of the kittens were doing when they watched the crew at work or followed them around as they performed their duties. He didn't tell the crew what he knew, though. It would freak them out.

Pshaw-Ra disregarded the crew most of the time and swept around the ship as if he were the captain. For Jubal, another advantage to shipping with this particular crew was that he didn't have to explain to any of them what Pshaw-Ra was. While Pinot bluffly declared that he was "a nice old cat," many of them were a little afraid of him, or at least respectfully gave him a wide berth.

Pshaw-Ra let Sosi pet him and ignored Hadley when he hissed at him, as Hadley felt bound to do since he was back on his own turf, even though he was sharing the *Ranzo* with a great many interlopers.

But Jubal knew Pshaw-Ra was constantly urging the kittens to try new things, especially things that involved using their paws in ways cats didn't usually use their paws.

Cabinet doors were left standing open. Lockers inexplicably spilled their contents onto the decks. More small objects went missing. Cat treat packets were scattered all over the galley deck until Jubal started locking them up and keeping the key with him.

The day a few kittens took the shuttle for a joy ride, under the direction of Pshaw-Ra, he decided he couldn't keep their new prowess a secret any longer. He went looking for Balthazar first.

"Look, this is out of control," he said. "Those kittens could hurt themselves or damage the shuttle or the ship. The crew is trying to find them homes, and if they are up to tricks like that all the time, no ship or space station is going to want them."

"His Excellency only tries to prepare the kits," Balthazar said stiffly.

"I know, I know, they're supposed to dominate the universe."

"Is that what he said? I thought rather that they would be its salvation."

"At the rate they're going? No way!" Jubal said. He hadn't meant to be harsh, and regretted it later, after his sleep shift, when he saw that while the shuttle was where it belonged, the pyramid ship was gone, along with Balthazar and Pshaw-Ra.

Jubal was still puzzling over that when Chester leaped onto his shoulder, put his cheek against his and rubbed. *Renpet went with them,* he said. *Pshaw-Ra told her it was time for her to lead her people, before they fell into error, whatever that meant. I think they were planning on visiting the planet where most of the Mau moved all those years ago. I hope she'll be okay.*

Me too, Chester. Me too, Jubal told him, stroking the nearest paw with his fingertip. To his surprise, he missed Pshaw-Ra already and knew that Chester did too.

I wonder what he's really up to, Chester said, yawning before falling asleep on the back of Jubal's chair.

Pshaw-Ra had not known exactly where the serpent Apep would manifest himself in his latest aspect, for the serpent was almost as wily and unpredictable as Pshaw-Ra himself. Such serpents occurred elsewhere in the universe, he knew, but no race but the Mau had ever learned what they truly were. Some conventional astronomers even considered their destructive transformation orgies as the crucibles of the galaxies. And so they were, once they had destroyed all other worlds anywhere near them.

The trick, as he knew, was to find them in their early stages, and so he had made his little forays away from the ships with the kittens to track the progress of the worm cloud.

The pirate ship had been utterly gone when he last returned to the site of the abortive hijackings by the unfortunate Mavis. He did not see the worm cloud at all and kept returning to look for it. It would not do to let something like that roam around loose. There was no telling what harm it might do, or to whom, so he kept returning until at last he had a sighting.

He could not tell if the hazy bit he saw in the distance was the worm cloud or some other substance until he was close enough to see it in the view port. It was not as if Apep had dreams he could enter.

He thought the cloud drifted toward him, and he withdrew the pyramid ship a bit. It drew closer, until he could see it tumbling its wormy bits inside its cloud. He pulled back a little more.

Suddenly, as if it had an engine of its own, the worm cloud came after him. He opened the mouse hole before it could catch him, or so he thought.

He hightailed it through the mouse hole and back out again, closing it behind him, his fangs bared in a fierce expression of triumph. Now he knew where it was, he thought, and how to get it.

That was until he entered the mouse hole again, this time with Balthazar and Renpet as passengers. Balthazar fortunately was studying charts, and Renpet was sleeping, as she did a lot these days.

He thought seeing Mau-Maat, the planet for which her ancestors had deserted the inhabitants of Mau, leaving them with little more than a shadow of their former greatness, might rouse Renpet from her lethargy.

How could he know that the worm cloud had entered the mouse hole with him on the previous occasion, and now, as he opened the hole into the Ra-Harahkty system, would follow?

With swift maneuvering, he evaded the cloud, but his small

ship no longer attracted it. The serpent chose as its new power source the star orbited by Mau-Maat.

Pshaw-Ra had not intended for that to happen, but he was not entirely displeased that those who had deserted his world were about to have theirs seriously disrupted if not destroyed. Since the people and cats on this new world had abandoned the ancient teachings of the sacred feline ancestors in favor of a place with less desert and more modern conveniences, he found it fitting that they were to be given a dramatic demonstration of the error of their ways.

Of course, this caused some friction with Balthazar.

You played with Apep as you would a mouse, seeking him out and tempting him to follow you through the mouse holes you opened, Balthazar scolded.

Pshaw-Ra regarded his old servant with a sideways and slitted glance. *I knew it was a possible risk. But I had to know where Apep was. Once the transformation has begun, old man, it will complete its destructive metamorphosis unless stopped. I had to monitor it, did I not?*

Balthazar snorted. *You have been drifting in space for how long, with no desire to visit Mau-Maat until now? But suddenly, when the worm cloud happens to have followed you into the mouse hole, you cannot wait to visit our estranged descendants to see how the immigrants are faring?*

Do not fuss, old friend, Pshaw-Ra told him. *If you wish to teach kittens to hunt, you must bring them live prey to catch. The ability to battle Apep is what separates our kittens from the house cats.*

Balthazar had looked pained and unconvinced. *After all the trouble you took to ensure that the kittens were born, you will now send them to be slaughtered.*

"Pfft!" Pshaw-Ra said aloud. *Naturally, there are preparations to be made beforehand. The young need training to succeed.*

And proper human companions to work with, Balthazar added. *Even though the sacred texts tend to belittle their role.*

192 ·, ANNE McCAFFREY AND ELIZABETH ANN SCARBOROUGH

You are too sensitive, old man. Now then, instead of visiting Mau-Maat, we—and by we I mean you, since they are no respecters of feline-kind, must alert the Galactic Government to this impending catastrophe.

They just happened to have brought with them from the catacombs the plans for the necessary weapons to fight Apep's current aspect. Now, Pshaw-Ra knew that all it would take was for Balthazar to use his considerable powers of persuasion to convince the military to build the small devices and employ cats to fight a battle that would daunt the bravest human warrior.

Once the battle was joined, either the catlings' deeds would command respect—and even reverence—from the two-leggeds of this galaxy, or they would perish in the attempt. He hoped that wouldn't happen, naturally. As Balthazar had pointed out, it would be extremely tiresome for him to start his campaign to improve the lot of his race again from scratch, as it were.

Finding homes for the kittens was a big job. Beulah was supposed to contact ships, space stations, the Galactic Academy, anyplace not among the ships already recatted. Jubal and Ponty took holos of each of the kittens being adorable and attached the kitten's pedigree papers to each holo. This made a sort of kitten catalog Beulah could send out to potential homes and employers. The response wasn't quite as wholeheartedly enthusiastic as they had hoped. Some people did not regard them as real Barque Cats and wanted to quibble about the price—or, worse, somehow had not gotten the news that the cats weren't infected with anything, and didn't want some "pest-ridden animal" in their ship, station, or compound. Ponty began looking shifty again, since his plan wasn't working out.

Meanwhile, Jubal was glad his mom was on the *Molly Daise*, in thrall to Chester's daughter Buttercup. She hadn't liked cats before, but now called Buttercup "Dori's darling girl" and cooed at and fussed over her as she never had with him. Even with Janina, a trained Cat Person, still onboard, his mom insisted on comming him as often as she was allowed, to ask him stuff about cat care and to hold Buttercup up to the screen to "wave to her daddy." He was glad to be away from the *Molly Daise* for that reason if no other. His mother had always been a hard-nosed and rather mercenary farm woman, a dedicated cat disliker. Was she being won over by having the same kind of close relationship with Buttercup that he had with Chester, or were the half-Mau kittens actually able to dominate the will of humans, as Pshaw-Ra had suggested?

"We have to find homes for these little buggers soon," Captain Loloma said after tripping over a box that had found its way into the middle of the bridge deck. "One ship's cat is a nice, soothing, useful, helpful sort of thing. Old Hadley never gave a moment's trouble. But all of these kittens are going to destroy us if we don't offload them soon!"

In spite of Jubal's and Sosi's best efforts, the ship was beginning to smell distinctly catty. The kittens had accidents sometimes, or "forgot," according to Chester.

They're unhappy, Chester told him.

Why? Jubal asked. *They have a place to live and food and the crew plays with them, and they have each other.*

Not like we have each other, Chester said.

Then there was the matter of the cat fur clogging up the ventilation system. That required Chester and Doc going in to herd out the kittens who had nested back there and then carrying in a vacuum tube attached to their collars to suck up the cat hair, which was seriously endangering the ship. That almost caused the milk brothers to mutiny. *Why can't Hadley do it?* Chester protested indignantly, mewing loudly and repeatedly. *I hate hate hate the way that monster sounds, and it is right next to my delicate ears, and the ducts make it louder.*

You know why, boy. 'Cause we can't make Hadley understand, whereas you and Doc do get it that if the hair stays in there, the ship stops working and that is not good.

They didn't think the kittens would stand for the noise either, but as soon as the motor started and Chester and Doc began walking through the tubes, Junior and three other kittens crowded in behind Chester, and Doc was joined in his ventilation tube by several more kittens, which made it hard to maneuver the hose and hard for the encumbered cats to back out.

"They're amazing," Guillame Pinot said, scratching his head. "It's like the little devils know somehow what will make things the most awkward and that's what they decide to do."

Jubal figured that was probably exactly what the kittens did, but he was supposed to be on their side so he said, "Naw, they're just curious. How are they going to learn if they don't see what the older cats do?"

But after that, all kittens had to be thoroughly brushed before they went anywhere near the ship's innards. And the crew started grumbling.

Pinot's remark was funny, but others now scowled when they tripped over a kitten, as someone did at least two or three times a day. "Little buggers were supposed to be my early retirement," growled the assistant engineer. "Instead they're going to give us all an early death."

When he wasn't actively herding cats, Jubal spent a lot of time at Beulah's com station. She had free time to chat when they weren't near a space station or within close com range of other ships. They still exchanged relayed messages with the *Molly Daise*. That ship's strategy was to spend an extended amount of time on each landfall, taking the kittens for outings. Of course, they had Chessie to keep the kittens in line, but Jubal bet she was exhausted. When the ship returned to Hood Station and Dr. Vlast went down to Sherwood, he found good homes happy to pay the price of the kittens, with two desperate farmers eager to have them. Mom and Buttercup had gone ashore to work for Mr. Varley, who was running for the Galactic Council.

At first, Jubal relieved Beulah on short breaks to go to the head or eat, and then one day Captain Loloma said to him, "How would you like a promotion?"

"I'm not assistant Cat Person anymore?" he asked.

"Well, in addition to being assistant Cat Person, how about being relief com officer?"

"Cool!" Jubal said. And after that, he and Beulah slept at different times so he could relieve her during her sleep shift. Her station was partitioned off from the others, and as soon as he took over, he had a circle of small furry observers, at first sitting attentively around his chair and then, as Chester allowed it, one at a time up on the com board.

There was always low-level chatter from ship to ship as well as government announcements and news. It was interesting and, he realized, a little scary. There was a lot of stuff Beulah hadn't mentioned to him before, though he was sure it was the kind of thing she must have reported to the captain. Ships had been disappearing—first in a certain sector and then in an ever-broadening area. He listened carefully for the names but none were ships he recognized. Elsewhere, a planetary system identified only as one containing some of the more recently settled planets was having strange weather problems—its sun seemed to be occluded by something causing climactic changes so disastrous to the orbiting planets that the GG had sent thousands of troops and humanitarian aid to facilitate massive evacuations. One thing about galactic news events, though: most of them happened far far far away.

Chester purred and spoke to him of home and generally chattered, which was unusual for him, but Jubal became aware of an undercurrent as he stroked fur and watched the screen.

Do it. Send. Now.

He knew Chester was saying it, but not to him. The kitten on the com's big mittened paw went out and brought up the cat holos on the little screen he didn't think Jubal was watching, tapped his own holo, and tapped the send button.

He kept quiet. The kittens loved putting something over on people, but if Chester was helping them, he wanted to know why.

"Watch the board, will you, boy?" he asked Chester aloud, as if the cat was *his* relief officer. "I gotta go." He pretended to head for the head, but when all feline attention was directed back to the board, he watched from across the cabin. None of the other crew on the bridge seemed aware of anything peculiar, but one by one each kitten jumped onto the board, brought up its holo and attached lineage paper, and sent it out. It was almost cartoonish, watching the kittens use the computer, but then, he had seen Chester and Pshaw-Ra operate the pyramid ship. Pshaw-Ra must have taught them to do this, and specifically to send their pictures out, though there was no need. He and Beulah had already sent the holos to every potential cat customer they could think of.

Where were the kittens sending them? he wondered.

He tried to look it up without being too obvious—he was still playing cat and mouse games with them—but found only a very odd assortment of destinations, most of them to individuals instead of ships or space stations. The kittens had pen pals?

He asked Chester. To his surprise his friend said, *Just help us, boy. They're turning on us.*

Who? he asked.

The other people. Kittens are a lot of trouble. With Pshaw-Ra gone and Mother on another ship, I can't keep all of them in line. The kittens need friends, like you are my friend, or they'll just go feral. They're very smart and can open anything. I smell fear on some of the crew.

Fear? Of kittens? Really?

Yes. Fear. We smell it and see it in their eyes.

I think maybe some people still want to think humans are the only sentient species, Jubal said. *They think really intelligent animals are unnatural or something. Idiots! Okay, then. When these ones finish sending off their holos, I think we have time for another group or two before it's Beulah's shift.*

But these kittens want to watch the com and see if replies come.

I'm sure they do, but fair is fair and you've convinced me. The situation is getting critical. He *had* heard crewmen calling the kittens little monkeys or demons, and he didn't like the sound of that. Time for them to go, for sure.

At Tao Station they got their first real break. A class of touring cadets from the regional space academy passed through just as Ponty and Jubal "happened" to be taking some of the kittens out for checkups with the station vet.

All of a sudden, a gray and white spotted male called Ciko began crying and scrabbling to get out of his cage. The class moved on, but one of the cadets lagged behind, looking back at the cage.

"Cadet Shinta, why did you break formation?" her superior demanded. Shinta looked a little younger than Sosi. She pointed at Ciko's cage.

Jubal smiled and waved at the commander and hoisted the cage. Ciko cried louder.

"It's him, Squadron Leader," the little girl squealed. Her shrill childish voice carried across the docking bay. She started jumping up and down. "It is my kitty. He's found me."

"Disobeying rules is no way to get what you want, Cadet Shinta," Jubal heard the squadron leader admonish her as he walked toward the woman, trying to hold onto Ciko's wildly jiggling carrier.

"But how can I be a Cat Person without a cat?" the young girl asked. "He says he is mine and, oooooh, look at him, Squadron Leader Kyuti, just look!"

For a two-pound kitten, Jubal thought the bouncing, mewing Ciko seemed to weigh a ton. Afraid that he might drop the carrier before he reached the girl—and make a bad impression on her superior—he set down the carrier and started to take the latch off. But before he could, a paw flashed out of the wire mesh, the door jangled open, and the gray and white kitten streaked to the little girl so fast his spots blurred.

Ciko jumped into her arms, purring madly while she giggled and stroked him. The squadron leader made a face and started to say something when the kitten looked up at her, making his eyes as large and bright as possible, as if to beam a command from them into her brain. The squardon leader reached out slowly and touched Ciko's head, and he arched into her palm.

"Well," she told Shinta. "For want of the right cat, we were going to have to change your specialty, but now that he's arrived, it looks as if he is ready for you to start learning the practical application of your lessons."

Jubal was relieved that Ciko had found a person, and was ready to hand him over on the spot when his father appeared behind him and said, "There's the matter of his price, Squadron Leader . . . Kyuti, is it? Our ship had to rescue him and his fellow cats at great personal danger and cost to ourselves, and understandably, the crew cannot give these valuable creatures away."

Jubal wanted to stomp on the old man's foot. Ciko dipped his head a little and looked up at them through sad, reproachful eyes, as if he knew exactly what was going on. Well, if Ciko and Shinta had the same connection he had with Chester, Jubal thought, then he probably did know, through her.

"The Crane Academy is an exclusive private educational and training facility for the children of distinguished families," the squadron leader said proudly. "Shinta's family knew of her wish and provided in their legacy the funds for the purchase of a Barque Cat." She turned to the other students. "Senior Cadet Mallory, you remember where the snack bar is? Please lead the other cadets there in an orderly fashion, and Cadet Shinta and I, and . . ."

"Ciko," Cadet Lin Shinta told her. "Silver Ciko Nugris is his name."

"Cadet Shinta, Silver Ciko Nugris, and I shall rejoin you as soon as our business is concluded."

But Cadet Mallory said, "There are other kitties on that ship, Squadron Leader Kyuti. May we not see them? It's been months and months since the others were taken away."

"Oh, ma'am, the kittens would love to meet your students— uh—cadets," Jubal said. "They haven't had much chance to be around young people. It would be a big favor to our ship—"

"Possibly worth a price reduction," the old man put in.

"—if you would all come aboard. The cadets could play with the kittens while you finalize the arrangement for transferring the credits for Cik—I mean, Silver Ciko Nugris."

The cadets bounced up and down in a very unmilitary fashion, and Jubal was sure that back aboard the *Ranzo*, the kittens were bouncing up and down too. Somehow he thought it was all part of their great feline plot—the one begun by Pshaw-Ra. But it would be so great if a home for Ciko was only the first, and the other kittens would soon find people as in love with them as little Cadet Shinta was with the spotted guy.

It turned out that Cadet Mallory had an ulterior motive for backing up Cadet Shinta. Some of the kittens ran and hid, but about ten peeped their little fur-fringed heads out from around doors or from under chairs and bunks. One saw Cadet Shan Mallory and let out a "Meh?"

"There you are!" the cadet cried. "Ice Cream, it's me, Shan!" That was the last she spoke aloud for some time, as another gray and white kitten, this one with a spot on his nose, snuggled into her arms and they communed—he purring, she stroking, but exchanging vital impressions and information, Jubal felt sure.

Meanwhile other ships that had been transiting near the station started docking, and visitors requested permission to come aboard.

"Why all the company all of a sudden?" Captain Loloma asked.

"It's the kittens' pen pals, sir."

"Their what?"

"These kittens are much like Chester—they can call to someone they connect with, as long as that person is within a certain range. They've been sending their holos out to the people they like on the nearby ships."

"They have? You mean you have?"

"Whatever you say, sir."

"Good work, boy. Good work."

In the days that followed, a dozen more kittens were collected by their own close personal friends from the ships docking at the station.

"Clever of the little devils to form their bonds with people who can afford the ransom," the old man said, rubbing forefingers and thumb together in a mercenary gesture. He leaned forward and said quietly into Jubal's ear, "Though I think if any of the customers had backed off, the crew would have made them an offer they couldn't resist."

"I wonder how long it will take those people to realize the little beasts are more trouble than they're worth?" the second assistant engineer growled when the new cat owners and their small partners had departed and their credits were deposited.

Jubal responded hotly. "You wait and see. These are going to be the best Barque Cats ever. They just need a job they can do and someone to love them."

The job was coming much sooner and was much more vital than anyone could have predicted.

CHAPTER 23

CHESTER ON THE RANZO

The crew and even Jubal had been blaming the kittens for the smell of cat pee that no amount of ventilation or vinegar spritzing dispelled. Although half of the little dears had by now found true love with their human partners, the pee smell just got stronger. By then I knew it wasn't all the kittens. It was Hadley.

Rather than rat him out to Jubal, I decided to take it up with the old boy myself. He was sleeping on Sosi's bed. "Hadley," I asked, when he opened one eye, "why are you peeing on everything? Are you jealous because Sosi is spending so much time with the kittens?"

"Uh—no," Hadley said, jumping down to go to his water bowl and refuel. He was coming back to sit down when he let fly all over the deck. "No, not jealous. Sosi is mine. She only loves me. I'd help her play with those pesky kittens myself but the truth is, Chester, I don't feel good. I'm tired all the time and—'scuse me, I'm a little dry. I need another drink." So he took another drink and then immediately had to pee again. Something was very wrong.

I contacted Jubal and told him Hadley was sick. He came right away, as I knew he would. He knelt and stroked Hadley, who cried a little.

Guillame Pinot, the ship's medical guy, came to Sosi's cabin. Sosi, for once not carrying a kitten, was right behind him.

"Sosi, when did Hadley start urinating in your bed?" Pinot asked her.

She shrugged and cast her eyes down. She sat on the wet bunk beside Hadley, stroking his fur. "I used to pee the bed too. He'll outgrow it," she said. "I did."

Pinot shook his head and petted Hadley too. I jumped up onto Jubal's shoulder so I could see better. "He's a grown-up cat, Sosi. He's older than you—a grandpa, in cat years. And when a well-trained ship-broken cat like Hadley starts peeing on things like this, it means he's probably sick."

She shook her head so that her shiny dark hair flipped back and forth. "No, he's not. He's just too tired to make it to the litter box all the time. I think the kittens wear him out," she confided.

"He's tired because he's sick too. I think we better get him to a vet soon."

"Dr. Jared," she said. "If Hadley is sick, he'll cure him."

The *Molly Daise* had docked at Hood Station a few days before, delivering Dr. Vlast and Janina. They were going to get married and run the clinic together. My mother was going to retire and live with them. We knew all that stuff already because Beulah had kept in touch with them. So the *Ranzo* changed course and sped to Hood Station.

I went with Jubal, Sosi, Hadley, and Captain Loloma to the clinic so I could tell Jubal to tell the doctor what Hadley felt like.

They set the poor guy on a metal table and he peed. They stuck something in his ear to take his temperature and he peed. The doctor stuck him with a needle and took out some of his blood and he peed. Dr. Vlast checked his boyish bits and got peed all over, but he just wiped his hands and continued the examination, taking a sample of the pee while he was at it. "Diabetes," he said.

"Is that serious?" Sosi asked.

Dr. Vlast nodded. "Adult cats are very prone to it and it can often be fatal." He said it gently but I saw Hadley's friend begin to tremble.

"You mean he'll die?"

I was okay with interpreting what Hadley said to the humans, which so far wasn't anything beyond "meow," but I was certainly not going to interpret what the humans were saying to Hadley. Not yet anyway.

Dr. Vlast handed him to Janina, who took him away, telling Sosi she was just going to clean up his fur. Then he wiped down the table and washed his hands. "He could. At one time it was a death sentence. But we have a good treatment now. Just make sure he gets these pills twice a day—but don't go too far. He needs to be stabilized on the meds before he travels."

That's how we all came to be there in the place where my journey began, when the Galactic Guard arrived with orders to requisition cats.

Second Lieutenant John Green had been assigned the unenviable mission of rounding up Barque Cats—again. He had been commissioned shortly before the Fairy Dust Incident, as it was now called, since it didn't turn out to be an epidemic after all. It had been a real test of his ability to follow orders and command, because he liked cats, and he still dreamed about the big sad eyes of the loyal little beasts who had protected their ships. At least he didn't have to re-collect them. Just the ones on these two ships. There were plenty left, according to recon, without having to wrench the ships' cats away from their crews again. Besides, it was the new ones they wanted, according to the informants, and most of those were on two ships conveniently docked at the same backwater station, sitting practically next to each other.

The captains and crew were unsmiling and hard-faced when he told them what was required of them, but the real opposition came from one young boy.

"You can't just draft our cats!" the youth declared. He stood with his arms crossed and his feet spread wide, blocking the soldiers' access to a cabin where as many of the cats as possible were hiding, all trying to crowd under the bunk.

A grizzled looking older guy with a strong family resemblance to the boy stepped in and said, "On the other hand, most of the cats you see here are for sale to the right homes. I'm assuming you want them because you have a lot of cat-lovers among your troops?"

"Some," Lieutenant Green said. He recognized the man and boy from the ID photos in their files. "Actually, we need to draft you too—Mr. Poindexter, isn't it? Am I pronouncing that correctly?"

"Close enough," Pop said. "But I didn't do it, whatever you're planning to arrest me for. Captain Loloma can testify that I have been a model crewman—and if you don't believe him, ask Captain Vesey of the *Molly Daise*. Or Dr. Vlast."

"The recommendation we have is from the captain of the late, unlamented *Grania*, sir. A lady named Mavis?"

"You can't listen to her. That woman holds grudges and she's angry because I refused to participate in illegal activities."

"I wouldn't know about that, sir. She did tell us that the *Grania* was the first ship the alien menace destroyed and that, although the *Ranzo* and the *Molly Daise* were responsible for introducing the menace to Galactic space, both seemed immune from destruction because of the special cats they carried. So we need your cooperation in assisting us with having the cats protect the affected areas in the Ra-Harahkty planetary system."

"This is all gibberish to me, General," Poindexter said. "Ra-Hawhatty?"

"These are almost all kittens," the boy said. "How can a bunch of kittens help you with some alien menace?" But the boy's voice shook as he said it, and he glanced back at the cats. His uncertainty verified the incident reported by the colorful lady captain of the dead ship *Grania* more than anything Green had heard so far. He swore to himself. They were just kittens and this was a harebrained plan and likely to get all of them killed.

"You'll all be briefed." He tried to make his eyes as steely as his father's and grandfather's and great-grandfather's had been in their official Guard portraits. He addressed Captain Loloma again. "Don't worry, you'll be there to look after them. We'll be giving the *Ranzo* and the *Molly Daise* as well as human captain and crew and livestock cargo a lift aboard the battleship *Quanah Parker.*"

"They're cats, sir," the boy said angrily. "Highly intelligent and very special cats, not livestock or cargo."

"I know that," Green said, apologizing quickly. His father would not have approved of the apology. "Sorry. Of course they're cats, and a really handsome breed of cats at that. I just have to call them something we have a category for."

"Cat—Sorry," Poindexter said, stifling a snicker at the pun.

The pile of cats under the bunk slid and shifted, and one pulled his way out from under the others, leaving them to tumble back on top of each other. It was a black and white kitten with a bushy tail, humongous white paws that resembled mittens, and wide bright green-gold eyes that looked straight at Green. *You're him,* a voice said inside Green's head. *You're my guy.*

Stay away from me, kitty. I'm here to arrest you.

Don't care. I'd go with you anyway. You're the one.

The one what?

My human. You're him. I can tell.

This is not the right time, kitty. You're undermining my authority. No, don't climb my uniform trousers.

He bent to pick up the kitten. Several of the other cats now ventured out into the corridor, including a fluffier adult version of the kitten. He hopped lightly onto the boy's shoulder as a mottled gray cat jumped onto Poindexter's. Both the man and the boy relaxed visibly as Green attempted to maintain his command presence.

The kitten purred like a well-tuned engine and rubbed his face against Green's, totally spoiling his attempt to look hard and purposeful. *I'm losing control of the situation here, kitty,* he told his furry stalker, who was trying to lick his nose. *I'll lose the respect of my troops.*

Not really, the kitten said. As if his takeover of Green signaled the attack for the other cats, they came out of the cabin—and others—to carpet the floor with wriggly but graceful bodies. Each soldier was visually inspected and then some were approached with mittened front paws on the knees of fatigue trousers, while mews of varying degrees of softness or insistence requested permission to board.

It occurred to Green—and he wasn't sure quite why—that relationships with these cats could make the mission easier. "Okay, you win, kitty."

Ishmael, said the kitten known to his father as Junior, sounding surprised. *Call me Ishmael.*

Those who were not Cat People either stood very still or advanced, shuffling, to the rear, back toward the hatch.

"Sir?" said Sutton, a female NCO currently under siege by a very large black kitten.

"Pick him up," Green said. "If we establish rapport with our—uh—new recruits, I believe it will be in the best interests of the mission."

"Yes, sir. Yessss, sweetie, come on up. Mugger, is it? You're a big palooka, aren't you?"

Green knew he was losing control of the situation. But both captains were cooperative enough about redocking aboard the *Quanah Parker.*

The *Quanah's* captain, not known to be a cat lover, nonetheless appreciated the advantages of the situation as revised by the cats. Human personnel were to carry on orienting feline personnel and would report, along with human and feline conscripts from the two ships, for orientation and training in addition to their regular duties. Watch rosters were rearranged accordingly.

CHAPTER 24

The humans watched the visual presentations with dismay if not horror. Most of the cats slept. They were shown films of a planetary system whose central star, Ra-Harahkty, appeared to be covered with a dense, shifting, growing cloud. Where the cloud covered it, the sun's rays penetrated only spottily.

"Holy cra—cow," Jubal's dad whispered to him. "Those wormy things are fast travelers. I guess they've given wormholes a whole new meaning."

But the instructor overheard him. "You think this is funny, Mr. Poindexter? You find those things comical? Perhaps that's why your party didn't think it necessary to report the first incident, when the earlier mutation, according to the *Grania*'s captain, devoured the hull of her ship and killed the crew still aboard?"

"No, sir," Pop said earnestly. "No, we just figured if it ate Mavis's ship and there was nothing else for it to feed on, it would die as soon as the food was used up."

"Did you wonder why it did not eat the *Molly Daise*, or the *Ranzo*, when according to the *Grania*'s captain the organisms were first attached to the hulls of the *Molly Daise* and the *Ranzo*?"

"Is this instruction or interrogation?" Captain Loloma demanded. "We had no knowledge that those organisms attached themselves to our hulls, or when it happened. When I boarded my ship before leaving the terraformed planet known to the locals as

Mau, my ship was clean. We have explained this to your superiors already."

But the instructor, who apparently had as many answers as they did but wanted to harass them because he thought he could, overrode him. "Do you know what happens to the planets in a system when, for all intents and purposes, its star or stars die?"

"Don't tell me the snakelets are eating the sun!" Pop responded.

"No—not as far as we know. Although they may be feeding off its energy, as they do keep multiplying. But the organisms have partially eclipsed the sun in spots to such an extent that formerly inhabitable planets are no longer. Oceans and rivers are freezing solid, plants we terraformed onto planetary surfaces at great expense have already become all but extinct, and the inhabitants who have been building new civilizations for generations have had to be evacuated . . . those that survived the first round of catastrophes."

Jubal didn't like where this was going. He raised his hand. "That sucks, sir. I mean, it's really a tragedy and a shame, but I don't see what we have to do with it. Maybe the organisms got their start on the same planet we just left, but I don't get why you wanted our cats—or us—to come here. It's not like there's anything we can do about it."

The instructor gave him a dirty look and shut off his equipment. "That information is classified. You'll know when we're ready for you to know."

"That's pretty high-handed," Captain Vesey protested.

"In case you hadn't noticed, you, your crews, and your vessels are under martial law. We get to be high-handed."

Jubal had the terrible feeling that this plan of theirs was not going to be healthy, especially for the cats. He saw nothing they could do about this emergency that could concern the kittens unless it involved sacrificing them in some way, which he got the distinct feeling it might well do.

Chester licked his earlobe, picking up on his anxiety for them.

It'll be okay. Green is good. Ishmael says he won't let them hurt us. And lots of the soldiers have turned out to be the people the kittens were waiting for. They are much happier now.

That's just great, buddy. But Lieutenant Green is a lot more important to Ishmael than he is to the Guard. He's very low in the pecking order—uh, not the alpha tom, by any stretch of the imagination. And our other friends here aren't exactly in control of the situation either.

There came the day when they were redirected from the classroom to another deck, one so huge that the kittens, cats, and crews of the two ships felt lost in its darkened expanse. "Please come forward," said the disembodied voice of the instructor.

Most of the humans did, but some of the cats were playing chase or hunting each other, enjoying the room to run. For a moment there was little sound but the pattering of paws and the occasional thump as a cat jumped and hit the deck again. Then someone coughed nervously and the humans began shuffling forward, to avoid stepping on unseen paws or tails.

A thin rope of light led, many steps away, to portable chairs. "Be seated," the instructor said. They did.

As soon as the humans sat down, making laps, most of the cats came scampering back and proceeded to find a likely looking lap or a chair to crouch beneath, a shoulder to perch on.

With a soft shooshing noise, the bulkheads slid back, uncovering a bisected ring of brilliance with a shifting, scroll-worked lacy pattern twining around the middle. It seemed to be all around them, as if they'd been thrust out into space itself, but Jubal realized they were on the forward part of the main deck. The actual bridge was a smaller space just above, but this section was where attackers and other vessels often sat—or landed, when the part that was now a viewing port became a wraparound hatch. It was configured like no other ship he'd ever seen, and was massive. And yet it was totally overwhelmed by the phenomenon menacing the star and the planets orbiting it. The swirling shape of the occlusion wrapping the star was in the form of the great snake, only much more enormous.

The movement inside the patterned part made Jubal feel queasy.

"Ladies, gentlemen, and animals, this is no simulation or feed from a probe. We have reached the Ra-Harahkty planetary system. Before you is the star at the system's center, surrounded by the phenomenon earlier described."

Someone whistled.

"This threat now circles the star, and the band continually grows in width and depth. If you will recall, the depictions I presented to you earlier on this voyage were only about a sixth this size."

"Are we too late?" Jubal couldn't see who had asked.

"No. We have, as a famous patriot once said, just begun to fight. But to do so we have called in—"

He's back, Chester told Jubal.

"—Ambassador Balthazar, head scientist of the planet Mau," the instructor continued, failing to mention Renpet and Pshaw-Ra, beside Balthazar, who winced at the omissions. "He alerted us to this threat and has provided us with schematics for weapons and calculations to combat it."

While Balthazar explains things to the humans that they won't understand, Pshaw-Ra will tell us what we cats really need to do to keep the serpent from swallowing the sun, Chester purred into his ear.

I thought they were headed back to Mau.

They were stopping at the new home of the Mau first, Chester said. *It is one of the planets in the Ra-Harahkty system. Probably it is no coincidence. I'll bet Pshaw-Ra made his mouse hole again and those snaky things followed him through it.*

So that's why he's being so helpful. Has he been here all along? I didn't see him before.

I didn't sense him before.

Being inside a cabin on a ship aboard another ship was not the best way to learn what was going on. The military ship was very stingy about sharing its com messages with the guest ships, to the disappointment of the kittens who still lurked near Beulah's com station, waiting for a chance to send their résumés to prospective human partners or to get a flash of intuition that told them which person on the other end of the com might be their particular telepathic match.

Balthazar said, "The fleet commander and the scientists I have been assisting from shipboard and from Mau-Maat at first questioned how we could know how to combat the evil that has befallen this star. I say to you that such a thing has happened before in our history, long before our sacred furred guardians came to Old Earth and showed us the way. With them they brought tales of the time when the great serpent Apep ate Ra, the sun, and how Bast the cat slew him with her sword. The young cats in this place are the descendants of Bast, and like her, are the ones necessary to defeat the serpent's new form. To that end my colleagues and I have provided the Guard scientists and technicians with the schematic for individual barques in which the sacred animals will ride to slay the serpent."

Jubal recalled the drawings he had seen on the tunnel wall beneath the City of the Dead, the ones with the cats and knives and snake bits and sun disks. That was all very well for an old drawing, but Balthazar was proposing to use real cats.

The instructor wore a guarded look, and Jubal reckoned he wasn't comfortable with Mauan mythology as a basis for a mission.

He wasn't the only one. Captain Vesey stood up, dumping two black kittens off his lap, and said, "With all due respect to you and the ambassador, Commander, and to cultural beliefs and differences and all that, this is the biggest load of kitty litter I have heard in all my days in Galactic space. You don't mean to tell me that you have this enormous problem and you intend to fling half-grown kittens at it? That's just plain cruel! What has this galaxy got against our cats anyway? First you try to destroy them one way, and now you want to throw them at a sun? For heaven's sake, man, have you no nuclear weapons, no lasers, no other kind of computerized electronic force you can exert to dispel this thing?"

"We've tried everything we've got, of course," said the instructor, who was in fact a commander as well. "Every time we fire on the damn thing it grows larger."

"Of course it does," Balthazar said. "These remnants of Apep, when dismembered, turn into more snakes. In this aspect, Apep reproduces by a very virulent form of mitosis. The resulting spawn feed on the energy of the sun, and your weapons feed them with similar energy."

"So you want them to feed on our cats instead?" Captain Vesey said. "I thought you people liked cats."

"We not only like them, we revere them. Precisely because they are known to be able to thwart such a threat."

Captain Vesey started to stalk off when Captain Loloma put a restraining hand on his arm and spoke to him. Then Vesey sat back down. He had not been on Mau, and Captain Loloma had picked up a little of the culture surrounding the cats during the time the crew was stranded there.

The wraparound view port closed and the lights went up. The view they had been engulfed in was now much reduced and shown on a screen off to the side of Balthazar and the instructor.

"These are the barques custom-constructed for the cats, equipped with weapons that may be operated by the merest flick of a toe."

The holo projected before them was shaped like a shallow bowl, with two extensions and what looked like suckers on the ends folded over the transparent covering like arms trying to meet across a full belly.

"Each cat will operate his or her own barque," Balthazar continued. And at that point, on either side of the crews, machines bearing large pallets covered with little objects similar to those in the picture of the barque drove in and deposited the flats on the deck.

As soon as the noisy machines had withdrawn, Chester jumped down from Jubal's shoulders and strolled over to investigate the barques. Before he had taken the first sniff, he was surrounded by the younger generation of felines, at first trying to sniff what he'd sniffed and then sniffing adjacent barques. He gave the barque a tap with his paw and it spun into two others, making Mugger jump out of the way. Whereupon Mugger smacked another of the barques and it went spinning into five more and made several other cats jump out of the way. The other cats joined in and soon there were barques and cats all over the deck.

The commander gave a phony chuckle. "At least we know they're durable."

"He'll never get the cats to stay inside them," Beulah whispered.

As if he heard her, Pshaw-Ra strolled up to the nearest barque, which at that point was standing on edge, flipped it over and patted the top with his paw. It lifted and he jumped inside and curled up in it as if it were a basket.

"And comfortable!" the commander continued in his new cheery tone.

Jubal stood up. "But are they safe? If they open that easily, how do we know the cats will be secure? And what about life support? Those things can't hold much oxygen or food and water. I don't see any weaponry either. I'm not letting you send Chester on a suicide mission."

"What I'd like to know is how you manufactured all of these things so darn fast," Captain Loloma said. "Research and development alone—"

"As I mentioned before," the commander said in a tone that implied *if you'd been listening*, "Ambassador Balthazar sent us the schematics and specifications by secure transmission shortly after the invasion began. We can move very fast when doing so means preserving trillions of dollars worth of terraforming on the inhabited worlds." Then he added, "Not to mention the lives of the settlers, of course. That goes without saying."

"And tell us, how are the cats supposed to survive in these crafts?"

"Each barque will be individually keyed to the ID chip on each cat so only that cat's paw can open it from the outside. There is an oxygen recirculating system built into the hulls that keeps the cat supplied with air as long as it is breathing. Water and liquid nourishment are fitted into a special compartment prior to each short journey. The barques also have homing devices so the barque will always return to its base, regardless of the state of the cat inside. That ought to be pretty good, since the material from which these are constructed was used in the lenses of the solar monitors operating continuously at a distance twenty times closer than the nearest planet to the central stars of each of our systems. They are heat, cold, pressure, and impact impervious."

Jubal said. "Maybe the ambassador's cat, Pshaw-Ra, could show us how one works and what our cats are supposed to do?"

"Such is our intention," Balthazar said. "But first each unit must be fitted to each of the noble felines. Pshaw-Ra's paws are not as dextrous as those of the new breed, but he will do his best to demonstrate."

The class was dismissed, though the cats continued playing shuffleboard with the tiny spacecrafts until someone noticed it was time for food.

Cuddled with Chester in their bunk, Jubal was still troubled. *Toy spaceships or not, I don't see what you and the kittens can do about all those acres of snakes.*

I don't either. Let's sleep.

No, I mean really. There's something fishy about all of this.

Where? Chester asked, yawning and curling his pink tongue back inside his mouth. *And is it in the form of a treat?*

Jubal smiled and scrunched Chester's thick soft black fur with his fingers. *You sound like your old self again.*

It was worrisome being a family cat, he said. *I'm glad the kittens have people of their own now and Renpet is going back to her people—if Pshaw-Ra doesn't get her killed first.*

I wonder about the kittens who don't have people yet, Jubal said. *I almost think they came for us because if we disappear, nobody will really know the difference, especially about the kittens. They don't have anyone.*

The soldiers are trying to make friends, Chester replied. *It doesn't really work that way, but they don't realize that.*

Or don't care. Jubal said. He lay his hand across the warm back of Chester's neck. *Don't worry, boy. I won't let them put you in any little flying saucer and send you into the sun to fight snakes. No way.* He'd steal a shuttle if he had to and go hide out somewhere where the GGoons would never find either of them. He didn't know how he could possibly save the other kittens, but he would save Chester.

CHAPTER 25

CHESTER: STRATEGY

Scritch scritch scritch. Someone was scratching at my door. Jubal was still sleeping. I jumped down and went to the door. Thanks to copying the exercises Pshaw-Ra had taught the kittens, I could now use my own paws in a much "handier" way, and I easily stretched up high enough to flip the latch.

Pshaw-Ra and Renpet stood on the other side of the door. I slipped out into the corridor. Renpet rubbed against me in a friendly way and Pshaw-Ra actually purred at me.

"What?" I asked, puzzled by the visit and especially by the purr.

"Catling—I must not call you catling any longer, for you have become the leader of our hope for the future—we are here to brief you."

"Oh really?" I sat down for a good clean under my tail. "Brief me on what?"

"On how you must conduct the mission to save the star from the serpent horde," he said.

"Jubal says we're not going," I told him. "And that suits me fine. Buttercup is back at the farm with Jubal's mother. My mother is with her Kibble. I might like to go hunt mice in the fields for a while and be with my boy."

Renpet looked at me with big sad golden eyes. "I would wish to be with my Chione too, Chester, but the serpent slew her. Please, for me, slay his new form in return."

My ears went back in annoyance. "Oh sure. Anything for you, fish breath," that being a private endearment between me and her. "How do you propose I do that? It's impossible. Jubal's right. The soldiers just want to kill us, and you two are encouraging them."

"No, no, you should know, catling—I mean, Chester—that I would never put our very special young in the path of danger for naught. There is a way, as Balthazar told the humans, based on the story of the first time the serpent sought to swallow the sun."

"Jubal says that was something called a myth, which is like a lie only really old."

"Just because Jubal does not understand it does not make it a lie," Renpet said softly. "Our kind had knowledge of space and its hazards long before we came to Earth, remember."

"I can't remember any such thing," I told her. "I'm not one of you, not really."

"But you are, mate. All cats are. The humans think we came from the forests, but before we were in the forests we traveled among the stars and brought to the humans of Mau the wonders of which you have heard, many now faded. But all cats spring from our divine heritage, including you. Adaptations occurred over the centuries, and the thousands of centuries: some traveled far, some grew furry, some grew large, some grew small, some grew the wonderfully spreading papyrus paws you share with the young. But all sprang from our kind originally. Think, remember, and you will know the truth of what I say."

I did feel *something*, some kinship, some hint of a memory, but it was very fleeting.

"If you know all about this mythic historic mission to kill sun snakes, Pshaw-Ra, why don't you lead this one?"

"Alas, neither of us have the paws to operate the new barques. The humans are nonconversant with our language, as are many of the new kittens, so the technology suitable for our paws in ships

218 · ANNE McCAFFREY AND ELIZABETH ANN SCARBOROUGH

like mine would be too difficult for them to grasp on such short notice. But the individual barques can be easily operated by the
papyrus-pawed, such as yourself, with the assistance of a human in
one of their small crafts. You and the other human-affiliated cats
must lead the way in the binding of the serpents."

"Binding?" I asked. "I thought we were going to kill it. Them."

"Apep is immortal but its fangs can be pulled—figuratively at
least," Pshaw-Ra said.

Renpet gave a little shudder, her fur rippling all the way down
her back, thinking, I knew, of the fang sunk into her Chione.

"I have with me the spell of binding," Pshaw-Ra continued.
"With it, you and the other cats will weave over, under, and
through the assembly of serpents."

"What? We just think the spell to ourselves and do a lot of flying
until it catches us? I don't think so. You want it done, Pshaw-Ra,
you do it yourself."

"No, of course, you do it with the sword of Bast," the old cat said.

"I thought if you cut that thing up it turned into more snakes."

"It does, but the sword you will use does not cut it asunder, it
cuts it together," he said.

Having done under my tail, I had only the top of my tail to wash
to show what I thought of this logic.

"Like all magic, there is sound science behind it," Pshaw-Ra
said. "The Sword of Bast is not, as has been translated, a short
sword, it is a *light* sword—a sword of fusion not fission. It will bind
the snakes one to the other as you weave them into this pattern . . ."

He showed me a complicated wrapping that looked like a
mummy wrapping.

"Me and all of these wild kittens?" I asked. "I don't see that happening."

"You don't understand how serious this is, Chester," Renpet
said.

"What's one solar system more or less to me, right?" I asked in a voice that would have scratched her if it had been a claw. "Of course I understand it's serious, but . . ."

"Should any of the serpents remain free, they can repeat this sun-eating throughout space, and the universe will truly go dark," Pshaw-Ra finished.

I tried to imagine that, and could not. "Meh," I said softly. "Okay, what are we supposed to do again?"

When next the wraparound view port opened, it looked onto a different sector of space, with no snake-infested sun.

"We are now at Nome Station, the Galactic outpost closest to the Ra-Harahkty system," the commander-instructor said. "The cats have been fitted with their individual barques and codes, and today there will be a test flight for them, and for you, their controllers."

"Controllers? This guy knows nothing about cats," Pinot whispered to Jubal.

"I heard that, crewman," the instructor said. "The little crafts containing the cats are not equipped to fly beyond a certain range. Some of you, however, have psychic connections with your cats. It is these pairs we are most interested in at this time. Jubal Poindexter, Carlton Poindexter, Lieutenant John Green, Chief Petty Officer Anne Sutton, Guillame Pinot, Felicia Daily . . ." He continued with a roster of all the partners the kittens had found for themselves, including, to Jubal's surprise, Captain Mavis Romero O'Malley, Cadets Shan Mallory, Shinta Lin, Daffodil Airey, and others with whom they had recently placed cats. At the last moment the names were joined by the recent arrivals of Dorice Poindexter, Jared Vlast, and Janina Mauer. Buttercup was with Mom, of course, but to his surprise it wasn't Chessie with Janina, but her brother Sol. Dr. Vlast carried one of the youngsters.

"Dr. Vlast will be on the mission not as the veterinarian but as the control for his feline friend Herriot," the commander said, apparently just in case anyone got the notion to approach the vet for worm pills or some other nonmission-related need.

Jubal realized that if this went wrong, not only would the cats be wiped out, but so could his whole family and all of his friends. He truly would have nowhere to go. But Chester had his mind made up that they were going through with this, no matter how nuts it sounded.

Mom and the old man had apparently been coming to the same conclusion. After the break, they were sitting in the chairs on either side of him, while Doc and Buttercup bumped noses with Chester and the three of them smelled each others' butts.

Mom took a hand off Buttercup to hold onto his tightly, and Pop rested his arm along the back of Jubal's chair. They were in this together, if separately.

Flying the specially outfitted shuttle was not too difficult for him — he'd seen it done often enough. It might have been, loosely speaking, rocket science, but it was easy rocket science.

The shuttle contained a custom-built bay to hold the kitty-sized barque, as well as extra scanners to give him a full view of the serpent band and help him eject Chester's barque at the right point for his friend to guide it into the target, and special controls to resupply Chester if he came back to the shuttle for a break.

The cat ships were rigged with rays of light to simulate the weapons that would be installed at the last minute, after Pshaw-Ra briefed the cats, he supposed. The commander said information on how the weapons were supposed to defeat the snakes was classified, and that the controllers did not need to know.

The weapons would be mounted in the extensions on the barques and manipulated by the cats' paws. The inner lid was sensitive to the touch of the large paws, and the barque extensions acted like the cats' own paws, striking, smacking, batting, and pouncing with both rays on a single target.

Jubal guided their shuttle out of the big ship's shuttle bay and into the sector bordered by larger ships pretending to be the snake band. Other shuttles popped out of the ship too, kind of like kittens being born. A couple of the little barques shot out early, their feeble light rays strobing in all directions while the cats got the hang of controlling the pretend weapons.

But Jubal waited until his scanner light blinked, then said *Ready?* to Chester, who answered with a yawn.

Then Chester said, *Go!*

This is serious, buddy. You could get killed. Me too. No sleeping on the job.

But it is very comfortable in here, Chester replied before saying, not to Jubal, *Hey, not me, small fry. The target! The target!*

But the kittens didn't see a target. There was no fun to be had in attacking humongous ships that didn't notice they were being killed. So the kittens attacked each other with their light rays and had a very good time making the entire area look like a traffic accident until the commander's voice on the com ordered the shuttles to collect their passengers. There was a button for that too, a homing device that pulled each barque back to its shuttle. With another button, you could rescue some other shuttle's cat if necessary, but since each shuttle only had room for one barque, doing that would endanger the shuttle's own cat, giving it no place to go unless— It was overcomplicated and to be avoided except in dire emergency.

Once the cats and humans had reassembled in the classroom, the instructor thundered at them. "What part of deadly menace don't you understand? These little cat boats are expensive, not playthings. Their fuel costs too much to waste turning them into carnival rides."

Lieutenant Green stood and said, "Permission to speak, sir."

The commander looked like he wanted to say he wasn't done bawling them out yet, but nodded and gritted his teeth instead.

"Ishmael was ready to attack a deadly menace, sir, but not a huge ship. He and the other cats who—uh—speak Standard were prepared for the mission, looking forward to it. But they needed a target, not a zone. They are cats, sir. They attack snakes, fish, birds, mice, rats, and bugs, not whales."

Jubal had to snicker, and saw the old man and his mom doing the same. He was not surprised when Chester said, *Way to go, Junior!* Green had obviously been transmitting his message from the kitten now calling himself Ishmael.

For the next training session, the larger ships were surrounded by small pieces of debris, making them look like they were under attack by a swarm of insects. This time the kittens eagerly attacked the balls of paper, packet wrappers, and bits of uneaten food with their rays of light, though when the light had no effect on the garbage except to scatter it, the kittens began to see how far they could scatter it instead.

Chester, that ain't gonna work, Jubal said, exasperated, but his friend was way ahead of him.

I know, I know. I'll tell them, and directed his thoughts at the other cats. *Pshaw-Ra says we'll have to use our new toys to mush the snake back into a big solid to kill it, not scatter the little ones.*

The barques swiftly changed tactics and began zipping out to retrieve drifting debris and herd it back toward the mass. Of course, the rays of light were no help whatsoever. And some of the kittens, especially those with no telepathic links with their controllers, still preferred to chase the space junk instead of herding it. One or two headed away from the mock battlefield and had to be drawn back to their shuttles.

It would have been amusing if it weren't so serious. What kind of weapon could kill something that was apparently not killable? Not only that, but in its diffuse form—countless smaller serpentine shapes writhing in space—Apep had expanded to be much much larger than it had ever been in the tunnels—large enough to obscure a sun from the planets orbiting it. How could the cats possibly cover so much space and zap enough snakes to neutralize the monster? It all seemed pointless, hopeless, and he would have said needless, except of course you couldn't have snakes eating up suns whenever they wanted to, not really. Not if Pshaw-Ra and Balthazar were right and they could be stopped.

All too soon, after not nearly enough practice, the commander announced that they were ready to launch their offensive.

CHAPTER 26

Before we arrived at what the noisy man at the front of the room called "the mission launch coordinates," Pshaw-Ra, Renpet, and I went around to every cat on the ship while Pshaw-Ra told them that I was in charge, especially of coordinating the cats who hadn't found a special human yet.

"Why should he be?" asked Metaxa, one of Zvonek's kittens by a Mau queen. "He's no better than us."

"Because I am the Grand Vizier and this is your queen, and if you do not mind Chester and yet somehow you survive, we will smack you. And that, my child, is why."

As the two of them turned, Metaxa gave a tiny snarl in their direction, but I put my paw around her neck, pinned her down and licked her nose. "Believe it or not, it is for your own good," I told her. "I don't like this either, but I'll try to keep you alive and get you back safe."

Two naps, a couple of mouthfuls of kibble, and a thorough grooming and petting session with Jubal later, we boarded the shuttle and got in line with the others to exit the mother ship. While en route, our weapons were installed where the light beams had been.

"What if the kittens don't understand the difference and use it on one of the other ships?" I had asked Pshaw-Ra. ·

"It is a snake-specific weapon," he assured me. "It would harm you and your craft no more than the beam of light you used in practice."

Meta was behind me, her shuttle controlled by a soldier. I sent out reassurances to her and all of others who were going out without their own person.

"Oh, stick it up your tail, Chester," Bojangles told me. "Cats have been hunting way before any humans could read any cat thoughts. Get over yourself. This is going to be fun!"

Then the bay doors opened and the shuttles streaked out into space, the central feature of which was the serpent-infested star, all blinding orange fire around the top and bottom with a black snake middle.

Even from back there—probably thousands of miles away by Standard reckoning—I could see those snakes wiggling, and it made my paws itch with the urge to smack some scaly tail.

The shuttles fanned out as they got closer to the snakes.

"Good luck, buddy," Jubal said as I patted the top of my barque and hopped inside. The lid closed after me. It was cozy in there, but it smelled a little different—the weapon, I thought. The weapon had a sharper smell than the light beam.

For another moment I was inside Jubal's head, hearing his heart beat fast and tasting his fear that I would never return, that he was sending me to my death, and then I was back out in space as I had been in practice, a free agent, a mighty hunter stalking something that had invaded this great vast territory that was mine to defend. I tried to take it all in but it was so enormous, just the enemy in the middle of that hypnotizing heat . . .

Engage, Chester, Jubal said inside my head.

What?

Sic 'em, boy. Those little boat things will sustain you only so long.

226 · ANNE McCAFFREY AND ELIZABETH ANN SCARBOROUGH

Right! I said, and shifted my weight to shoot forward, as we'd been shown.

My vessel obeyed and homed in on the target, just as I did. How far it was exactly, I had no way of knowing, nor how close to the sun we would have to go to engage our foe. The snakes feeding on the sun's light and heat did not dull its power nearly enough to suit me.

The shuttles were positioned about halfway between the *Quanah Parker* and the snakes, close enough to stay in thought and radio communication with our barques but far enough away to be out of the fray and away from the sun's heat that was not being absorbed by the snakes.

The barques were the swiftest things I'd ever been aboard, and they covered the distance between the shuttle and the snakes so fast that Jubal was just at the end of thinking *Good* and hadn't yet thought *luck* by the time I arrived at the target.

I flew right into the mass of wriggly things, quivering with the thrill of the hunt. Snakes surrounded me, big ones, little ones, snake heads, snake bodies trying to wrap themselves around my craft.

Up go my front paws into sunbeam-batting mode, but now it is not the warm and life-giving motes of sunlight I slap around but the slithery things leeching life from the sun itself. *Bat. Smack. Batabatabata!*

The weapons elongated and smashed the snakes together, right snake, left snake, all one snake.

The snake wrapped itself around the extension and tried to pull. These little ones were as cunning as the big ones. Another head was coming toward me. I pulled it in with the unencumbered weapon rod, zapped it, and smacked it into the other head, zapping them both. The loose snake pulled, flopped, welded face-to-face with the one that had tangled my weapon arm. With no head guiding it, the body fell away and drifted off.

That was it! A tactic!

Fuse them head-to-head, I told the other cats in thought-talk.

Three snake heads struck the top of the barque. To me a snake looks like a very angry if ugly cat, with flat ears, slitty narrowed eyes, fangs bared, and tail lashing. Venom floated up from their open mouths and they bit down again and again. A fang broke off. I automatically ducked back from their furious faces, my paws frozen by their glaring eyes. Their wiggling tails caught my own eye, though, and the paws came up, the barque paws shot out and fused their tails together. They fell back away from my craft.

I didn't wait to be attacked again but waded in, fusing tails together and heads together over and over again. Little snakes strung into big snakes, tails tails, heads heads heads heads tails tails flip the barque and do the ones trying to climb it, double flip and attack a new area, pouncing the barque sideways to duck clutching coils.

Mrrryowwww help! Yow yow yow! It was Buttercup.

Where are you? I asked, already leaning the barque.

Here! she cried. *It's got me!*

Except for Pshaw-Ra, cats don't do coordinates, and in space, direction doesn't make a lot of difference—but I headed for my daughter as if she were a magnet drawing me through the wiggling coiling serpentine masses.

I saw her then, between a snake's jaws. The snake was enormous—not as big as the serpent of the tunnel but large enough to stuff a barque in its mouth with a cat inside. My poor kitten, her green eyes wide with horror, her paws pressing against the clear dome of the barque, her little pink mouth stretched into a long oval with cries I could hear only in my head, stared out at me as venom dripped down the front of the barque and the snake gathered itself to open and swallow. Suddenly, on her other side, Junior was there too.

Can you make yourself heavy like Pshaw-Ra showed us? I asked Buttercup. Would his gravity-increasing trick work in space where there was only freefall?

I can't I can't I can't—

Do it! I said, slapping the inner surface of my barque and fusing two passing heads together as I did so because the weapons followed the swipe of my paw. I used one of them to pluck the things up, and fused them to the inside of the hinge of the big snake's jaw. Junior flipped over, fused two snakes, and brought them back to do the same thing on the other side.

The fused lower jaw sagged as Buttercup stomped as hard as her mittened paws could stomp inside their enclosure. The jaw snapped downward and the barque floated free. Buttercup zoomed off and I thought she would be returning to her control shuttle, but she returned in a moment with a collection of snakes fused together into bundles in each barque extension, and fused these to the larger snake's mouth, partially filling it. We worked together, trip after trip, to fill the gaping maw of this dangerous specimen.

When it was done, we kept working together, our backs to each other as we rolled and spun, fusing any snakes that came near any of us. When my front paws were limp with exhaustion I flipped onto my back and kicked with my back paws, also bearing dextrous extra toes, fusing more serpents that way.

I called to the others to work in teams with the barques nearest them, wrapping the fused snakes like a bandage around the smaller ones within, confining them. We looped around and around the snake, fanning out and joining up our links of fused serpents, weaving diamond-shaped patterns around the mass. It took a lot of flying. The thing had spread to circle the sun, so we too had to circle it in our pattern.

I don't know how long we fought before I became way too warm and the searing light blinded me to more snakes.

Most of the other cat pilots reported being affected the same way until they could loop back over to the shadowy side of the snake chain.

So I didn't actually see when some of the larger ones that had not been joined with others broke out of the serpentine cylinder to attack the control shuttles. I only heard Jubal cry my name once, and what I saw was with his eyes as he stared out the shuttle's viewscreen at five serpents each at least the size of the one that had attacked Buttercup, their tails propelling their bodies forward through space, swimming toward him.

Jubal had watched with pride and excitement as Chester and the other barque pilots bound the snakes together and wove them into a loose sausage that contracted in mass as they fused it together. Though it hardly seemed possible, within a few short hours they had opened diamond-shaped holes in the lacy writhing mass through which the sun blazed. He cut the transparency of the screen until it was almost opaque, but the brilliance was scary and painful to his eyes and he looked down, back, from side to side, anywhere but directly into the action, which was how he missed seeing the snakes until it was too late to evade them.

Unlike Chester, Jubal experienced no arousal of his hunting instinct as he watched them close on him, pass him, and then whip a coil directly over the screen, then another and another. A face dipped into view, and once more fiery eyes glared hungrily at him as a fanged mouth opened in a silent hiss—but this time he could not see anything within the mouth but more fire—the snake seemed filled with it. Light leaked around its scales, barely contained by them.

Back on Mau, the snake, despite its supernatural reputation, had seemed like an overgrown anaconda or something—mortal if monstrous, a flesh and blood reptile. And as a cloud the creatures had an amorphous look to them—he couldn't really see Apep in that mass of what seemed to be earthworm-sized particles of the snake that had killed Chione. But the creatures that had him in their grip now were just *wrong*, nightmare serpents filled up with solar energy until they were about to fly apart. And yet they had the single-mindedness, even at this stage, to break away from their main body and evade the cat ships by coming after the control vessels—or at least his.

The hull creaked and groaned and, he thought, buckled as the coils tightened. The backlit scales rippled and surged, and the head reared back as if to strike through the viewscreen. He was sure the heat from the core of the beasts was penetrating the shuttle's shields. He would have checked the gauge but was paralyzed by the hypnotic, horrible gaze of the serpent head that filled his mind as much as his field of vision.

His heart boomed in his ears and it seemed to him that the booming spoke his own name, "Ju-bal, Ju-bal," but it was nothing but background noise compared to the compelling will of the snake, which told him he was about to become one with the cosmos. It made it seem like a good thing, and yet . . .

"Jubal? Son?" His father's voice sounded panicky.

"Jubal Alan, are you still in there? Answer me!" His mother's voice was an annoying buzz.

He tried to answer them, but his mouth was dry and his tongue felt thick and heavy. The snake's forked tongue, on the other hand, flickered like a flame as it hungrily licked at the viewscreen.

What will happen to me if you let yourself get eaten, boy? Chester demanded directly inside his head, cutting through the serpent's spell. *I am almost out of fuel and snacks and I'm very tired. You're supposed to take me back to the ship.*

Jubal looked down at the control panel, snapping the snake's hold on him. Not that it did any good. *Buddy, I'm sorry but I seem to be tied up right now.* He thought he was making a joke, but it came out anguished and despairing. When the serpent killed him, unless one of the other shuttles could pull Chester in, he would be doomed to death from exposure, once the fuel cell in the little barque was exhausted. He might have oxygen, but the temperature controls would fail, and other life-support functions too. Any shuttle that took him aboard would be dooming its own cat pilot to that fate instead of Chester.

I'm sorry! he told Chester. He'd never felt more helpless.

In the background he heard his mother complaining. "I told them these damned things should have weapons."

Stay alive, boy, Chester said.

He didn't dare look back out the viewscreen again but felt as much as saw Chester approach, and experienced his relief when Ishmael, Buttercup, and Doc joined him.

The light shifted, and when he looked up, the snake's coils were falling away and the head was gone, fused to the head of another serpent. He could watch then as the three cats harried the snakes together until they could wrap them all into a big fused knot like one of those designs he'd seen in old books about ancient Ireland, slowly being drawn back into the orbit described by the larger fused serpent.

Two barques peeled away from the snake knot then and disappeared, but he heard a noise against the hull.

Does this hatch still work? Let me in! Chester said. Jubal got the mental picture of his friend scratching at a door.

CHAPTER 27

CHESTER RETURNS TO THE MOTHER SHIP

I lay inside my barque limp with exhaustion, both my body and my mind frazzled with my exertions. Then the hatch opened and my barque nestled into its slip. The barque lid sighed and slid back. Jubal lifted me out and cradled me on his lap as he flew the shuttle, which fortunately was sturdier than it had felt to him, back to the mother ship. After a few minutes I sat up and washed my paws, but his hands trembled on the controls.

Two of the kittens had been lost. Despite what Pshaw-Ra said, their barques did not return to the shuttles when called. I hadn't known Trixie or Greyling well, hardly at all, and they never found their own humans, so their shuttles were controlled by a couple of soldiers.

We found that out when we returned and popped out of our shuttles. Some of us, including me, were carried. I'd had enough exercise for the moment and felt I deserved a lot of carrying and cuddling. Most of the others were strutting proudly. Mugger said, "I wish I'd been able to bring back one of those snakes to carry around a little, show these humans what a real hunter can do."

"I guess we showed them, didn't we?" other kittens called to each other.

"You bet we did. They never saw us coming."

"That was fun! Do you think they'll let us do it again?"

They did, of course.

But not right then. We were all pretty tired, but the humans were exhausted. Jubal lay down on his bunk to sleep but stared at the wall and quivered. I snuggled close to him, butting under his chin, inserting my head into his palm. I walked on him, increasing my gravity until he had to pay attention to me. His mind was still crawling with snakes.

Come on, boy, forget about them. They're gone.

But they came after me, Chester. They act like they're some sort of natural disaster—like a tornado or a hurricane—but then they came after me, because they knew you and I were together. I could see it in the way that snake looked at me. And—he's got eyes again.

Pshaw-Ra said Apep's injuries wouldn't last. And of course he knows we're together—we've defeated him twice, you and me. He's scared of us and trying to think how to get around me by going after you. It won't work, though. Don't worry, Jubal. I'll always protect you.

Yeah, sure, buddy, but you're a ten-pound cat and I'm a human. I'm supposed to protect you.

So we watch each other. Are you hungry yet?

We stayed on the Guard ship long enough for them to repair and service the barques and shuttles. Since Jubal wasn't up to it, I suggested through Doc and Ponty that some kind of charge be rigged in the hulls of both shuttles and barques to dislodge clingy coils.

Meanwhile, once the humans had eaten and slept, the noisy man who stood at the front of the room prattled on about the birth of something called quasars and how they never knew what caused it, but now that they'd seen the snakes in action, they thought that must have happened before and that the snakes were responsible for other such holes in space.

Pshaw-Ra looked up at the man with total disdain. "What does he think we have been telling him all this time? Has he no ears? No eyes?"

Before we flew again, I had a chance to talk to each of the other cats about tactics and warn them that some of the loose snakes might attack their control shuttles and to let the rest of us know if they did so we could help. But the next mission went far more smoothly, and the one after that, though Jubal was still unnerved and his hands shook harder and his eyes stared farther—I had more trouble getting his attention to let me back inside on the third trip.

Once Apep was thoroughly fused, however, the snake was recondensed to the size it had been in the tunnels—not sun-spanning or even obscuring—and the big ships were able to trac-tor beam it and haul it away to the farthest, unterraformed planet from the sun, where it was buried in the frozen underground of an-cient lava tubes.

There, Pshaw-Ra assured everyone through Balthazar, it would be dormant in perpetuity.

"I have heard him say that before," Renpet told me somewhat bitterly. She still mourned Chione but had a new task. The Mauans of Mau-Maat had been displaced by the disastrous effects of Apep on their sun and needed a haven. Balthazar, speaking on behalf of the new queen and her vizier, offered them shelter once more on Mau. I think Pshaw-Ra felt that they could use a refresher course in their native culture.

Buttercup and Ishmael would remain with Jubal's mother and Lieutenant Green, but they came to see their mother off.

"Isn't it funny how the snakes arrived at the star here on the far side of the galaxy at the same time we did?" Buttercup asked.

"Yes, that is funny. Good thing we were ready for them," Ishmael said.

"I hate to think what would have happened if we hadn't been."

But I suspected that I knew what would have happened if we hadn't been ready to carry out Pshaw-Ra's master plan. The snakes wouldn't have been there either. Once our reputation as defenders of the star system spread throughout the galaxy, there were not enough kittens to go around to all of the humans with high psychic ability that were willing to pay all of the credits they had to be paired with one.

Jubal, weary and a little jumpy, but better, came down to the docking bay to say good-bye to Balthazar and give Renpet a stroke too. She nuzzled his hand hungrily and licked it. She missed a human touch. Pshaw-Ra put a paw on Jubal's knee in farewell, though of course petting was not something he ever solicited.

Before they boarded, however, the lift descended from the upper decks, and Beulah, carrying a pack, joined us. Renpet spurted a purr and stretched up with her front paws for Beulah to lift her. The communications officer told Jubal, "I always wondered what it would be like to be a lady-in-waiting. I guess I'll find out."

"But the *Ranzo* . . . ?" Jubal said.

"You are ready to take over my job. And we'll be in touch. Count on it," she said.

We watched silently as the pointy nose of the pyramid ship drilled its way into space, Jubal stroking my hindquarters and tail.

Funny how in spite of everything, Renpet has put on weight again, he said.

I licked his earlobe. *Now that we're all heroes, there's a kitten shortage again. I decided to help Renpet out. As queen, it was her duty to set an example, you know.*

Don't you want to go back to Mau too?

No, not really. I washed my paw. *I'm sure Pshaw-Ra will have plans for the new litter, so I expect we'll be seeing them when he's ready.*

Jubal sighed. *Not that I don't want to see your kittens, Chester, but I hope the universe can survive that old cat's next scheme to dominate it.*

I hoped so too, but we'd had psychic bugs, sentient rats, solar snakes, and warrior kittens already. What could he do next? It made me tired just thinking about it. Time for a nap.

PHOTO: © ORLA CALLAHAN

ANNE MCCAFFREY, the Hugo Award–winning author of the best-selling Dragonriders of Pern novels, is one of science fiction's most popular authors. She lives in a house of her own design, Dragonhold-Underhill, in County Wicklow, Ireland.

www.annemccaffrey.net

PHOTO: © ADRIENNE ROBINEAU

ELIZABETH ANN SCARBOROUGH, winner of the Nebula Award for her novel *The Healer's War,* is the author of twenty-one solo fantasy novels. She has co-authored eleven other novels with Anne McCaffrey. She lives on the Olympic Peninsula in Washington State.

www.eascarborough.com

ABOUT THE TYPE

This book was set in Electra, a typeface designed for Linotype by W. A. Dwiggins, the renowned type designer (1880–1956). Electra is a fluid typeface, avoiding the contrasts of thick and thin strokes that are prevalent in most modern typefaces.